I0712779

# SANDY FLASH

## AND THE

## TRAIL OF HISTORY

## BY GENE PISASALE

Front cover image: Sandy Flash reenactor at the Colonial Pennsylvania Farmstead event

Title page: Artist's depiction of Sandy Flash courtesy of *The Sunday News* March 3, 1935

Back cover images from left:
*Painting of Humphry Marshall* by Adrian Martinez; *Walking by Light of the August Moon* by Adrian Martinez; Painting of Bayard Taylor as a young man

# Dedication

To my wife Phyllis Recca, I am so very thankful for your love and support in this and all of my books, articles and other works written over nearly two decades of exploring Chester County's fascinating history. Without your help and timely, insightful comments, this book would not have been possible.

To my parents Salvatore and Ida Pisasale, I thank you for giving me a wonderful foundation in life which has allowed me to pursue many different goals and achieve them. You provided a loving home and guidance when I truly needed it.

To our good Lord and our Father in Heaven, I thank you for giving me this life which has taken me on many adventures and for bringing four beautiful kitties to us- Dadcat, Momcat, Francis and Frankie- who became our family, our very best friends and beloved soulmates. We found you all living in the forest behind our home 17 ½ years ago and somehow we knew you were destined to become a precious part of our lives. To our kitties- we'll always love you and we thank you for your affection, being with us for all these years, walking with us around our home and through the forest. You have enriched our lives immeasurably… and *you will forever be with us…*

*"Those we love don't go away…*
*They walk beside us every day…*
*Unseen, unheard, but always near…*
*Still loved, still missed and very dear…"*  -Alex Maclean

Dadcat

Momcat

Frankie and Francis-
Forever Friends

# Acknowledgements

I want to thank Connor Munzert and Library Manager Gillian Hayward at the Longwood Gardens Library and Archives for their kindness and generosity in providing a large array of materials for review. Many thanks to Doug Miller, Site Director at Pennsbury Manor for providing a private tour of William Penn's estate. Thanks go out to the Hagley Museum and Library for their kindness in allowing use of an historic photograph related to the book. I also thank Ellen Endslow, Curator and Wyatt Young Librarian at the Chester County History Center who both supplied valuable sources for examination and images for inclusion in this work. I thank Paul Hewes, Director of the Delaware County Historical Society and the Team there who were very kind in providing numerous references related to the Revolutionary War outlaw James Fitzpatrick. I am also grateful to Cliff Parker at the Chester County Archives who made several documents from the 1770s era available for review as references for this work. I thank the Team at the Pennsylvania State Archives who provided period materials related to Thomas McKean and the trial of James Fitzpatrick. All of these persons donated their time and effort helping me produce this 'walk through history' and I thank you all for your contributions.

# Chapter 1

*"A kiss from my mother made me a painter."* -Benjamin West (1738-1820)

*The young boy did not want to be kept alone in the room with his infant niece, but had no choice, as his mother had left him with the toddler temporarily. Seeking some form of distraction, he noticed a bottle of black ink on the table near him. Nearby stood a quill pen, which he grabbed and started to dip into the bottle, testing its pointed edge on a rough scrap of paper, drawing lines and shapes. Just then, the toddler let out a whimper- and he turned to walk over towards her. The angelic face captivated him. "So innocent, my little girl, a new member of our family…" he thought as he brought the paper and ink near where she lay in the crudely fashioned wooden crib and started drawing. After several strokes of the pen, the girl came to life before him. "There… I think I have your smile in these lines. Those beautiful eyes and luscious cheeks for us all to enjoy." Just then the door to the cabin opened; his mother walked over to him to see what he was doing. She took the paper from his hand and examined it, then looked over at the newborn and exclaimed "Why, it's Sally!," bringing her lips to his face in thanks for the infant's portrait.*

***********************************************************************

The first rays of the morning washed the katsura and giant arborvitae trees in the back yard with a shimmering glow as Jim raised the cup of Earl Grey to his lips. Just then, he sensed something rubbing up against his right leg and looking down toward the oak floor in the kitchen, noticed the grey and white tabby next to him. "Hi Frankie! Mom's not up yet- just you and me, but she should be here soon." The cat's head moved toward her left and she gazed for several seconds toward the foyer, then swerved back around, as if she were looking for something- or someone who should be there. She stared again toward the foyer and then back, slowly, all around the room, then finally up at Jim's face with a sweet *'Meoww.'* "Yes, my girl. We *do miss Francis*- we miss him every day. Momcat and Dadcat, too, but they *are* here. They'll *always* be with us." He set the Laurel Burch mug down on the counter and scooped Frankie up in his arms. "I love you so much- so does Mom… and here she comes."

"There's my beautiful kitty!" Natalie strolled toward Jim and leaned in for a kiss, then bent down toward Frankie and gave her a long hug. "Good morning. Looks like you two have a head start."

"Just a bit. Coffee?" He went to the silver and black Cuisinart coffeemaker and waited.

"Sure. Let's go into the Conservatory. I have an idea I want to share. Come on, Frank."

Jim filled the cup to her preferred three-quarters level and quickly followed. "I'm always open to new ideas. What's up?"

"We both love old structures and I read that The Square Tavern over in Newtown Square is opening up for public tours. It dates to around the mid-1700s- and the historical society there apparently has kept it in wonderful condition. Ready for a drive?"

Jim thought for a few seconds. "Isn't that off of Route 3- West Chester Pike? I think I know where that is."

"Yes, it's not too far, maybe 40-minutes. They've also restored an old paper mill near there which hosts events. The Tavern opens at 12 Noon, so we can have a snack here and then drive over."

"Sounds fair. I'll check it out before we go and see what it looks like." Jim sat next to her on the olive-green couch and just barely missed the cat as she jumped up next to Natalie's side.

"Yes, go to the Newtown Square Historical Society's website. I looked at it briefly and they seem to be pretty active, with a lot of events throughout the year" said Natalie, before sipping her coffee.

Relaxing on the couch as Frank took her favorite spot on Natalie's lap, Jim nodded in approval. "I will." The trio sat there as the morning light filled the room. "Weather looks good- we can relax for a while here then make it a fun day." They both took turns petting the kitty, who seemed to smile each time she felt their hands. After more than an hour, Jim got up. "I'm checking out the Society website."

Sitting for a long while at his computer, paging through their historic structures and list of events, Jim finally glanced at the clock. "Hey, sweetie- it's later than we thought." He moved into the kitchen and put two English muffins on a plate resting near the toaster on the black granite island, cut both open and put one in to toast. Natalie came in just as he was buttering the first one, then he inserted the second one.

"I'm hungry. I hope you don't mind if I start." She took a quick bite as she watched him.

Jim finished buttering his and sat down beside her at the glass and wrought-iron breakfast table. As he finished his tea and took the last bite of his English muffin, his Eddie Bauer watch showed it was already 11:15 a.m. "We should probably get going soon."

"I'm way ahead of you. Let's move."

Route 926 in southern Chester County gives riders a pleasant view of 'the way things used to be': multi-acre farms, horses grazing in large meadows, sometimes bumpy side roads with not a car in sight and rustic stone barns from more than two centuries ago whose walls have survived the Mid-Atlantic Winter snowstorms and occasional Spring torrential downpours. Turning onto Route 3 (West Chester Pike) brings you 300 years forward into the 21st century, with cars whizzing by on smooth blacktop at well over the posted 55 mile-per-hour speed limit.

"Wait! Weren't we supposed to turn *back there?*" Natalie's yell pierced the air inside their SUV.

"Don't *do that*. You almost made me drive into the other lane!" Jim steered the car left onto Providence Road. "No, we turn somewhere up here." Passing Marlborough Road, the blue Subaru Forester *SWERVED* sharply as a huge branch from a white oak tree crashed just feet in front of them along the edge of the thoroughfare. ***"MY GOD!! That was a near disaster!*** We just avoided about a $5,000 repair job.**" Jim looked over at Natalie and saw her shuddering, turning around to survey the scene as they drove around the edge of the 10-foot long, leafy limb.

"That was *way* too close for comfort." Natalie straightened her hair which had slumped forward onto her forehead.

Jim took a deep breath as he tried to focus on the road ahead while scanning the trees on each side. "Who'd have thought a tree might take us out?" He guided the Forester at a reduced speed as his instincts told him that things other than traffic could be their undoing. A few minutes later, as they cruised further down the street, a tractor-trailer abruptly turned left right in front of them, inches away from *HITTING* their car, Jim *jamming* on the screeching brakes. ***"HOLY CRAP!! That guy almost killed us!*** This isn't a public road- it's an obstacle course." Jim kept his now shaky eyes glued to the stretch ahead to avoid any further mayhem, then mumbled: *"I guess I passed my driving test."*

"Drivers today *are crazy!!* These winding roads are too dangerous."

"Hey- *take a chill pill*. Yes, that *was* almost a calamity, but having a coronary won't help. Huge trucks should *not be allowed on these back streets!* They come through here just to take short-cuts to the main roadways. Now… *I think we missed our turn."*

*"Again."* Natalie's tone was proof of her irritation.

Jim took the first side street, which after a few hundred yards didn't look promising. "We need to somehow circle back to get to Marlborough Road, which intersects Goshen Road. That'll take us to the tavern, which is at the intersection of Goshen and Route 252." He kept driving and driving… and finally slowed the car down. "I think we're actually in *or on the edge of… Ridley Creek State Park? I know*, I know, we don't *want* to be in the Park. Well, you know what Yogi Berra said."

"What?"

*"We're lost, but we're making good time."*

Natalie managed a slight smile despite the cataclysms they'd avoided. "This reminds me of the night of our very first date. I was driving in the heavy rain and fog from Bryn Mawr towards Chadds Ford. The storm brought some trees down and several of the better roads were closed with 'Detour' signs, so I had to go on these tiny back streets taking me in unfamiliar territory. I had no idea where I was, but I kept driving and reached Route 202 South, went down to Baltimore Pike and finally made it to The Chadds Ford Inn."

"Where you were 20 minutes late and I was almost finished my glass of chardonnay, standing on the porch, looking out into the fog thinking *'Well, 30 minutes means you've been stood up, pal…'* Then… *you arrived.*"

"Speaking of arriving- **where the Hell are we?**" Natalie's voice became shrill again as she turned all around, looking up at street signs. "Now that's a strange name- Sandy Flash Drive. I think I've heard that name before."

Jim glanced over at her. "He was a Rev War era outlaw who robbed people around Chester County. I'm thinking we're south of Providence Road. We should probably turn up there. Yes! That's Providence. This'll get us to Goshen Road." The car turned as they approached the Route 252 sign. "Here we go. Should be up there on the… left." After a few minutes, the red brick structure came into view: The Square Tavern sign with a man in Colonial-era garb painted on its front. "I think we can park in back." He cruised slowly into the gravel parking lot.

"*Finally!* I was ready to give up a half-hour ago." Natalie's smirk was quite visible as she exited the car.

"O.K., let's just *enjoy ourselves.*" As they entered the tavern, several people dressed in late 1700s clothing greeted them.

"Welcome! Where you folks from?"

"We drove up from Kennett Square. This place looks very well preserved." Jim walked up to a stout gentleman with a silvery mane and beard. "I'm Jim- this is my wife Natalie. We're new here, but recently joined on-line."

"Excellent. I'm Tom Weathersby- a volunteer here and also a professional sculptor. I'm working on one of a well-known local artist and if you come back into this room, I'll give you the presentation on Newtown Square's most famous resident, Benjamin West." He led the two into a side room with numerous lithographs, paintings and artifacts all around. "This tavern dates to 1742. Benjamin West was born in 1738 on the grounds of what is today Swarthmore College, but his family later moved to this area. His father ran The Square Tavern for a while in the 1740s and 1750s. West showed exceptional artistic skills as a young boy, later studied in Philadelphia and started creating portraits which he sold to earn money. He left the area in 1760 and went to study art in Italy, then later ended up in London and became King George III's favorite artist. Too bad the King didn't always pay him for his work." Weathersby clicked forward through the PowerPoint slides detailing West's life.

Jim's eyebrows rose as he heard this. "King George *stiffed him?*"

"Well, he paid him for *most* of his works, which the King truly enjoyed. Gave West a good living, but he eventually did owe West some money. Benjamin West was the very first American artist to move to Europe and ply his craft; others like John Trumbull, Gilbert Stuart and John Singleton Copley were his students, studying with him there, later becoming famous in their own right. Interestingly, even though the colonies were at war with England, West and the King really hit it off… and they shared something unusual."

Natalie looked right at him. "What was *that?*"

Tom glanced first at her, then back at Jim. "Benjamin West and King George III were *born the same year… and died the same year.*"

"That's interesting. West left Pennsylvania for England. How did he stay neutral while his colony was later fighting *against England*? Seems like a thin line to walk."

Tom grinned. "Somehow he managed to keep his sentiments to himself, which we believe *were* in support of the colonies. His painting '*The Death of General Wolfe*', a famous British officer caught the eye of the King and others in positions of authority and really started his rise to fame."

Jim nodded. "West painted '*Penn's Treaty with the Indians*', based on the Treaty of Shackamaxon, made with the Lenape under a tree along the Delaware, which I think captured a lot of attention in the late 1700s, right?"

"That's correct. He completed it in 1771-1772 when he was a rising star in London. It quickly became one of his most popular works. There are several things in the painting which are not quite accurate, though. He includes large red brick buildings in the background which didn't exist there in the 1680s. Also, it seems to depict an older William Penn- perhaps in his 50s, but when the event occurred, Penn was only about 38. Still, a wonderful painting- one which thousands of people had copied for them and made into a print. The original is at the Pennsylvania Academy of Fine Art in Philadelphia."

Jim's interest was piqued. "It's ironic that the painting depicting friendship and cooperation between Penn and the Indians was, I believe, commissioned by William Penn's son Thomas, whose actions took us in the *other* direction: confrontation and *taking lands from them*, as with the notorious 'Walking Purchase.'"

Tom nodded in sad agreement.

Jim thought of other paintings by West and quickly remembered '*Benjamin Franklin Drawing Electricity from the Sky.*' "His painting of Franklin with his kite in the rainstorm is one I've always loved."

"Oh, yes- also quite popular in the states, completed in 1816 just a few years before he passed away." Tom turned off the presentation and pointed to objects around the room.

Jim followed him. "As I understand it, he didn't completely shy away from painting scenes related to the Revolution. His *'Treaty of Paris'* shows the American commissioners, including John Adams, John Jay and Franklin among others in Paris negotiating the Treaty which ended the war. It's got to be one of the most famous *unfinished* paintings ever created." Jim's glance meandered to nearby walls where other items honoring West hung.

"That is right. Begun in 1783, but never completed. The British commissioners refused to sit for the portrait. So, West decided to leave half the canvas blank."

"Very good discussion and presentation. Can we tour the building?" Jim headed toward the entrance area as Natalie followed close behind.

"Of course. Go upstairs. You'll see several displays- all done by Historical Society members."

Jim carefully climbed the creaky wooden steps behind Natalie and entered a room with a bookshelf on the left, paintings and prints across the walls. "Hey, look here. Some books on… *Sandy Flash.*"

Natalie walked over to the bookcase and leaned in to see some of the titles. "Oh- the guy they named the street after? Maybe he was telling us something, leading us on the drive." They viewed the numerous displays there and in the adjoining room before heading back down the narrow stairway to where the Society members were standing. "You've done an excellent job preserving this building. So, West actually lived here?"

A woman in Colonial garb nodded, then answered. "Well, West's father ran the Inn. It's possible they lived here starting in the mid-1740s, but likely most of the time in a house across the street. Benjamin was young when he left for Europe- only 22 in 1760. He never came back."

"Interesting. Never made it back home to Penn's colony 'across the Pond.'" Natalie admired the rustic fireplace and Colonial-era utensils. "We love this place. We'll be back."

"Glad you enjoyed it. We've also restored the old Paper Mill House and have events there. Check our website for details. Thank you for coming by."

As they walked hand-in-hand to the parking lot, Jim looked back at the structure. "It's a lovely building. We'll have to visit the Paper Mill sometime." As the car weaved its way out onto Route 252, Jim knew it was coming and thought "I bet a hundred bucks she says *'Don't get us lost'*" as he waited at the stoplight.

"Let's not get lost this time, O.K.?" Natalie kept her eyes along the side of the road, where several large trees towered above them.

"Just won $100."

"What are you talking about?"

"*Oh… nothing important.*" Jim couldn't hide his laugh. "Look, we know the way back, so don't worry- we don't need Google Maps and won't end up in Wyoming."

"That name Sandy Flash still sticks in my head for some strange reason. You said he held people up right around here?"

"Yes. I know a few things about him. Real name was James Fitzpatrick; it's believed he became a bandit sometime after he went AWOL during the Revolutionary War. Apparently he was furious with the way the Army had treated him and wanted to get back at the rebels fighting against England- even though he was previously *one of them.*"

"Story sounds intriguing. Maybe worth digging into." She calmed down as the SUV reached West Chester Pike. The car's occupants did not know they were traveling the exact same route the notorious outlaw had traveled centuries before…

**Chester
County
Landscapes**

## The Square Tavern

*Penn's Treaty with the Indians* by Benjamin West

*Treaty of Paris* by Benjamin West

*Benjamin Franklin Drawing Electricity from the Sky* by Benjamin West

*The Death of General Wolfe* by Benjamin West

Benjamin West self portrait

# Chapter 2

Frank Robinson, Tony DiAngelo and Sal Esposito sat at the cheap Formica table inside Frank's Coatesville apartment. All three had done time in prison. In their late 30s- early 40s, they wondered where their lives were leading them, to some form of success or… back to confinement if they didn't find some money soon. Tony fidgeted with a plastic PEZ dispenser he'd found abandoned in the parking lot. Sal was trying to get his watch to work, banging it onto the table in hopes of making the mechanism kick into gear. Frank stood up to command their attention.

"O.K., I got it all figured out. I heard from some of my buddies on the street and they say this'll work. It's easy. We drive around rich neighborhoods and keep our eyes out for all the mailboxes with their 'FLAGS' up. That means they have outgoing mail and some of them have checks to pay their utility bills, checks going to charities, basically money waiting to be lifted. So, we go to those mailboxes, open 'em when nobody's lookin' and take out everything that looks like it's a bill or might have checks. We get back here, open the envelopes and get the checks, change the dollar amounts and *make 'em out to us!* They got these Ink Erasers now that can take off almost anything written down. I just bought a few. I'm tellin' ya, we can pull in *a TON* of money!"

Sal wasn't anywhere near convinced. "So, where do we cash 'em?"

Frank was ready for questions. "We cash the first ones at each of our banks- where we already have accounts set up- then use part of the cash to open up *new accounts* at banks around the area, where we cash other checks if things seem to be gettin' hot. Hell, we can even go to those check-cashing places- *who cares if they take 10%?* It'd be 10% of money we never had anyhow! The other 90% is for us. It's a cinch!!"

Tony started to grin. "Sounds good. When do we start? I'm broke."

Frank patted him on the back. "That's what I wanted to hear! We start tomorrow around dusk, when most people put stuff in their mailboxes for next day's pick-up. I know a lot of rich neighborhoods to cruise where we'll have some good pickins…"

# Chapter 3

*"Be quick, now! Hand over the money!" cried Fortune, thrusting the pistol an inch nearer.*

*With his wicked eyes and shining teeth, Barton imagined that he beheld a devil.*

*"Did you ever hear of Sandy Flash?" said the robber.*

-Bayard Taylor (1825-1878), *The Story of Kennett*

******************************************************************

Natalie walked out onto the patio surrounded by the coneflowers, cleomes, impatiens and Solomon seals she had planted, which thrived under the two cherry trees flanking the outdoor chairs they'd recently purchased. As she bent down to peer into the small Fairy Garden tub standing at the patio's edge, she could hear footsteps approaching from the basement door.

"The garden's glorious- in full bloom. You get an A+, sweetie." Jim strode up to her and gave her lips a brief kiss.

"Thank you. It's been a lot of effort. Weeds never sleep." Admiring her work, she looked right at Jim. "What did you think of The Square Tavern?"

"I like the place. Rustic, very historic. They've done a superb job maintaining it. I'd go back."

"I was thinking, since in some strange way a 'Flash' seemed to be *guiding us* there- I'd like to check out that shelf filled with books on him. Another visit sometime?"

"Sure. When do you want to go?" Jim walked over to the sculptures of the three kitties on the upper patio and bent down to touch each one.

"We said that we wanted to visit their other site, the Paper Mill House and maybe we could do both in one day. They're pretty close to each other." Natalie held the hose as she sprayed water all along the edge of the garden, making sure she reached each plant and the hanging baskets nearby.

Jim nodded. "Let me check out Futhey and Cope first. They might have something on Flash- actually Fitzpatrick. Want to do a late breakfast at Floga, then head over?"

"Sure. I'll be out here; you can do some quick reading and then we'll go."

He headed up the stone steps to the terrace and went directly to the large bookcase in the Family Room. "Futhey and Cope: *History of Chester County*- the 'Bible'. Let's see what you've got on this guy." He pulled the heavy, black leather-bound oversized book from the shelf. "I could get Schwarzenegger biceps just *doing curls* with this thing." Two full pages described Fitzpatrick. Born in Doe Run, working for a time as an apprentice blacksmith, joining the militia in 1776 to fight alongside the Continental Army, but later deserted while in New

York after being flogged for insubordination, swam across the Hudson River and made his way back to Chester County. A footnote states:

*"The readers of Bayard Taylor's 'Story of Kennett' will remember the personages who figure therein under the names of Sandy Flash and Dougherty. These characters appear to be based upon those of two celebrated bandits who flourished in Chester County during the years 1777 and 1778, bearing the names of James Fitzpatrick and Mordecai Dougherty, and who were for a considerable time the terror of the Whig citizens of the county."*

Jim held the leatherbound book open, then flipped ahead a few pages, hoping to see a sketch of the man- but there were none and he thought for a few seconds. *"That's* where I know this guy from! It's been a few years since I read *The Story of Kennett.* This is the *real-life* outlaw that the character Sandy Flash is based upon. I assumed it was total fiction, but he was an actual person." Jim felt energized and walked out onto the terrace. "Hey hon- let's go to breakfast. We'll check out this bandit."

Natalie put the hose down, turned it off and started walking up the stairs, along the clematis vines, petunias, sage and Angelonia spreading their lavender and pale aqua flowers along the edge of the wrought iron banister. *"What* bandit?"

"Sandy Flash- formally James Fitzpatrick. Futhey and Cope have a good summary; now I'm charged up to find out more about him and read some of the books on him at The Square Tavern, which is where we're heading right after we eat."

"Hold your horses! I thought we said we'd check out the Paper Mill House first, then go back over to the Tavern."

"O.K. Paper Mill first, then the Tavern. I actually like the idea of going to a tavern first thing in the morning. They did that often in Colonial times to discuss business, crops, the weather, politics."

As they entered Floga Bistro, the raven-haired waitress with a friendly face and Greek accent said "Hello! Sit wherever you like."

Jim nodded and walked over to the third booth from the door, then waited for Natalie to take her seat first. "We can make this a quick breakfast. I'm craving… **Scrapple!**"

"You know how they make that, right?"

"Delectable, prime cuts of filet mignon, pork tenderloin and veal?"

*"Not… exactly.* It's all the scraps of meat leftover from the cuttings. The stuff they normally throw away. They grind it all up, add some spices and press it together in a big vat, then cut it into little blocks, kind of like another delicacy- Spam. That's what you'll be ingesting." Natalie waited for his response.

"They should just take away the *'S'* and be up front about it."

*"Very nutritious…"*

"Point taken… but here they make it *just right*: a nice, big slice, really crispy on the outside, still tender inside. I only order it as a treat every once in a while."

Just then, the waitress came up to them, laying the menus on the table. "Good to see you. Anything to drink- coffee, juice?"

Natalie spoke first. "Just ice water for me, but I already know what I want- biscuits and gravy." She glanced up at her and waited to make sure she had it written down.

Jim was quick. "I'll have coffee, the veggie omelet with cheddar cheese, rye toast- and a side of… *SCRAPPLE!* You folks make the best Scrapple in the hemisphere." He gave her a quick grin as she giggled. The waitress jotted down the order before walking away to the kitchen. Looking at Natalie, he became more serious. "So, do you think we'll find out much about Sandy Flash from the books there at the Tavern?"

"I hope so. I noticed at least four or five of them, maybe more. The shelf was overflowing with books. Must be something there of interest. I also saw a side room with several displays on local history. Not sure, but I believe one was on him. After we see the Paper Mill House, we'll go over and explore a bit more." She glanced around the restaurant where only two other tables were filled with diners. "Pretty slow here today."

Jim noticed the waitress coming back from the kitchen with their orders, placing the ice water and coffee first, then their meals on the table. Jim took a long sip from his mug, looking right up at her. ***"Honey, THAT'S a great cup of coffee!"***

"Ignore him. It's from a television commercial *about 50 years ago*."

Jim laughed. "Great service and good food: a nice combination."

The waitress smiled at him as she walked back to the kitchen. They both dug into their food, Jim looking around to the other booths as he sipped his coffee. "We're here at a good time- a quick serve and… we'll be out on the road soon." As they ate, a few more customers entered and sat near a beautiful painting of a scene from Venice hanging on the wall.

"Here's your check; pay whenever you're ready." The dark-haired waitress started to turn around, but Jim was already pulling out his wallet. "Here, this'll cover it- and thanks so much for the prompt turnaround." The cash he laid down included more than a 20% tip. Then his eyes met Natalie's. "You ready?"

She nodded as they both got up and walked out the door.

The historic three-story tan and brown stone building constructed nearly two centuries ago stands along Darby Creek, its walls still strong after decades of wind, rain, hail and snow, providing a home to families who worked at the Crosley Woolen Mill and nearby Garrett's Union Paper Mill. By the 1980s, the structure was in ruins, its roof gone, the building abandoned, ready to collapse. A group of local citizens realized its importance and dedicated themselves to restoring and preserving the site, their effort the spark for what became the Newtown Square Historical Preservation Society. They created a replica of a mid-19th century General Store inside and included numerous artifacts and paintings telling the story of the area.

As Jim and Natalie walked through the pale-yellow wood-framed doorway, he grinned seeing an oversized, 6-foot square framed map of Philadelphia and vicinity dating to the mid-1800s.

"Welcome to the Paper Mill House. Have you visited here before?" The chestnut-haired woman in a flowery dress had a welcoming smile which made them feel right at home.

"No, but we recently joined the Society and took a tour of the Tavern last week. We thought we'd see this before going back there today." Jim liked the map and inspected it up close before turning around to peer into an adjoining room.

"That's our General Store. Feel free to wander around."

Natalie was first in, strolling past a black, cast-iron wooden stove, then stopping at a counter holding dozens of items from the mid-19th century. "Jim, look at this: an old grain grinder, probably used for corn. Bottled honey, tins of cocoa, Mason jars of every size. This place is wonderful." Pots and pans hanging from the rafters nurtured the thought that the place was a workingman's store meeting the needs of the community.

"I love it. This must have taken quite a bit of work." He strolled into the room off to the left and stopped before a series of yard-high posters on the wall illustrated with stories of local history hanging above well-preserved signs from centuries ago. Nearby clear-glass cabinets showcased utensils, tools, pottery and items used by citizens who lived by candlelight and horse-and-buggy. "Hey hon, check this poster out. 'The Legend of Sandy Flash: The Highwayman of Castle Rock.' Here's our guy."

She came and stood beside him. "Nicely done. Says he was an itinerant blacksmith who worked in several locations around southern Chester County. Maybe there'll be a lot to explore." After admiring the posters describing the heritage of Bartram's Bridge, the Octagonal Schoolhouse and other sites, she smiled. "These displays are superb. Wish the Society near us had things this good for visitors." After wandering out toward the small gift shop, she looked at her watch and turned toward Jim: "Want to get moving? We should try to get over to the Tavern."

"Sure." Jim nodded to the woman who greeted them. "Thanks very much. You've done a great job here. We'll come back for another visit sometime." As they got into the car, Jim thought of the irony. *"Some thief who robbed people deserves a poster in an historical society? Must be a lot more to this story..."*

Natalie was already buckled up. "I want to check out those books upstairs on Sandy Flash. That's where I'm going first when we're in the Tavern." Knowing the way from their previous trip, she was more relaxed on the roadway. As they approached the building, she wondered. "Maybe as Members, we might be allowed to borrow the books to do some research." The car came to a stop in the parking lot; she got out and quickly walked toward the back door with her hand in Jim's.

"Hello again. We were here last week and wanted to check out some things up on the second floor-like the bookcase. Is that O.K.?" Jim waited for the man in the tri-cornered hat to reply before he went toward the stairs.

The gentleman looked a bit puzzled, but managed a quick "*Uhh- sure… go ahead.*"

Natalie preceded him on the stairs. He was just a few feet behind her as she entered the second-floor room where they saw the bookcase the previous week. "Where *is it?* There's **nothing here!**" Natalie's bewildered eyes looked first to the left along the wall where she had seen it, then all around the room and into the next one. **No bookcase.** *Anywhere.* "I *swear* there was a bookcase here filled with books- for sure four or five on Sandy Flash. I can picture the book covers in my mind; they were brightly colored, with images on the front. I **know it!!**"

Jim peered all around the room, then walked into the adjacent room and explored the entire space. "No bookcase. No *books.* This is… *very strange*" He thought back to last week. He definitely saw the same bookcase Natalie had seen and knew exactly where it had stood. "I'll go downstairs and check; they *must* have moved it." He rushed back down the creaky wooden steps and went right up to the man they'd just seen as they were entering the place. "Excuse me- we were looking for the bookcase upstairs. Did you take it out- move it somewhere?"

The man was just as confused as he'd been when he first spoke to them coming in. "There's *never* been a bookcase up there. We don't even **own** a bookcase- although I wish we did. I have some great books on history I'd like to bring in." The other Guide standing near him nodded her agreement. She eyed Jim's face, which showed complete disbelief.

Jim thought for several seconds… then quickly turned and *ran up the stairs* to stand in front of Natalie. "I don't know how to explain this, but the Guide downstairs says there has **NEVER** been a bookcase here." He could see Natalie racking her brain to explain the mystery.

"I am **absolutely certain** there was a bookcase here. **You saw it! I saw it!!** Either someone is playing a strange trick on us or…"

Jim cut her off as he chuckled. "*… or maybe Sandy Flash doesn't want us to dig too deep into his past…*"

Natalie was clearly flustered. "O.K. This is *way* too bizarre. We're logical people. We both agree there *WAS* a bookcase here. This must be some kind of clue. Maybe in some strange way… something- or someone- is guiding us to find out more about him and local history. This might take some effort, *but it could also be interesting*."

"One rises to meet a challenge." Jim grinned as Natalie shook her head. "I want to ask the Guides a few questions. Let's go downstairs." As he came up to the same man who he spoke with a minute before, he stopped. "Look, I'm sorry for the confusion. Maybe we were thinking of someplace else, but I have some things to clear up. One- did Benjamin West's family run the Tavern when Sandy Flash was terrorizing the area?"

The Guide spoke quickly. "No. They ran it over 20 years *before* his robbing days."

"Thanks for that. Did Flash- James Fitzpatrick- ever stop here at the Tavern?"

"Well, we don't have specific documentation, but Bayard Taylor's book mentions him being here at least once. According to Taylor's story- remember, that was *a novel*- he supposedly stopped in for a drink at the same time that dozens of armed local militia were relaxing here as they were trying to track him down. Held them all at gunpoint, had his drink, then left. **He got away!** The story goes, everyone there was completely befuddled as to what had happened."

Jim eyed Natalie, then the Guide. "We appreciate the information."

"Sure. You're welcome here anytime. Thank you for coming by."

**The Paper Mill House**

## The Paper Mill House General Store and Exhibit Room

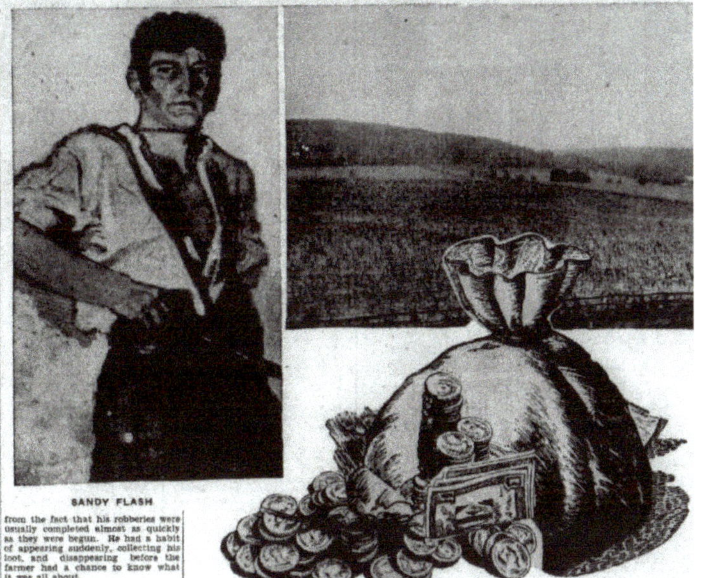

Article on Sandy Flash in *The Sunday News* March 3, 1935

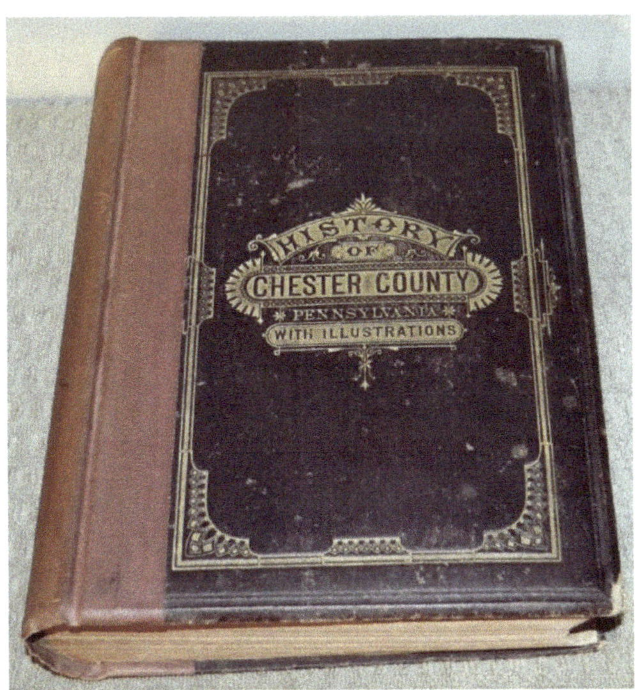

*History of Chester County*
by J. Smith Futhey and Gilbert Cope

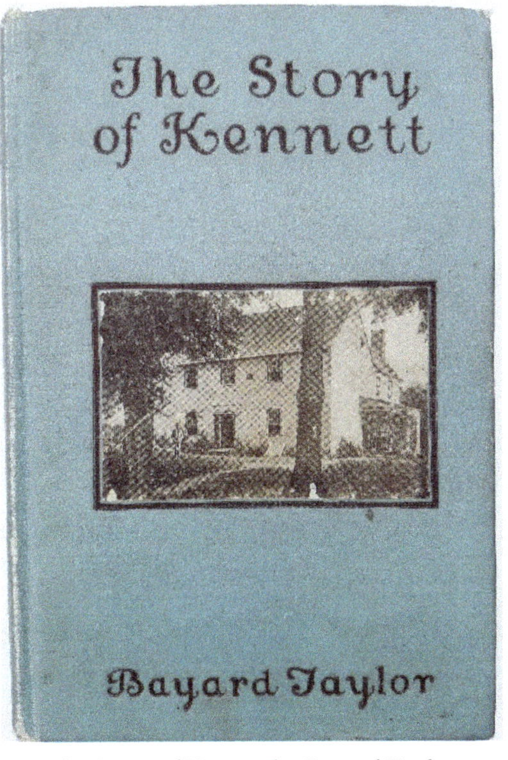

*The Story of Kennett* by Bayard Taylor

# Chapter 4

As the evening approached, the sun close to the horizon, Frank was in the best mood in years. "O.K. Tony, you're gonna' drive. Sal, you're in the front seat, lookin' all around to make sure nobody sees us. If you see somebody, tell Tony right away and we get outta' there. I'll be in the back seat. I'm in good shape, so I'll be ready to run out to each mailbox and grab the letters."

Sal was still skeptical. "Whose car do we use? Somebody might see us- get our plate and model to rat to the cops."

Frank's smile denoted a confidence far above his cohorts. "No problem. My pal Vinny Delgado runs an auto-body repair here in Coatesville. All legit- except in the back. He has a chop-shop where he takes in old clunkers after offering top dollar for 'em- and gives each seller an *extra $500* so he can keep the license plate: far more than they'd have to pay to get a new one on their next car. You'd be surprised at how many people take him up on it! Vinny's a master mechanic, a damn good welder and auto-body repair guy. He can fix anything; takes in dented fenders and crunched side doors and makes 'em new again. Then he uses different body parts and fits 'em onto other cars. Takes off the hood ornaments and brand logos from each one, so you can't tell what kind of car it is! He uses the license plates, which are still good- and puts 'em on each re-made car. He's a *friggin' genius!*"

Tony shook his head. "So? It's still a car people can recognize, right?"

"Nope. I've seen some of 'em. You can't tell if it's a Ford, a Chevy or a Toyota. The guy does great work!"

Tony still wasn't convinced. "Yeah... but if we use the same car every time, somebody'll report it to the cops!"

"*Think I'm stupid?* Vinny chops dozens of cars, rents 'em out to people for each 'occasion'- if you know what I mean. He owes me *big time* for some favors I did for him couple years back, so he'll give us a different car- no charge- each time we need one." The troops followed Frank out to the grey, 4-door sedan parked out in front of his building.

Tony was starting to become more optimistic. "Hey, Frank- what kind of car is *this?*"

"That's what I'm sayin', numb nuts. I can't tell. The *cops* can't tell. Looks like a cross between a Honda Accord and a Toyota Camry, but don't quote me on it. Anybody who sees us won't have a clue what kind of car it is. Get in- we're leavin.'"

Cruising around West Chester at dusk, Frank called the shots. "O.K., slow down. Tony- drive up to that tan house on the right. See the 'FLAG' up on their mailbox? Stop right out in front- **NOW!**" The car skidded to a quick stop. Seeing no one around, Sal gave him the go-ahead.  Frank jumped out, sprinted up to the mailbox and grabbed every long envelope which looked like a bill, then jumped back inside the car. "See- *it's easy!* There's another 'FLAG' up at the end of this block- over there. *Let's hit it!!*" Tony gunned the engine, then came to a quick stop again. Frank exited the car, ran up to the box, grabbing just about everything inside and got back in the car. The team robbed five different mailboxes easily, like they were stealing from children. Arriving back at Frank's apartment, he took their haul up the stairs, opened his door and laid their winnings out onto the table. "Now, here's the tricky part. We have to each wear a pair of these plastic gloves. I hate 'em, but they're useful- so *we don't leave prints* on the checks for the cops to find. Whenever we handle checks- **you gotta' wear gloves!**"

Sal was waiting to see how it really worked. "So, exactly HOW do we change these checks? Somebody's gonna' see the writing and know it's fake- *and turn us in!!*"

Frank was ready for that. "No, they won't. These Ink Erasers work like a charm. Watch this." He took out one of the checks, put it flat on the table, dabbed its narrow tip gingerly on the writing, erasing both the dollar amount and payee easily, with no trace of a 'missing margin' to alert the viewer. "Here's the trick: you don't want to change it to a really *big* number. I say just $1,000… $2,000 tops. That avoids suspicion- *and the $10,000* limit the Feds are always lookin' for. Then we just write in *our* name, like this- *with the right color ink*- and take it to the bank! One thing- *ALWAYS WEAR A HAT*- and some kind of regular-type gloves when you cash the checks. Leave no prints. Best hats to use have a brim on front, like a baseball cap, so they cover not only your hair, but part of your face. That way, nobody- and none of the cameras- get a good look at you…"

Tony grinned. "Hell, we can deposit checks by phone now. No one even sees you." He stared as Frank did the same trick with two other checks, adding $11,000 to their pool of funds. "I gotta' hand it to ya', Frank. This looks damn good. Easiest money I made since I worked Summers at Gino's and 'lifted' almost $100 every week from their cash drawers. We're back in business!"

Frank wrapped his arms around the crew and spoke. "We *ARE*… back in the money… and I got a list of at least 20 different neighborhoods not too far from here we can collect from."

**Mailbox thief courtesy of iStock**

# Chapter 5

*"When we take a survey of Mankind in general, and of the several requisites by which life is rendered comfortable and desirable, the productions of the Vegetable Kingdom are amongst the foremost; as affording the principal necessaries, conveniences, and luxuries of life."*          -Humphry Marshall (1722-1801), *Arbustum Americanum*

*The man in his 40s walked through the room which held his hundreds of seeds and plant specimens, each identified with its genus and species, along with a brief description of its biological characteristics, size, color, shape and potential practical and medicinal uses. He knew there were dozens of people here in the colonies, Benjamin Franklin and many others in England and throughout Europe who wanted samples of these to plant in their gardens. As he strolled past the table which also held his prized microscope and a new addition to his collection- a telescope to scan the Heavens, his face broke out in a wide grin.*

*************************************************************************

As they sat on the couch talking, Natalie was still in disbelief. "You're not joking with me, right? You *did* see the bookcase there last week, correct?"

"Bookcase? **What** bookcase??"

"Don't be a bean-brain! Seriously- you saw it. I didn't hallucinate this." Her eyebrows were raised to their upper limit.

"No, we're not hallucinating, although I knew some guys in college who rearranged their chromosomes that way a few times. Me: *never*."

"Stop joking!"

"Not my cup of tea. Drank a fair amount of beer, though."

"Will you be *SERIOUS*??"

"O.K…. O.K… No, you and I were *NOT* hallucinating. I saw the **same bookcase** you did. It was *THERE*. I am **absolutely certain**- and I did see some books about Sandy Flash on the shelf."

"So- *what does this all mean?*" She was shaking her head, trying to find some logical explanation.

"The Lord works in strange ways. For some reason, He brought us onto the trail of a late 18th century highwayman and *I guess* wants us to dig into local history. Hey: Flash worked as a blacksmith around the area and *we* know a wonderfully preserved 18th century blacksmith shop not too far away."

"In Marshallton?"

"Exactly. Let's go there, take a look around and ask Linda some questions. She's probably familiar with this story. Who knows? We might even find something interesting stuffed away amidst all the artifacts there in her shop."

"Sounds good to me. I think they're open right now." She got up after petting Frankie's head as the kitty slept next to her. Jim was already in the kitchen grabbing his car keys.

The weathered stone face of the old Blacksmith Shop in Marshallton reminds visitors of its longevity, the rustic fieldstone façade enlivened with maroon-painted wood trim around the seven windows, faced out towards the street where riders once brought their horses in for a new pair of shoes. The horsehair within the walls reveals its link to pre-Revolutionary War days, where James Woodward and Thomas England worked their hammers from 1750 up to 1809. The structure stands just up the road from Martin's Tavern, where travelers could quench their thirst and some guests in 1777 spotted British troops approaching before the Battle of the Brandywine.

"Linda- how are you?" Jim approached the desk where she sat inside the shop greeting visitors from behind a stack of newly arrived items donated for sale there.

"Wonderful.  You and Natalie both well?" She didn't stand because of the ankle injury which still affected her stability.

"Doing great. It's good to see you!" Natalie moved to the edge of the desk and gave her a brief hug. "You've gotten a bunch of new things in- a lot to sell for raising funds."

"Always. People are very generous- and I'm grateful for all *your* donations. If you see something you like, I'll give you a good price."

Jim ambled over to the side room where two newly donated pianos stood. "You take *pianos?*"

"Anything that might sell, to raise money in support of Martin's Tavern. Those came in not long ago; I think someone will buy them. I know you're interested in old maps. We got some in recently- over there to the right, past the large desk."

Jim maneuvered gingerly around the mass of items stacked all around him- pottery, plates, silverware, framed lithographs, paintings, old books, candlestick holders, glassware- all from a bygone era. Lying on an antiquarian wooden table, he saw what appeared to be tattered pieces of heavy paper barely held within cracked wooden frames. Leaning down, he examined each one, picking them up, hoping his grip did not break them apart. "Hey, these look interesting. One is a map of Chester County dated 1847. Another with no date looks even older, maybe… around 1800?"

Linda glanced over at where he stood. "Yes, those are all quite old. I wasn't able to get an estimate of their value, so if one interests you, just let me know."

Natalie wandered around the other side of the shop. "Do you have any pewter? We're trying to furnish the old Eusebius Barnard house, now called Barnard Station and they're looking for pewter plates." She picked up one small grey metal plate which had the appearance of pewter, but could tell from its light weight it was not.

"We do occasionally get in pewter, but I don't think we have any right now. I'm sorry."

"Oh, no problem. If you get some dinner sized pewter plates, roughly 8-10 inches diameter- please let me know." Natalie examined the side wall where each table held dozens of fragile mementos from the last century.

"Hey, I found one I like." Jim held up a dilapidated map of southern Chester County which had the earmarks of having been produced centuries ago. Its weathered pine frame was barely holding itself together, so he held two corners gently. "How much?" as he strode towards the front desk.

"For you, I'll do $20. Is that O.K.?"

"Oh, of course." He took out a bill bearing Andrew Jackson's face from his wallet and laid it in front of her. "You're very kind. This might be worth *ten times* that much."

"I really don't know, but I don't have the expertise to accurately value everything that comes in. We're really short on help. Most days, it's just me. I know some things about antiques, but I'm not an expert. I think that's a fair price. Enjoy it!"

"You've probably heard of the Rev War outlaw Sandy Flash, right?" Jim watched her place the money in her drawer, hoping for an answer with helpful information.

"Sure. The highwayman- terror of Chester County way back when."

"It was 1777-1778, I believe… I've learned a bit about him as we're digging into his past. Apparently he was indignant after being harshly punished for insubordination, went AWOL- and dedicated himself to robbing people- especially tax collectors and anyone who appeared to support the patriot cause fighting against England. He was trained as a blacksmith and I've read that he worked all around Doe Run and the surrounding region- as a journeyman. Do you think he could have made it here to Marshallton?"

"Quite possibly. This blacksmith shop was started around 1750… so it would be the right time period."

"What about Martin's Tavern, down the road? Wasn't that here… around the 1760s?" Jim raised his eyebrows, waiting for confirmation.

"Yes, 1764. Here before the Revolution. If Sandy Flash traveled around this area, there's a decent chance he stopped in for some sustenance. I don't have any specific information on that, but perhaps letters from people like Squire Cheyney who were there right before the Battle of the Brandywine might shed some light."

Jim's curiosity was piqued, knowing the area was so steeped in history. "Isn't the house of Humphry Marshall- the famous botanist- right down the road, too? I know there's an historical marker by the side of what looks like his property, but the area is surrounded with trees and bushes, so you can't really see the house."

"Yes, Marshall's home is still standing there, built in the 1740s. I know the people who live there today. He's buried across the street in the yard of the Bradford Friends Meetinghouse. I can take you there if you like." Linda cleared some candlesticks from her desk and put them on a cabinet nearby.

"Absolutely. I'd enjoy seeing the spot where he's buried. I'd love even more to get into the house." He noticed Natalie was walking towards the door to meet them both.

"Well, I could give you the contact information for the family who lives there, but don't get your hopes up. They're very private and rarely interact with people. We can walk down to the Meetinghouse now; it'll just take a few minutes. Marshall's father Abraham was one of the founders of the Meeting. NOTE- most Quakers did *not* use a fancy tombstone. They were very plain, usually with just their name and the year they passed away. Marshall doesn't even *have* a tombstone; we just know roughly where he was buried. I can't stay there long, because I'll have to come back to the shop."

As they advanced down the paved street, Jim imagined characters who roamed what were then dusty, poorly defined dirt roads, many of them Indian paths, more than two centuries before. "In my research, I've come across several interesting characters who were all around here at about the same time: Humphry Marshall, the outlaw James Fitzpatrick, a native American they called Indian Hannah…"

Linda's eyes perked up. "Yes, I believe Indian Hannah stayed on Marshall's property at one point. She lived from around 1730 to 1802; in her later years, she was unable to care for herself, so several of the local Quakers formed a group to take care of her."

"I know they made a pact titled *'Kindness Extended'*, pledging support for her. They have a copy of it at the Chester County History Center." Jim peered over at Natalie, who seemed eager to get to the cemetery. All three exited the Blacksmith Shop and headed towards the Meetinghouse property.

"They did. We won't go *into* the Meetinghouse, but over there is where a tree once stood, under which Marshall was buried. There's no gravestone, so the precise spot is not clear." Linda pointed to a patch of grass as she glanced over at Natalie standing near her.

"It's strange: wasn't Marshall one of the most famous botanists of his day- yet they didn't even give him a simple gravestone?"

"Fair point- it doesn't seem right, does it?" Linda watched as Jim strode to the spot where Marshall's remains were likely buried. "Remember, Quakers- especially way back then- were people who believed in a very simple life, no pretensions, plain clothes…"

"*Nuthin' fancy…*" Natalie laughed as she said it, looking over at Jim- who nodded with a grin.

"What are the chances I can get into his house?" Jim stared directly at Linda.

"Between slim and none. A well-known artist, Adrian Martinez helped celebrate Marshall's 300th birthday a few years back. He painted a lovely portrait of Marshall and I believe met the people who live there. You may want to contact him."

"Yes, we were there at the celebration and we've met Adrian- wonderful guy and really outstanding artist. I believe we have his contact info, don't we Natalie?"

"Of course- I bought one of his paintings, *remember?* I enjoyed meeting him and his wife Leah- very nice people." Natalie peered over at their host, wondering if she needed to get back, signaling quietly to Jim for them both to get moving.

"Well, this was wonderful, Linda. Thank you for taking us here. I'd like to go inside the Meetinghouse at some point as well. I'm sure you're ready to go back to the store."

They proceeded back to the Blacksmith Shop, but before they reached it, Jim said "We'll be in touch. I'm going to have this old map re-framed and I'll let you know if I can get hold of Adrian."

"Great to see you both!" Linda proceeded inside the store, her cane assisting her.

As Jim and Natalie got inside the car, he thought about Strode's Mill on the way back- another historic structure- which was also there at the time of the Battle of the Brandywine.

Natalie glanced out the window as the car rolled past the Marshall historic marker, wondering as Jim did about all the personalities who lived around there hundreds of years ago… and she started to daydream about meeting Marshall, Hannah and others who knew them. "I wonder if it's even remotely possible that we can actually get *into* the Marshall house? Your estimate?"

"From what Linda said, about ZERO… but maybe… we can just get *onto the property to see* the house. That would be good enough for me." As they drove West on Route 162, Jim thoughts paralleled Natalie's… and he imagined Hannah and Marshall together by the side of the road they were now on.

**********************************************************************

In Frank's seedy apartment, the crew had dozens of envelopes laid out on his cluttered table. After they each put on their gloves, they got to work. Check after check was 'doctored', with almost no trace of what they had done. The ringleader smiled as he saw each of his guys complete their work.

"*Frank, you're the man!!* I count right here… $17,000- all for me. That doesn't include what Sal has… or yours!" Tony's grin widened as he recounted all the checks.

"I say we're gonna' clear well over fifty grand – *easy*- this month alone. Can't wait to see how much we can pull in after a year doin' this! Best con job I ever pulled- and I say nobody finds us out: no prints, no paper trail, nuthin'. We're on our way, boys…"

Sal was ecstatic. "Hey, Frank! You're a history buff, right? Way back when, they had a word for guys like us. We make our money *on the road*. We're whatcha' call… '*Highwaymen*…'"

"That we are."

**Blacksmith Shop, Marshallton, Pennsylvania**

Bradford Friends Meeting, Marshallton, Pennsylvania

Martin's Tavern, Marshallton, Pa.

*Meeting at Martin's Tavern* **by artist Adrian Martinez**

*Humphrey Marshall*
**by artist Adrian Martinez**

# Chapter 6

*"This day my country was confirmed to me… 'Tis a clear and just thing, and my God that has given it me through many difficulties will, I believe, bless and make it the seed of a nation…"*     -William Penn (1644-1718)

*The man in his late 30s sporting a tri-cornered hat walked towards the marshy area filled with cattails and meadow grasses along the river to the East, surveying the beginning of construction of the country home he had personally designed. Standing along the great river which separated it from the Jerseys, the house, farm and gardens would be a refuge, a blessing from the Creator which his cousin William Markham had purchased from the local Lenape Indians for 2,164 British pounds worth of goods and supplies. He had great plans for his estate that he hoped would provide respite from the bustle and noise of his 'Green country Towne' 26 miles to the south. He did not know then, in the Year of Our Lord Sixteen Hundred and eighty-three that the land granted to him from King Charles II- and the system of government he planned to establish- would dramatically alter the course of American history.*

********************************************************************

Jim sat at their table flipping through *Pennsylvania: The Colonial Years* by Joseph J. Kelly, Jr. A page showing two antiquated documents laid before him: the top one, dated August 3, 1681 written by the first council of Penn's new colony, promising to run *"true and well… the Government of the sd* (sic) *Province…"*; the lower one stating *"… Penn's first written treaty with the Delaware Indians made in 1683."* The word *written* grabbed his attention. "I know there's been a long-running dispute as to whether another treaty made by Penn guaranteed the Indians land ownership rights along the Brandywine, for one mile on either side, from a spot in Chester County all the way down into the state of Delaware, but no one has ever found it."

"Reading anything interesting?" Natalie came up to his side and gave him a hug.

"I was just thinking- to understand more about the local settlers and their relations with the Lenape, we really have to go all the way back to William Penn and *his* interactions with them. As I understand it, several books have been written on whether the local Indians were given legal rights to land along the Brandywine by Penn himself- land which was later taken from them due to the onslaught of settlers. Unfortunately, there appears to be no proof of the Indians' claims, even though they apparently fought it in court for years."

"I've read the same thing; nobody seems to be able to prove it, but it would be wonderful to *find* that document… if it exists." Natalie sipped her coffee watching him at the table pouring over the book.

Just then, he looked up. "Idea: Penn's home still exists; it's called Pennsbury Manor, in Bucks County- and they're open for visitors!"

"What- you're going to *drive out and see it?*"

"Why not? How often do you get to walk the same ground and stroll inside the house where William Penn lived? It's along the Delaware River."

"… and *when* are you thinking of doing this trek?"

"Today! I'm up for a drive; it's not that far. If I leave soon, I'll be back before Happy Hour. What do you think?" Jim got up from the table and wrapped his arms around her, hoping for a "YES."

"You probably have to take the Turnpike, right? You know how much I *hate* it when you're on roads like that… and I-95."

"I know. I promise ***I'll be extremely careful***, O.K.?"

Natalie's grin remained cautious. "One thing you can count on…"

"What's that?" Jim's eyebrows perked upwards.

"Most people out on the roads today are *whacked out.* No way to be safe."

"Wait a minute. I checked up on that. You **can** drive safe- in a Bradley Armored Fighting Vehicle. Six-inches of steel plate all around. Not a problem."

Natalie shook her head, but could tell from his tone that he was quite intent on going. "I used to love going out driving. Not anymore. People drift into your lane while they look at their cell phone and nearly kill you."

"I used to like driving, too. It was a chance to take in some nice scenery- not the Emergency Room."

"All right… but *PLEASE* watch out for those maniacs. It's not *you* I'm worried about- you're an excellent driver. It's *THEM.* They're the ones who are reckless and cause accidents. Give me a hug." Her frowning face revealed her uneasiness.

"I'll be good. Hey, *gotta' go* if I want to be back by 4:00 p.m. for cocktails." He grabbed the binder which held his notes. "Love you- and I love the kitties. See you soon."

The red brick structure with 12 windows facing the Delaware River sits on 42 acres out of an estate originally more than 8,000 where the founder of the Keystone State lived beginning in 1683. Pennsbury Manor was Penn's peaceful haven away from his newly created Philadelphia. Today managed and run by the Pennsylvania Historical and Museum Commission with the assistance of the Pennsbury Society, the site with more than a dozen structures including a boat house, the kitchen house, the manor house, stables, blacksmith shop and outbuildings was once nearly lost to history. Left to deteriorate into a state of near total collapse in the decades following his death in 1718, Pennsbury Manor was reconstructed beginning in 1937. It was reopened in 1939 as a center honoring the legacy of one of the most important statesmen of the Colonial era, whose ideas encapsulated in Pennsylvania government preceded many principles enshrined more than a century later in the *U.S. Constitution*. Today the site stands as a shining monument to the man who helped forge what would be called the 'cradle of liberty' in a colony which became a major force in the development of the young nation.

As Jim advanced toward the Visitor's Center at the front of the complex of buildings, the door opened. "Hi, I'm Doug, the site Director. Welcome to Pennsbury Manor."

"Jim Peterson. Great to meet you. I've done some reading on William Penn and have long wanted to come here. Can we actually go through the house he lived in?"

"Sure. There are several buildings we'll walk past, but you're talking about the Manor House, which is open. Follow me. Do you have any questions right up front?" Doug turned into the hallway of the Visitor's Center after shaking his hand, pointing to the Library and nearby gift shop. "We can stop in there, if you like, after the tour."

"Well, yes. I have some questions regarding Penn's relations with the local Indians- the Lenni-Lenape and the 'treaties' they signed. In my research, they appear to be closer to agreements of *cooperation* and uses of land, is that right?" Jim watched Doug's face for an answer.

"There were several so-called treaties, but they weren't exactly the same as what we understand today, as between two nations generally focused on resolving a conflict of some sort. They were usually intended to promote peaceful interaction between Penn and the Lenape, often regarding a particular tract of acreage."

"That's what I thought." Jim followed him as they walked outside on a gravel path fringed with trees. "So, where did Penn live?"

"That's up ahead- the Manor House. Over to your right are stables and the blacksmith shop. On your left are the Kitchen House and Garden. You'll see his home as reconstructed in the late 1930s. We can go inside."

The two men entered through the white door which was fringed by solid red brick all around. A warm, welcoming feeling hit Jim as he followed close behind his guide. "I can kind of sense… *him here…*"

"A lot of people say that." Doug started his narrative. "This was William Penn's country estate- and it was a fully functioning, working farm. Situated along the Delaware River, its rich soil supported the growing of wheat, barley, rye and oats. The river was teeming with fish, including herring, perch, bluegill and shad. The immediate area at the time had a nice assortment of trees, including red maple and tulip poplar."

Jim glanced all around as they went from room to room, filled with items and artifacts from centuries ago. "A lot of people today would be surprised to know that Penn only spent about two years here in Pennsylvania, from 1682-1684, then he left for more than a decade and didn't return until 1699. He went over to England two years later- and *never came back.*"

"That's correct. He had a house in downtown Philadelphia as well, although that hasn't survived. There are several rooms to see here: we're walking now into the Parlor, which was a reception room for notable guests. You'll see Penn's ornately carved wooden chairs with 7-inch cushions surrounding the lovely late 17th century table. Through here you'll see the Governor's Withdrawing Room, used for more intimate get togethers with his guests… and over here… is the Great Hall, used for group dinners."

"This place is wonderfully restored. You really *do* feel like you're walking back in time 300 years…" They strolled into adjoining rooms, including one holding a huge tub. "What did they do with this?"

"Make beer. Homemade beer was a common beverage back then." Doug continued to walk ahead.

"Wait a minute- I thought Quakers frowned upon alcohol and rarely consumed it."

'No, that's not quite correct. They *did* consume beer and other alcoholic beverages that were brewed or distilled, *in moderation*. Those beverages were safer than drinking water, which often could be contaminated. You may know that Benjamin West's father, who was a Quaker, ran a tavern. They drank very lightly and highly condemned drunkenness."

"So, did Penn meet with the local Indians to make treaties, maybe over a beer?"

"Yes, he met with the Lenape a few times while here and at other locations. Evidence of them generally being very friendly meetings is the now famous 'Wampum Belt' from the Treaty of Shackamaxon, depicting an Indian and a colonist holding hands in peace. The original is in the PA State Archives; we have a replica here."

Jim leaned close to the display case. "Yes, I've seen photographs of that. It's a wonderful symbol of Penn's essence: peaceful relations between all peoples."

Climbing the staircase to the second floor, Doug motioned toward other nearby rooms. "There are the chambers for women and children, often used for Penn's daughter Letitia or others. Here is the Best Chamber, where important guests slept… and… over here is Penn's Chamber, where he and his second wife Hannah slept. The items in these rooms are largely period pieces, ones they actually used or similar items of their era." Doug preceded him downstairs and out the back door which took them to the overlook of the Delaware River.

"Nice view. Today it'd be worth millions. Can we go down there?"

"Sure." He led Jim down the rear steps toward the river, standing back, allowing him to take in the entire scene.

"Very impressive. You've done a superb job here. I do feel like I've had a walk through his life, getting to know him up close." They headed back through the house, then out to the Visitor's Center. "I do want to get a book on Penn. Is there one you recommend?"

"Yes. *William Penn: A Life* by Andrew R. Murphy. It's an excellent and detailed review of him and his many accomplishments. I highly recommend it."

Jim walked into the gift shop and saw the book on the shelf. "I'll buy a copy. Thank you." He paid the attendant and walked toward Doug.

"If there's anything else you have questions on, here's my card. Shoot me an e-mail and I'll be glad to help."

"Doug, thanks so much. This has been a wonderful visit. I'll be in touch." Jim turned back to look at the property once more before he got into his car. Pulling out onto the access road, he felt a soothing sense of peace suddenly come over him, his body relaxing as if he'd laid back onto a plush couch. As he reached I-276 for the drive home, despite the heavy traffic surrounding him, he was feeling *completely calm*, unlike most times on the highway where drivers constantly shocked his nerves. He thought about what just came over him. "I don't do massages, but this is what people tell me they feel like after they've had one- *totally relaxed…*"

He focused on the road ahead. "Whoa!! ***That was close!!****,*" shaking his head after a huge Cadillac Escalade SUV cut *right in front of him…* but the irritation he normally experienced wasn't there. None. He couldn't explain the sense of calm which wrapped its arms around him, but it felt… good. Suddenly, he perceived a *'presence'* in the car. He looked to his right, then felt his heart racing as he quickly glanced into the back seat. "Thank God. For a minute I thought someone had gotten in here." He kept driving West on the turnpike, staying in the right lane, obeying the speed limit, allowing most cars to pass. Again, the feeling of an intruder came over him. *"What is going on here?"* The radio was off- there was no sound distracting him. He looked all around the inside of the car and saw… nothing, but his body told him there was something near him. Then he heard a voice, very faint, but distinct, as if it came from far away.

*"I welcome thee… and thank thee for your kind visit…"*

***"What?!"*** Jim's eyebrows were raised to their limit and he started shaking. He didn't believe his ears, but it happened again. "What is going on? This *is* **strange**. I ***know*** I heard a voice."

*"There is more for thee to see… You will find it."*

As he shuddered and tried to control the steering wheel, Jim was certain- there *was* someone ***in*** the car. He attempted to slow down and pull over to the shoulder, but there was a car right on his rear fender tailgating him within a foot or two. ***"DAMN IT!!"*** He tapped lightly on the brakes to reduce his speed with no luck, cars racing all around him at more than 75 miles an hour. "I always thought that if I ever experienced a ghost, it would be a peaceful one… If you are a ghost, I can't see you, but I *CAN* hear you, whoever you are." Then he ruminated carefully about the specific words he'd just heard. "Visit? The only place I visited today was Pennsbury Manor." He thought quickly about what he was experiencing. "Somebody… is speaking to me. I don't know how or why." Then it hit him. "The only people I know of who spoke using 'Thee' were… *Quakers* and today I visited Penn's home. **Could it be…?"**

The faint voice came back. *"Continue your search… thee will be rewarded with something of great value."*

His entire body started shaking again, but he tried desperately to maintain his composure and steer the vehicle. "O.K.- this is **VERY, VERY STRANGE**, but I don't know why I'm *not… really… scared*." He hesitated before he spoke. "Are you… *William Penn?*"

Dead silence. The car became completely quiet.

The sense of calm lingered, but slowly over the next few minutes it started to leave him. He shook his head in disbelief, but knew for sure he had experienced something 'other worldly.' As he got close to Kennett Square, he understood that he had to tell Natalie. "She's gonna' say I'm making this up… but I'm **NOT** making this up. It **HAPPENED!** I'm a former analyst- very scientific; I ask lots of questions. Was I *dreaming?* No, **you're awake, driving a car- BONEHEAD!!** I know I *HEARD* a voice- that is *certain*. I just visited Penn's home and someone using 'thee' was speaking to me. If I had to count this as a *real* experience, I'd say it somehow *was…* Penn's spirit, but *what was he talking about?"* He pulled the car into their garage and turned off the engine. "O.K., you're gonna' need to explain this to Natalie. I will, I will… but… **How the Hell do I do that?"**

*William Penn* by Frederick S. Lamb

Interior room at Pennsbury Manor

**Reproduction of wampum belt given by the Lenape Indians to William Penn as a sign of friendship**

**Kitchen area at Pennsbury Manor**

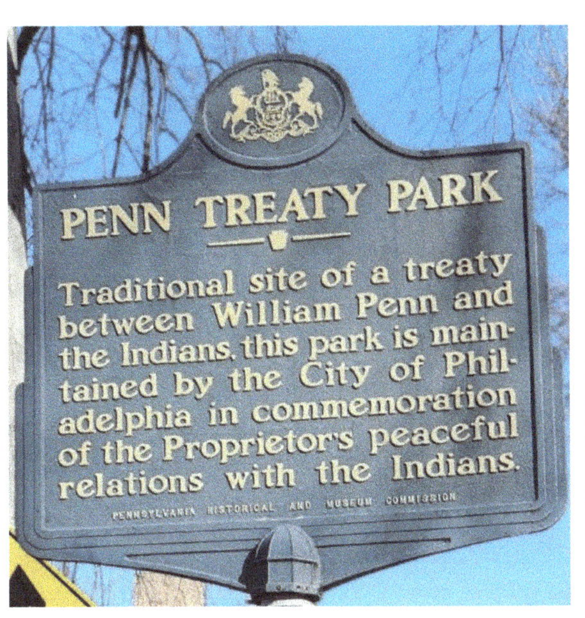

Sculpture of William Penn at Penn Treaty Park

Historical plaque at Penn Treaty Park mentioning the Treaty of
Shackamaxon between William Penn and the Lenape Indians

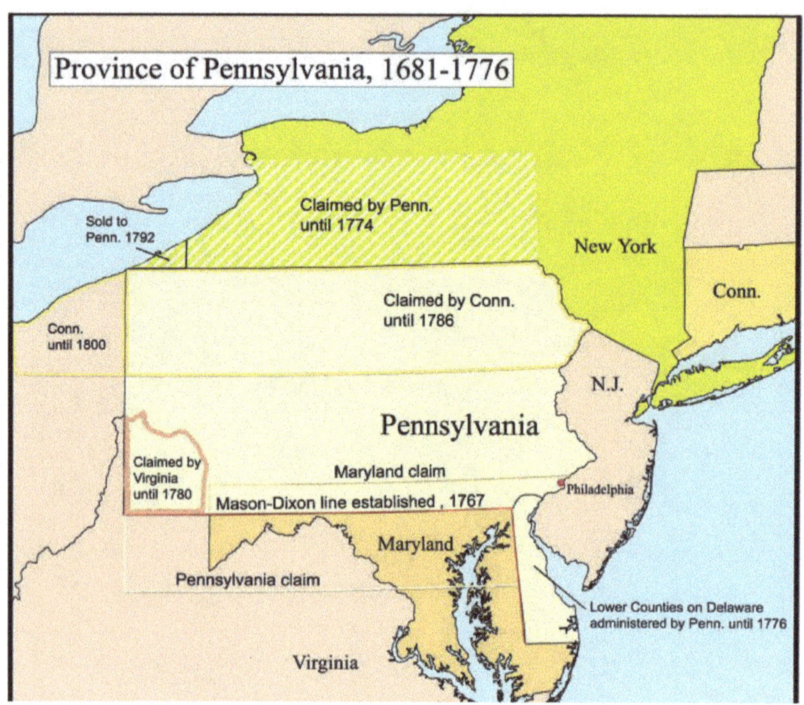

Map of the Province of Pennsylvania
with regional land claims and boundaries

Lithograph of William Penn
artist unknown

Gravesite of William Penn at Jordans Friends Meetinghouse,
Ruscombe, Berkshire, England

# Chapter 7

*"We will live in peace with William Penn and his children as long as the creeks and rivers run, and while the sun, moon, and stars endure."*
-Lenape Indian Chief Tamanend (1625-1701) in his response to William Penn's Treaty of Shackamaxon
**********************************************************************

"So, how was your trip?" Natalie was holding two wine glasses. "It's almost Happy Hour."

Jim hesitated, but didn't want her to think something was wrong. "Oh, it was a nice tour. It's a beautifully restored late 17th century house. Right along the Delaware River. Great view. Prime landscape. Penn was centuries ahead of real estate agents today."

*"How's that?"*

"Location. Location. Location."

She chuckled. "What was the house like?"

"Absolutely lovely inside- elegant period furniture, quite regal, as Penn was the Governor. The tour was great." Jim walked over to the refrigerator to grab the bottle of Chardonnay for her and noticed she'd already put the Cabernet out for him on the counter.

"You seem… *short on words*. You normally chat quite a bit about these places you visit. Anything *happen?*"

He thought for several seconds, pouring her glass, then his. "Let's sit down in the Conservatory." He led the way, sat on the olive-green couch and waited for her to sit beside him.

"O.K., more about your visit!" She sipped her wine and waited.

"All right. It was a wonderful tour. I learned a few things, but first I want to tell you that something strange DID happen on the drive back."

Her attention was glued on his face, waiting for a joke.

"I was driving home and despite the wild traffic on I-276, I felt a sense of calm wrap all around me."

"Is there a problem with that? Sounds good to me."

"Let me finish. Yes, it was good, but I'm going to tell you something. I am being *COMPLETELY* serious. I am *not* joking. I heard a voice inside the car." Jim glanced at her to see if she was starting to crack up.

"You had the radio on, silly."

"I did NOT have the radio on. I was driving, paying attention to everything around me, but I sensed a 'presence'… in the car. I looked all around; there was no one there with me… but I felt something. I couldn't explain it. Regardless of the heavy traffic, I had a feeling of total calm, like something enveloped me with peace. Then- I heard a low voice. It said *"I welcome thee… and thank thee for your kind visit…"*

"O.K., now I *KNOW* you're joking. You always do this with me! Can you just be *serious* for a change?"

"Hon, I am *totally serious*. This is *NOT* a joke. I am telling you I heard someone speaking to me in the car, a soft voice, very distant, but I could hear it clearly. It sounded like a man. I know this is very strange, but I heard it." He looked over at Natalie and saw her face beginning to go from disbelief to intense listening mode. "After those first words, he said: *'There is more for thee to see… You will find it.'*" He glanced at Natalie, expecting her to either burst out laughing or stare in amazement. Her face was very serious.

"I don't know how to respond to that. Either you're playing one of your 'I'll be cute and funny with Natalie' jokes or… you really *ARE* serious?"

"YES. I couldn't be **more** serious. I am telling you with 100% honesty- this *HAPPENED*. You can imagine- I was driving at 65 miles per hour on I-276 with cars racing all around me and I hear some strange voice talking to me. I could've had a *heart attack*- but somehow, I was totally calm. Well- to be honest, I did shake a bit… but it was as if that person's sense of peace enveloped me, trying to make me calm and listen."

"Did he tell you to pull over for a bathroom break?"

"Now *YOU'RE* being silly." Jim shook his head and started again. "Then this voice said: *'Continue your search… thee will be rewarded with something of great value.'* He stared directly at Natalie and gave his analyst's initial impression. "O.K.- just to review: the first words thanked me for my 'visit'. The only place I *visited* today was Penn's home. Second- he used the word *'thee'*. Nobody uses those words today; they're from the 18th century. Who used them regularly? Quakers. Who is the best-known Quaker in American history? William Penn. I can't prove anything- but if I had to make an educated guess, I'd say that after my visit to Penn's home, his spirit thanked me. Maybe he really *was* there in the car with me. Who knows? Some people claim that when they visit a person's grave or touch something that was connected to someone they know, they experience a sensation, perhaps a manifestation of that person's spirit. Was it Penn's ghost? I have no idea, but I think it might have been him."

"You know if you tell people about this, they're going to think you're joking and just laugh it off."

"I don't care. I know what I experienced. Look- you have to stand up for what you believe to be true. I was trained to always look for and evaluate evidence objectively as a scientist, but I also have a sense of the Divine. I believe the souls of all living things are eternal- they never die. Those of all who came before are still with us, in some form, perhaps in a manifestation we just don't understand. I think Penn's spirit was with me in my car today, speaking to me…"

"O.K.- fine. Maybe he *was* speaking to you, in some way and it was not your imagination. What was he trying to tell you?"

"Damn good question. I think it's linked to the last words he spoke: *'Continue your search… thee will be rewarded with something of great value.'* Somehow he must know we're checking out some characters from the past. Penn's one of the most important persons in Pennsylvania history, so maybe he's trying to tell us to keep digging and… we'll find something significant. That's what I make of it. What do you think?"

"Normally at this point, I would say you've carried this joke way too far, but I can see that you're totally serious, so I'll just say… if everything you said *is* accurate- you experienced something not explainable with the science we understand today. *Who knows?* Maybe it *WAS* Penn's spirit. All the words spoken to you would seem to indicate that the voice is likely linked to Penn. Since you had just been there visiting his home, I'd say that's my best estimate. Somehow, you came into contact with… the spirit of *William Penn.*"

"So- the cereal box *was* right." Jim started to grin.

"What are you *talking about?*" Natalie sipped her Chardonnay and glanced at his face.

"*'Nothing is better for thee than me.'* It was in Quaker Oats commercials when I was a kid."

"So- you're saying **oatmeal** is now a clue?"

Jim couldn't help but roar with a laugh. "No. In some strange way, maybe I had to visit Penn's home to 'link up' with him, to find out something critical- I don't know what. Remember- you didn't even want me to go, but I went there. I'm glad I did. Now I'm determined to find out *exactly* what his message means. ***I am definitely going to FIND it!***"

"*…and exactly how do you plan to do that?*"

"I have *no idea.*" Jim sported a wide smile. "It'll be fun, though. Want to join me- on a little adventure?"

"You know I do… and *always will.*" She smiled as Jim leaned over and gave her a long kiss. After their many times together exploring abandoned houses, strolling by gravestones of long-forgotten soldiers and delving into local mysteries, she knew this would be one to remember.

"Hey, not to change the subject, but want to take a look at that map we got at the Blacksmith's Shop?"

"Sure." She took another sip as Jim went into the kitchen area where the map was sitting on the counter.

As he came back into the Conservatory, Jim put his face closer to the weathered old document, trying to read what was in front of him. "When I bought this, I thought it depicted the Chester County area, because I think I see what look like the two branches of the Brandywine here." He held a magnifying glass as they sat together on the couch. "Yes, that does look like the two branches… and this shows it going down into northern Delaware… but what in the world are those?" He held it in front of Natalie for her to see it more closely.

"Let me hold it- I can't really see what you're pointing at. Could I have the glass?" She grabbed the magnifier and brought it close to the surface of the old map. "I'm no expert… but those look like Indian-type symbols of some sort. What do you think?"

She handed the map and glass back to Jim. "I know I've seen those somewhere… Yes! *Red Men on the Brandywine,* the book by C.A. Weslager. Came out in 1953 and was a review of the local lands inhabited by the Lenape and their interactions with settlers. He's got a few maps which show symbols just like these. Wait- let me go to the Family Room. I have a copy on the bookshelf." He got up and as he approached the bookcase, the reddish-brown leatherbound volume seemed to jump right out in front of him. "There it is." He opened it to the first few pages where all the maps were listed. "This looks quite similar to…" He stopped as he made his way back to the Conservatory and sat next to Natalie. "Here- what do you make of this map? Doesn't that look a fair amount like the one we just bought?" He gave the book to her.

"Well, yes, it does, but what does that mean? There were lots of maps made of this area over many decades. What makes this one so special?" She gave the book back to him and sipped her wine.

"Did you notice the very small symbols on it? They're hard to see without the magnifying glass, but here- take this and look again." He handed it to her and she examined the document more closely.

"Yes. I see what looks like… a *turtle*?"

"Exactly. Turtles were a symbol the Lenape in this area used. Now look at this page in the book. It says 'Reserved land: one mile on each side of Brandywine reconveyed to Indians after purchase in 1685 by William Penn.' Not sure about the year; Penn had already returned to England in 1685- so it could have been a year or two earlier. The treaty's never been found; some historians say it never existed, but the Lenape tried like Hell to get their land back. They received many promises, but were eventually driven out of the area."

"They could've used F. Lee Bailey in the courtroom."

"Right, but here's the crux of the problem. Indians lived, hunted and fished in areas for periods of time, then left and dwelled in other regions which offered similar resources to support them and their families. They often were gone for many months at a time, which means the lands were essentially vacant when settlers arrived who found… *land with no signs of anyone living there*. Totally vacant. So, what did the settlers do? They started to build cabins and took over. Indians did not understand the concept of land ownership as we know it today. They never heard of a 'deed'- that was foreign to them- whereas in modern society, all land ownership comes about with the transferral of property rights via a deed. Back then the settlers usually called them patents, but they were the same as what we know today as deeds. Add to that the fact that the Lenape thought land was a gift from the Creator which *all* could enjoy- and you can see how 'rights' to property could be misunderstood back then. Who *REALLY* owned the land- the Indians who lived in the area for centuries, but left for long periods of time… or the colonists who showed up later and developed the property? It's not an easy question to answer."

Natalie nodded in agreement. "You've heard the phrase 'Possession is nine-tenths of the law', right? Well, those who were there, on the land, 'in possession of it'- by our legal system had at least *some* claim to the rights for it. If the Lenape 'used it', then **left** for long periods of time- it's difficult to argue they truly 'owned' it in a permanent sense." Natalie looked more closely at the old map. "Hey- Isn't this the word 'Lenape' near the turtle, pointing with arrows to nearby land?"

Jim grabbed the map and the magnifying glass. "Yes, it is. Now I'm looking at the bottom corner and it's really hard to read, but I think it says… *1685!*" He looked at Natalie for several seconds. "It would take a professional archivist and Colonial-era map expert to know if this is genuine, but from this I would guess that the map either dates to 1685 or not too long afterwards- making it *more than 300 years old*. Who knows? It could just be a copy, but I got it for twenty bucks! Not a bad deal. Whether what's printed is accurate- who knows? I'm definitely going to have this framed. I'll bring it over to Strode's Mill Gallery next week."

"So, you know what's next?" Natalie looked at him intently.

"Going to the Pennsylvania State Archives in Harrisburg to look at their Indian files?"

"No- forget that. Too much driving. You can give me some more chardonnay- with ice."

He smiled as he took her glass and headed to the kitchen. Coming back, Jim had a hunch where the trail might be leading. "Who did Penn interact with quite a bit? The Lenape. That's where we should be going with this."

"Sounds fair. Sit here with me and Frank- and relax. She wants you here with us. No more running around. It's Happy Hour! Let's chill out… and enjoy the day."

The late afternoon amber rays shone into the Conservatory, illuminating the two landscape paintings on the wall. "My favorite thing to do."

"What's that?" She sipped as she waited for his response.

"Being here with you and Frank. That's home for me. Tomorrow I'll be eager to get back on the trail… and find out what Penn was trying to tell me."

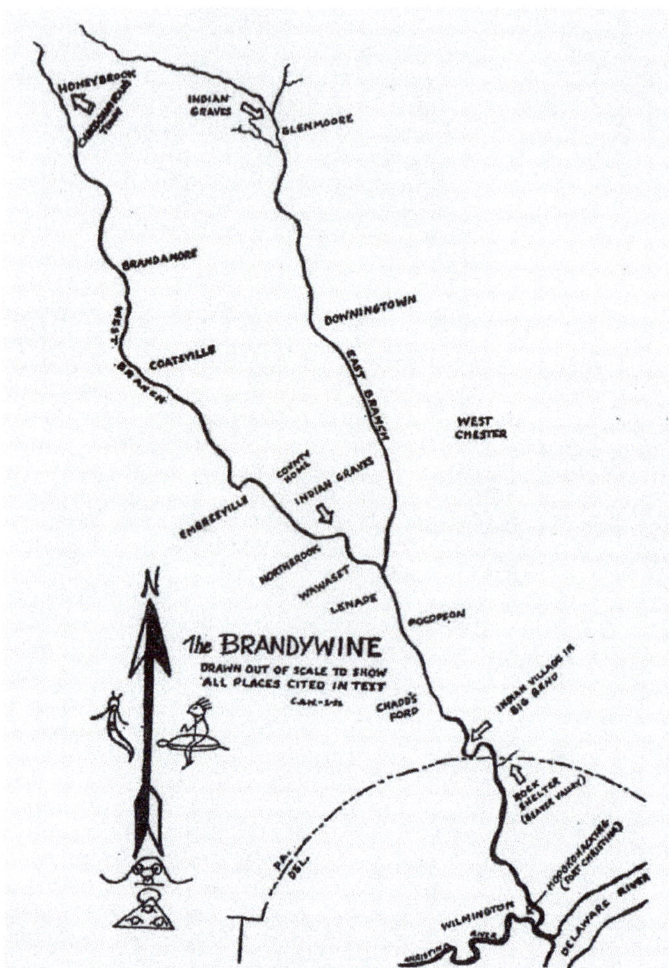

Old map of the Brandywine with Lenape symbols and lands from C. A. Weslager in *Red Men on the Brandywine*

*Red Men on the Brandywine* by C. A. Weslager

*Portrait of Lenape Chief Nicóman* by George Catlin

*Lenape Chief Lappawinsoe* portrait
by Gustavus Hesselius 1735

**The various tribes of Lenape Indians along the mid-Atlantic**

**Delaware Tribe of Indians Lenape symbols**

**Lenape turtle symbol**

# Chapter 8

*"I am much obliged by your kind Present of curious Seeds. They were welcome Gifts to some of my Friends. I send you herewith some of the new Barley lately introduced into the Country, and now highly spoken of. I wish it may be found of Use with us."*
-Benjamin Franklin (1706-1790), letter to Humphry Marshall, April 22, 1771
****************************************************************************

Jim proceeded out to the mailbox on the driveway, passing the maroon-leafed plum tree which they were trying to nurse back to health. He held the letter in his hand as he approached their box, then put it inside, shutting the black metal door. As he strode back to the house, he noticed a car which he'd not seen before slowly turning the corner onto their street, but he kept moving to the side door and went in.

Natalie was in the kitchen unloading the dishwasher. "Drop off a letter out front?"

"I did. A card for my sister; it's her 80th birthday and I want to make sure it gets to her in time, so I'm mailing it over a week early." Just then, he had a strange sensation of a 'visitor' in the area- and he rushed to the front door, peering outside.

At that moment, a grey Audi sedan screeched to a stop in front of their mailbox and a 20-ish woman in jeans and a hoodie jumped out. She ran over to the mailbox, opened it and grabbed the card, quickly getting back into the car before it sped off down the street.

*"DAMN IT!! Some jerk just took my card right out of our mailbox!!"* His yell could be heard in the kitchen. He stormed in and saw Natalie's face.

*"What?!* Someone literally *STOLE* from our mailbox, right out front? You've gotta' be kidding me."

"No- *I saw it!* You've got to be pretty desperate to steal from people's mailboxes. This is outrageous. They're probably trying to find money. *It's crazy!* I'm going to report this to the Kennett Police." Jim grabbed the phone and dialed 9-1-1.

"Thank you for calling 9-1-1. *What is your emergency?"* The woman's monotone, matter-of-fact voice paused as she waited for a response.

"Well, it's not exactly *an emergency-* I just want to get through to the Kennett Police. Could you connect me?"

"That number is 610-925-4475. You can contact them directly. Is there anything else I can help you with?"

Jim shook his head. "So, you *can't connect* me?"

"No, sir. Please call them directly. You will get their switchboard and you can report your incident to them. Thank you."

Jim looked over at Natalie and shook his head. "Our tax dollars at work- you have to call two different numbers to get to the police! Now I'm wondering… is it worth it?" as he thought for a few seconds.

"Well, it was just a card, right? No money or anything valuable inside?"

"Just a card, but this really *ticks me off!* We can't even put something in our mailbox without it getting *stolen?* What the Hell's going on around here?"

"Calm down. Just send her another card, O.K.? What does that cost- a few bucks? It's not worth involving the police." Natalie put her arm around Jim's shoulder. "Let it go. It's nothing."

"It *IS* something. I never thought our own mailbox would be a crime scene. I'll… *get another card.*" Jim walked over to the closet on the side of the kitchen, opened the door and took down the small plastic bin which held all their greeting cards. "This one I'm taking *directly* to the Post Office." He took out a birthday card, started filling it out, then sealed and addressed it and put a stamp on the envelope.

"My mother told me to let the little things go without getting stressed out. Stress is hard on your body. I avoid it at all times, but… *I'm* still O.K. using our mailbox."

"That's *your* call. I'm going to the Post Office." He thought for a few seconds. "I want to do some food shopping, I need cash and also need to fill up my tank, too. I should be back in… not too long." Jim grabbed his car keys. "See you soon."

"Not too long means 2 ½ hours. Love you, sweetie." Natalie went into her office and sat before her computer. "I have some bills to pay- well, at least one. The electric bill." She pulled out the envelope which she smartly kept in her desk, opened it and wrote out the check. "Let's see, is that it? Yes… that's it for this week." She put the check into the envelope, sealed it and walked back into the kitchen, where she opened the drawer with stamps. "There we go." She thought for a few seconds, then walked outside, up to the mailbox and put it in.

Strolling back to the side door, just to be cautious- she glanced back out front. "No cars coming. It's fine." She walked inside the garage and thought about her "To Do List" for the day. "O.K.… I know I wanted to… right- wash the car! It's a beautiful, sunny day and I can hose it down right outside and let it drip-dry." She grabbed her keys and got into the black Mercedes SUV, pulling it out about 15 feet from the garage door.

"Glad we set up the long hose with the spray nozzle outside here." Natalie knew she'd have to pull it way out in back and around the car to give her plenty of room to maneuver, so she unwound the garden-green hose more than 40 feet. "Good- ready for a bath?" She gave the entire car a generous washing, paying close attention to the front and back windshields, side mirrors and wheels. "I can't believe they charge over $10 for this at the car wash." She walked all around the SUV and made sure it was liberally sprayed up close, getting off stuck-on mud and grime from the past few months.

"Now, that's much better!" Natalie strode all around the car twice, making sure every inch was clean and well-washed. "Pretty good: saved some money and maybe even a little water for the reservoir." She walked over to the house and turned off the water, then re-wound the hose onto its circular housing. "With this sun, it'll dry in less than an hour." She positioned herself behind the car to see it from the edge of the driveway, then moved over towards the driver side just as she heard a car pull up near the front of their house.

"Who is that… and *WHY* are they going toward *OUR MAILBOX?!*" As she viewed the front yard, she saw a white Chrysler mini-van pull up and stop sharply in front of their yard, a 40-ish man in blue jeans and a tan T-shirt jump out of the passenger side. He ran right up to the mailbox, opened it, grabbed the envelope- and jumped quickly back into the car, which started to speed off.

"*WHAT THE…?? I cannot believe…*" Natalie thought for a half-second: "They're *NOT* gettin' away with this!!" She had her car keys in her hand and jumped into her Mercedes, tearing down the driveway after the other vehicle. The mini-van was only about 40 yards in front of her, but the driver was ripping it at over 60 miles an hour down the street. The Chrysler made a roaring turn at Woodview, then rushed to the intersection with Rosedale where it almost took out a mailbox as it turned left and raced onto the main road.

"*No WAY, Jose!* I am *ON* it." Natalie gunned the accelerator as she made the turn following the car onto Rosedale Road. She tried to read the license plate, but the mini-van was weaving a bit, almost going off the street which had no shoulder. "This guy's going…what-75…80…?" He's gonna' *kill somebody!*" She leaned forward and again tried to make out the plate ahead. "That's an… L…. is that an R or… is it a *K*? He's going so fast, I can't read it without getting into an accident."

The white mini-van sped down Rosedale, past the historic wood and stone barn which had stood for two centuries at the corner of Bayard Road. Jamming on its brakes, it made a sharp right at the intersection, the car nearly going up on one set of wheels as it maneuvered the turn. The minivan's driver floored it past the towering pin oaks and maple trees which lined each side of the road leading toward the incline for the railroad tracks, then literally went *airborne* over the three-foot hump before it *SLAMMED HARD* down onto the black macadam roadway.

Natalie stared ahead in disbelief. "He's a *LUNATIC!*"

The mini-van slowed slightly approaching the four-way intersection at Hillendale Road. Its driver checked the rear-view mirror to see if the black Mercedes was on his tail, but noticing it was more than 100 yards behind, he gunned it through the intersection without stopping, just barely missing an oncoming brown Toyota Land Cruiser, which hadn't fully come to a halt at the STOP sign. Up over the hill, it turned a screeching left onto Woodale Road.

"Now I've got him! He had to slow down for that turn. He probably lives near there and thinks he can lose me on one of these back streets. He ***won't!***" Natalie decelerated to make the turn, then saw the mini-van speed past the greenspace up ahead on the left. She gunned it up to 60 miles per hour, closing the distance between her Mercedes and the Chrysler to just 20 yards, then *JAMMED* on her brakes. ***"My God! This guy's a menace!"***

The mini-van skidded into a U-turn on the narrow road, nearly flipping on its side before completing a 180-degree arc, flying back down the road *past* Natalie's car, nearly scraping off her driver's side mirror. The driver gunned it back out onto Bayard Road, turning a sharp, *SCREECHING* left and escaping.

Natalie came to a complete stop as she caught her breath and looked around the intersection with the side road. Her eyes meandered slowly upward toward the sign: 'Sandy Flash Drive.' "This must be a dream." She turned her car around and headed back to Bayard Road, turning right to go home. "All this- just to steal a stupid check! *Unbelievable.*" As she made it back to the house, she clicked on the door opener and slowly entered the third-bay of the garage. Turning off the engine, she looked over and saw Jim's car beside her before going into the house.

"Hey- I beat *you* home this time. Where'd you go?" Jim sipped his organic Bigelow decaf green tea.

"I'll tell you, but you're not going to believe me." Natalie shook her head as she put her keys onto the counter.

"Try me. I like mysteries."

"Well, this *was* an adventure, but *not* a good one. After you left, I put the envelope with my check and the utility bill in our mailbox. I know- you don't trust it after your card to your sister was stolen. Turns out you were right. After that, I decided to wash my car out in the driveway, so I pulled the Mercedes out and started washing it with the hose. It's sunny, so I figured it was a good day to let it dry outside. I finished washing it, turned off the hose and was admiring how good it looked. Just then, a white mini-van pulls up out front and some jerk jumps out, rushes over to our mailbox, takes the envelope and runs back to his car."

"This is a joke, *right?*"

"I am *not* kidding, check the mailbox. Our utility bill is gone. So, the car jets off down the street, but I had my car keys in my hand. I wasn't going to let him get away with it! I rush after him as he turns down Rosedale, then onto Bayard, almost flipping over as it skidded to make the turn. The guy was flying like a wild man, going at least 70 miles an hour!"

Jim shook his head. "This is *outrageous!* Two mailbox thieves in *ONE* day?"

"I know, it's *nuts*, right? It was a different car than the one you saw, so this means it's an epidemic. Well, I see the car race up over the railroad tracks and come *crashing down* on the other side, but that didn't stop him. He turned left onto Woodale Road, but I was hot on his tail and thought *'I got him.'* Well, he gunned it down Woodale and even though I was fairly close behind him, he jammed on his brakes, skidded into a U-turn, then flew *BACK* past me! He almost hit my car."

"Did you get his license plate? If you know it, you can report it and they can arrest the guy."

"Only a partial plate- like an L and maybe an R- I'm not sure. He was going so fast, I couldn't make out his plate. Now this part you won't believe."

"What's that? *Were you hurt?*" Jim came up and put his arms around Natalie.

"No, I'm fine… but the intersection where he screeched to do a U-turn is at… **Sandy Flash Drive.**"

Jim thought for several seconds. "That *IS* bizarre. So… we have a Sandy Flash Drive *right here in Kennett Township…* and a modern-day highwayman robbing mailboxes for their checks- 247 years after Fitzpatrick terrorized this same area."

"The guy was driving like a *wild-ass maniac!* He almost T-boned a Toyota Land Cruiser at Hillendale. I thought for sure it was going to be a horrific accident… all to steal a check. I guess if you live long enough, you get to see everything… but some things you don't *want* to see."

"Look- you're not hurt. That's the most important thing. So, he got away. Just put a 'STOP payment' on the check; he won't get a dime out of all this… and you know what?"

Natalie shook her head again in disbelief. "What?"

"If this is the *worst* thing that happens to you in your life, you're a lucky woman." He wrapped his arms around her, bringing his lips to hers. "I love you- and I'm glad you got through this without a scrape. O.K.?"

"I love you, too. I'm just thinking… this is a *very strange* coincidence. First, the bookcase at The Square Tavern with books on Sandy Flash vanishes into thin air. Now some highway vandal takes me on a wild chase and leaves me at… *Sandy Flash Drive*, not far from our home? This is way too weird. I can't explain it."

Jim was silent for several seconds. "I can. These are *NOT* coincidences. They must *mean* something." Jim's eyes stared directly into hers. "Let's do some exploring and find out clues about him… and some of these other characters who were around at the same time. I have a gut feeling that Penn, the Lenape, Fitzpatrick and others are somehow, in some strange way… linked. Just not sure how, but some roadwork might just tell us. You ready to get back out there?"

Natalie breathed deeply, then nodded. "*Let's do it.*"

Sandy motioned sharply, his pistol cuddled close to the cape
over his right arm.

**Illustration depicting the outlaw Sandy Flash from *Sandy Flash,
The Highwayman of Castle Rock* by Clifton Lisle**

**Artist's depiction of James Fitzpatrick (a.k.a.
Sandy Flash) flogging a Whig captive courtesy
*The Philadelphia Inquirer* November 30, 1997**

**Sandy Flash Drive sign in Kennett Township**

# Chapter 9

Natalie was relaxed sitting in the Family Room with *The Chester County Press* in her hands and saw the headline: Fraud Ring Operating in Chester, Bucks and Delaware Counties. Her eyes were glued to each paragraph describing a series of mailbox burglaries all around the region. "Hey, Jim! Look at this- here's what happened to us! There's a crime ring robbing mailboxes around the area- and we were just one of them!"

Jim strolled up to the couch and grabbed the newspaper from her hands. "Oh, my God… this is worse than what I'd suspected. It's happening all around the region- and they say it's getting more common. Over 200 houses have been robbed just in the last few months. This is pathetic. We can't even trust our own mailboxes out front anymore."

Natalie stared right at him. "It says to contact the Kennett Square Police and even the PA State Police if we have anything to report. I'm going to call them."

"With what? My card didn't have a check in it- and you put an immediate STOP on your check- so it never went through."

"I don't care- we need to report this. Even if we didn't lose any money, it's something the police need to be aware of, so they know it's happening right here in Kennett."

"You're right. If you have knowledge of a crime, it's the duty of a good citizen to report it. Otherwise, the system breaks down and we all suffer the consequences. Go ahead and make the call."

Natalie strode into the kitchen, picked up the black cordless which always sat on the side island and dialed. "Hello- is this the Kennett Square Police?"

"Yes, Ma'am. Who is calling, please?"

"I'm Natalie Peterson. I want to report a crime."

"I will get an officer on the line. Please hold…"

"Hello. This is Captain Wallingford. To whom am I speaking?"

"Captain, it's Natalie Peterson. I've lived here in Kennett for almost 20 years, but just a while back experienced something really disturbing. On two separate occasions, someone drove up to our mailbox and stole items from it."

"Did you report the incident?"

"No, we didn't."

"… and *why not?* We expect people to report these things when they happen- not wait a while, when the criminal can get away and perhaps avoid capture."

"I am sorry. You're right. We should have reported both events which amazingly happened on the same day. The first one was just a birthday card which didn't have any money in it, but the second one was our utility bill which had a check. After I saw the car pull up I chased them, but they got away. I put an immediate STOP PAYMENT on the check, so we didn't lose any money."

"I can come over to your home and get a full report. Are you available now?"

"Yes, please come over." After giving the Captain her address and telephone number, she felt some reassurance that the authorities were at least alerted. "He's coming over now- said he'd be here in about ten minutes."

They both stood in the Foyer watching for the Police car to drive up. After nearly 20 minutes, one arrived and stopped in their driveway on the side of the house. The Captain walked resolutely on the stone path to the front door, then knocked.

"You must be Captain Wallingford. I'm Natalie; this is my husband Jim." They both shook the officer's hand and invited him inside to the Family Room.

"You have a very nice home. Even more reason to be careful about possible theft."

"Thank you. I agree- we should have contacted you a while ago." After giving him the details of the mailbox incidents, she and Jim were both curious as to the extent of the thefts occurring in the area.

"So, just for the record, the first incident was with a grey Audi sedan, with a 20-ish woman in jeans and a hoodie. The second incident- the same day- was a white Chrysler mini-van with a 40-ish man in a tan T-shirt and blue jeans, correct?"

"That's right officer."

"… and you didn't get a plate on *either* vehicle?"

Natalie sat up. "Sadly, no. He was driving too fast in the mini-van. All I could get was an **'L'** and maybe an **'R'**, but that's about it."

"Well, to let you know- this type of crime has been happening more often in the last year or so. The Pennsylvania State Police estimate these robberies statewide are responsible for over $500,000 in fraudulent checks being cashed in the last few months- and it's not just *one* ring. We think there are several operating throughout the Commonwealth; some of them may be linked together in some kind of a syndicate, we're not completely sure. Unfortunately, there are likely a few different theft rings operating *right around this area*, near your home- and we're doing our best to track them all down. This appears to be the latest craze among thieves- they think it's a fool-proof way to get money."

Jim's eyebrows were raised in amazement. "I am *stunned*. We had no idea it was anything like this. How the Hell do they get away with it?"

"Sadly, it is not easy to detect. With technology comes more opportunities for theft. We know that these people are using so-called Ink Erasers to change checks, then they take them to either their own bank or one of these check-cashing places where they pay a fee to get their cash. Either way, the institution is often clueless as to what is going on- until it's too late. One good thing is these crooks are not always smart. Some leave fingerprints on the checks- which we can identify- and a few of them go to a well-known financial institution- specifically banks- stupidly not realizing they are being recorded on closed-circuit camera. We can thank God for their stupidity. We've arrested several people in the last few weeks all around the region."

"That's good to hear. What would you recommend we do going forward?" Natalie had some ideas, but waited for a response.

"Always try to make a note of the person appearing at your property- sex, height, weight- if possible- along with the make and model of the car they're using. Many people use outdoor cameras- like Ring or other services- which record all movement from people, animals or other things right out in front of their house. We don't officially recommend those services, but it may be worth considering- not only to avoid another incident, but for your general safety."

Jim held Natalie's hand on the couch. "That is an excellent idea. I never thought I'd have to set up cameras around my own house to feel safe, but..."

"... *that's the world we live in today*... I say we do it." Natalie clutched his hand tightly and nodded her approval.

"Well, that's about it folks. I appreciate your contacting us and I'll make a full report. I will also alert the PA State Police with the details of your mailbox theft, but since no monetary loss was involved, you may not get a call from them. We here in Kennett will be your go-to for reporting anything in the future. Thank you." The Captain got up and strolled toward the front door.

"Thank you so much! If anything comes up, we'll definitely be back in touch."

As the Police vehicle drove away, Natalie looked into Jim's eyes. "I'm ordering outdoor cameras tomorrow. Should have them by the end of the week. We can set them up at the front door, on the tree out front near the mailbox, as well as the side and basement doors... so we can start feeling a bit more secure."

*"Amen to that..."*

# Chapter 10

*The old woman's weathered, loose-fitting clothes barely covered her brown skin, its wrinkles the roadmap of many years wandering the Brandywine Valley. Her shawl was homespun, her dress tattered and slightly stained, but respectable. She looked outside the small hut that was her home, which stood on the property of a settler named William Webb in southern Chester County. She knew the man well and respected him. Mostly she appreciated his ongoing kindness, giving her bread to eat and water when needed, shelter inside his stone-walled house in inclement weather. Yet she felt a keen sense of pride looking at her crude structure which sheltered her from the wind and most of the rain, so she could weave baskets to sell and collect the plants and herbs she knew had healing properties, sharing them with Webb and other Quakers. They all respected her independence and appreciated her home-made remedies. Hannah gathered several small piles of plants she'd roasted and dried on the hot-stone fireplace in front of her home and placed them in the small basket she'd woven from the reeds found along the creek not far away. She was ready to go out on her daily trek around the area, offering healing plant remedies to those who felt ill and selling baskets to support her life… an often lonely life, but a proud one.*

*******************************************************************

Natalie loved this time of the day: Jim was downstairs working out on the CrossTrainer while she and Frankie sat together on the couch. Frank's favorite spot in the whole world was right in the center of her lap, where she was most secure and could fall asleep. Natalie petted the kitty gently just a few times, trying not to wake her. "Yes… you're my beautiful girl…" Frank looked up and gave her a silent *"Meow"* in agreement before going back to sleep. Natalie waited to hear Jim's footsteps coming up the stairs from the basement as she sipped her coffee. "Good workout?"

"Great. As I was watching the news, I got some ideas."

"I hope you didn't hear any more voices."

"No voices- just some interesting paths to go down."

*"Paths?* Are we going into the forest?" Natalie's mug was almost empty. "Before you tell me- could you give me a refill? I don't want to wake up Frank."

"Will do." Jim returned from the kitchen beaming with energy. "We know the Lenapi lived all around this area- and they interacted with Penn several times. We also know that Adrian did extensive research on them for his portrait of Indian Hannah- the best known of the tribe. I'm researching all the places she lived, traveled, gathered food and generally spent time. I'm going to try and 're-trace her steps' to see where they lead me."

*"… and you're doing this because…?"*

"For one, I want to nail down *exactly where* she spent time around here. We do know from going to Longwood Gardens that she lived somewhere on the property where the Webb house stands. In my readings, it's clear she did quite a bit of wandering- from northern Chester County down into Delaware and even over the river into New Jersey. Some materials *do* indicate she was up in Marshallton and interacted with Humphry Marshall. One highly detailed genealogical review by a gentleman named Marshall J. Becker indicates she and members of her family were literally all over southern Chester County, Newlin Township for sure a few times, even down in Centreville, Delaware. Apparently Hannah was a traveling saleswoman offering her wares and her skills to anyone who wanted or needed them. Now here's a novel idea: *did a local Lenape Indian give one of the most famous botanists in America vital information about medicinal plants and herbal remedies?* The Indians were here for centuries and *knew everything that grew around the region*- what it looked like, the properties of the bark, roots, leaves, stems, berries and fruit, specifically if they were helpful in healing- even curing- certain medical conditions. Wouldn't it be fascinating to find evidence that Marshall actually *learned* some important things about plants *from Hannah*- who many historians say was a practicing 'herbalist'? I've never read anything that states this, but I say it's a real possibility."

"I won't argue against that. It's a good theory. How do you propose to find out?"

"By digging into her 'roots.' There's an Indian Hannah Drive up in Newlin Township, there's that Indian Hannah marker on Route 162, there's also the one that used to be on Route 52, now near the Longwood Fire Station; even the white cross marker for her off the walking path inside Longwood Gardens. I bet they have some materials in their Archives about her, since she lived on the grounds there. I think she's all around us, practically begging us to learn about her life."

"Agreed. So, *what's the plan?*" Natalie sipped her coffee as she slowly petted Frankie.

"I'm ready to head out on the Lenape Trail. She probably wandered through the forests right here in Kennett *near our house*. Maybe she even ran into James Fitzpatrick at some point."

"Now, wait… *that's a stretch*. What evidence do you have for that?"

"Just a strong hunch. I learned long ago: 'Trust your instincts. They're right about 90 per cent of the time.' I've read up a bit on Fitzpatrick- and the legend of Sandy Flash. I also re-read parts of *The Story of Kennett*, along with several newspaper articles written over the years. He robbed people everywhere around here, back roads, private homes, taverns, known thoroughfares, just about every place people traveled, all the way from Lancaster to Coatesville and Philadelphia. At least one of the legends mentions him trying to rob an old woman wandering along the road in this area, demanding her money, but when she spoke and pleaded for mercy, Fitzpatrick realized she was very poor and he actually gave her some of *his* money. Could that old, poor woman have been Indian Hannah? It's quite possible. They traveled the *same roads and paths* here in Chester County on a regular basis around *the same time period*- the late 1770s, when Flash was on his robbing spree. They were *both* well-known fixtures on the scene. I think there's a reasonable chance they did meet at one point."

"I like your thinking, detective." Natalie's smile was glowing.

Jim sipped his green tea. "Thank you. Want to do some prowling around?"

"Sure. We can drive around Newlin Township, also on Route 162 to her marker, then have lunch at Northbrook Marketplace. It's not too far from there."

"That's the best recommendation I've heard all day. Let's go, after coffee."

"Deal, but let's stay here with Frankie for a while. This is her special time… with us."

Jim smiled. "Sounds fair."

"So, here's the question- how are we ever going to *prove* that she ran into Fitzpatrick? I've never read anything about that."

"Think about it. Most cases in court are won or lost based largely on *circumstantial* evidence. Rarely do people actually *see* someone directly committing a crime. The attorneys have to piece together all the information, like a huge puzzle. The jury evaluates often unrelated bits of data to create a logical 'chain of events' and the most plausible answer. Since we're not trying to prove something criminal, this is more like a civil case, based on '*the preponderance* of the evidence.' As we gather more information, do more research on their travels and where they spent time, I know we'll be able to evaluate it more accurately. I think it may lead us to some very interesting conclusions, my dear."

"I'll have to trust you on that one. Let's get this show on the road." Natalie finished her coffee and gently moved Frankie to the cushion beside her.

"*Saddle 'em up… and ride 'em out.*" Jim was already heading into the kitchen to get his car keys. "We can check out a few spots- Indian Hannah Road and vicinity, the historical markers on Route 162 and then on to lunch."

"Done." Natalie grabbed her sunglasses and got in the dark blue Forester where Jim waited.

"Since it's close by, let's go over to the Hannah Monument near the Longwood Fire Station first, then head up north."

"O.K."

As he pulled the car to a stop behind the Fire Station, he noticed the building next to it had changed. "Hey- this used to be the Brandywine Valley Tourism Center, but the sign's gone."

"I think Longwood Gardens bought the building and may turn it into a museum. Not sure."

They walked up the paved area to the greenspace which held the monument that had originally been on Route 52, erected in 1925 by the Chester County Historical Society. The weathered brass plaque gave Jim some information he'd not considered before. "Look, it says:

*'INDIAN HANNAH 1730- 1802 The last of the Indians in Chester County was born in the vale about 300 yards to the East on the land of the protector of her people, the Quaker assemblyman WILLIAM WEBB...'*

"I never knew Webb was considered their *'protector.'* That implies a very friendly relationship between Webb and the Lenape, contrary to the relationship between the Quakers and Hannah that book by Marsh kind of implies."

Natalie leaned closer to the plaque to read the full inscription. "Yes, when I read *A Lenape Among the Quakers*, I had some doubts as to her conclusions, as Marsh seems to imply the locals were all trying to get rid of Hannah just so they could take over the land along the Brandywine. This plaque- if accurate- says something quite different about Webb. 'Protector' denotes someone helpful, concerned about another's welfare and safety."

Jim stepped back to take the entire boulder in view. "Pierre S. du Pont was here for the dedication in 1925. He paid for the monument. I read that it cost $600 and he donated the land that this monument originally stood on, as it was part of his holdings that later turned into Longwood Gardens. He wanted to preserve two things- one physically, one in memory: a sacred old growth forest which became Longwood Gardens and... Indian Hannah's legacy. The plaque says 'The last of the Indians in Chester County'- but she really wasn't. Perhaps she was the last well-known of the local Lenape- but there are people around the area *today* with some Lenape bloodline. In a way, it reminds you of the book *The Last of the Mohicans* by James Fenimore Cooper, which came out in 1820 as the Indians around the U.S. were being pushed out of their ancestral homelands."

Natalie nodded her agreement. "Not exactly our finest hour."

"I concur... but we *can* do something for them. We can keep their memory alive by delving into their history and sharing it with people. This plaque tells just part of her story. We've seen the cross inside Longwood a mile or so from here. We'll check it out next time we walk at the gardens. Descendants of the Peirce family who owned the land wanted to honor her that way... but next stop- the Indian Hannah marker on Route 162."

The tan, solid quartz boulder displaying the plaque sits several yards back from the road, out of sight of motorists as they cruise by. A short hike brings the visitor to the spot where some claimed Indian Hannah was buried in 1802, but since the plaque was installed more than a century ago, historians now believe she lies somewhere in the general vicinity, the exact gravesite unknown.

*"Here lies Indian Hannah the last of the Lenni-Lenape Indians in Chester County who died in 1802. Marked by Chester County Historical Society 1909."*

Jim leaned closer to touch the stone. "This is where Adrian and the D.A.R. had that event a while back! Adrian displayed his work *'The August Moon Lights My Way.'* It's one of my favorites by him."

"That's precisely why I *bought the painting*, remember?" Natalie looked up and all around the hillside, deep in thought.

"I know that. It was just such a special moment with him, talking about Hannah…" He glanced over and saw Natalie lost in a reverie. "Whatcha' thinking?" Jim strolled past the boulder, wondering if there was anything nearby which might produce some clues.

"Just that it's unfortunate. She wanted to be buried with other Lenape in their burial ground not far away- but what did they do? They put her over here, in an unmarked grave."

"She's not forgotten. Linda and other locals determined to preserve history wanted to keep her in front of people, so they had a ceremony in 2009- exactly a century later- and placed a new, prominent plaque on the boulder down the hillside. Let's check that one out." As they walked toward the road, it came into view. The other boulder more appropriately sits *directly facing* Route 162 where it is easily visible, the distinct black and gold plaque shining in the sunlight.

*"INDIAN HANNAH 1730- 1802 The last of the tribe of Lenni-Lenape in Chester County. Marked by Newlin Township Historical Committee 2009."*

"*Hey!* We **may** have discovered something. I've read that Humphry Marshall's nephew Moses was responsible for overseeing the poor in Chester County back in 1797. He interviewed Hannah to determine whether she might be eligible for assistance from the county, in what would be an 'almshouse' or poor people's home when it was built. She *was* ruled eligible- and when the Chester County Almshouse opened on November 12, 1800, Hannah was the first resident admitted, her age given as '69 years.' If she was 69 in the year 1800, that would mean she was born in 1731, **not 1730** as nearly *ALL* the historical markers state. Maybe we can get her birth year correct."

Natalie thought for a few seconds. "You're probably right. Perhaps the record needs adjustment."

"Remember when we toured through the old, abandoned Embreeville Hospital near here? I believe that was the successor to the Almshouse." Jim glanced over at Natalie for confirmation.

"Correct. Glad we got in there; they tore it down a few years ago. It's gone."

"Like so many other historical structures around here. We need to get photos of these places as we do our exploring so there's at least a record of what *used* to be here. There are two other spots to see- off the beaten path: where her cabin was *and* the Lenape Burial Ground. Cabin site first- it's on Indian Hannah Road, just off of Route 842. Isn't that also called Unionville-Wawaset Road?" He clicked on the remote to unlock the car as they approached it.

"Yes. Many people don't know that Wawaset is an old Lenape word, one they used to describe the Brandywine and its vicinity. A well-recognized name today: the WaWa stores all around the region. WaWa is based on an old Native American word for wild or snow goose, which are shown on their logo." Natalie perused the rolling hills of the Chester County landscape as the Forester wound its way onto Route 842, then turned onto the road named for the best-known Lenape in the region.

"Gotta' keep our eyes open. These old historical markers are often so overgrown with shrubs and vines, you can't see them." Jim steered very carefully on the narrow back road, watching for both oncoming traffic and the elusive marker. "*Whoa!!* It's right over there- almost passed it." He pulled over to the right side, slowly onto the dirt shoulder which barely allowed oncoming traffic to get by.

"Yes, I can see it. Be careful when you get out- I don't trust people on these back roads. They come flying by without paying attention."

Jim's door closed as he ran across toward the marker. "There it is."

***"In a rude cabin across the vale lived 'Indian Hannah' who died 1802. Last of the Lenni-Lenape in Chester County. Erected 1909 by the Chester County Historical Society."***

"Well, at least we found it. Says a 'rude' cabin- that shows how dated the sign is. Rude was a term used decades ago to describe something rough or crudely made. You rarely hear the word used that way today. Met a lot of rude *people*- no rude cabins. Can you get a photo?"

"Yes, but let's make it quick. I don't want to become two-dimensional."

Jim chuckled, then got back into the car. "O.K., we're heading toward West Chester, to Brandywine Drive. I think it's less than a mile from here."

"Yes, turn up there… that's Brandywine Drive ahead. Just be careful. It's another narrow, winding road."

"At that time in the late 1700s, almost EVERY thoroughfare was a 'narrow, winding road.' Hey, that's it over there!" The car moved onto the shoulder and they both got out quickly.

"This is what I was talking about earlier. Hannah wanted to be buried near her Lenape kinsmen *right here*." Natalie took a quick photo before running across the roadway.

*"In the wooded knoll above… sleeping their last sleep… rest the Indian owners of these lands before the white men came. Erected 1909 by The Chester County Historical Society."*

"Notice something? The Chester County Historical Society was extremely active in 1909. They put historical markers all around the region that year- some of which we've seen today. Gilbert Cope founded the Society in 1893 and was their Director and Secretary for 27 years. That was a time I wish I were around here to witness all this history being preserved. A golden age for Chester County." Jim perused the historical marker and his thoughts drifted back in time… to the 1800s. "Do you think they're… *still with us?*" His eyes turned toward Natalie.

"Who are you talking about?"

"All these people from the past. Humphry Marshall… Indian Hannah… Benjamin West. I sometimes think they *are* still here, in some form. Maybe just remembering them rekindles their spirit…"

Natalie's eyes almost popped out. She saw the dark brown, four-foot long snake within 6 inches of Jim's leg, curled up, seemingly ready to pounce at him. "*JIM!!* Stay right there- don't move. There's a big snake **right next to you**… so just… *slowly… back… away…* do **NOT** make any *sudden moves* with your hands or arms."

Jim looked down at his right foot and saw the viper poised near him, as if it was about to strike. Taking a deep breath, he first moved his left foot away… then his right foot even further… and took off running down the road. Looking back, he yelled "***That thing was ready to bite…*** *and it looks poisonous. Should we kill it??!!*"

"**NO!** Let me shew him away with this branch that broke off the tree." Natalie grabbed the 6-foot long limb with both hands and swept it right up against the snake, pushing it off the edge of the roadway. It slithered into the underbrush.

"Thank you. **I HATE SNAKES!! HATE 'EM!!** They remind me of a guy I used to work with… a real reptile. Look- we got some photos; *let's get outta' here.*"

Natalie threw the branch onto the side of the road. "The Indians knew how to handle snakes; I believe some American tribes ate them and used their skins. They didn't waste anything."

"Remember we got that rattlesnake skin out at the Clear Creek Trading Company in Sedona years ago? That's the closest I ever want to be to a snake, especially a rattler. They're all over out West."

"Oh, don't kid yourself. There are snakes all around us, in the forest *behind our house.* I've seen several, but they weren't anywhere near this size." She got into the car just before he gunned it to take off. "What's next?"

"Lunch. Traveling gives me an appetite. Our destination- Northbrook Marketplace. We can chat about Hannah, Sandy Flash, Humphry Marshall and all these characters with some good food and nice atmosphere." He steered the car back onto Unionville-Wawaset Road and cruised up to the parking lot flanking the large red barn structure with its white roof. As he pulled into a space, he noticed two men playing banjos out front on the porch. "We might even have some entertainment." As they exited the car, a familiar song rang out from their instruments. "That's… *Foggy Mountain Breakdown?* YES!! Earl Scruggs!! I *LOVE* that tune!! One of the best bluegrass songs ever written." Jim smiled and gave a hearty clap, then dropped a $5 Bill into their Tip Jar as they passed the two men and went inside. He took the booth closest to the door as Natalie walked up to the counter to order.

She eyed the hand-written menu on the wall and then noticed the small sign on the counter for the 'Soup of the Day- Potato Corn Chowder.' As the young, bearded man walked up, she said "I'll have The Shepherd- that's lamb, right- with a bowl of your Corn Chowder."

"Yes. The Shepherd is lamb. Is this all together?" He smiled as Jim came right up.

"Yes, and I'll have The Backwoods as a Wrap with extra mayo- *extra mayo.*" He felt Natalie's foot kick his shoe. "I'll also have the Corn Chowder and add in a bag of Uncle Harold's Barn Good Chips. They're delicious!" He took the order sheet with prices from the man and turned to walk toward the bakery. "Hon, I got us our favorite booth by the Jackalope under the Bearskin on the wall. I'll get us some water… and I'm having coffee. I'll be right back after I pay." He strolled over to where the Apple Cider donuts were being freshly made and stopped to take in the aroma. "If I worked here, I'd have them every day."

The smiling middle-aged blonde woman behind the counter laughed. "They *ARE* delicious. People come from all over to buy our donuts. Want to try one?" She grabbed a freshly made cinnamon-dusted donut and handed it to Jim.

He looked over at Natalie as he bit into the delicious brown ring and knew what he would hear. "I know, I know-don't worry- I *won't* buy a dozen. Maybe… *TWO* dozen?"

"Jim, *NO.* As much as I'd love them, we have to try and keep a healthy diet."

"I agree. Unfortunately, after you turn 55, you *LOOK* at food and gain weight. I work out six days a week just to *stay even.* If I was 20 years younger, with all these workouts, I'd look like Jack LaLane. Donuts won't help any, but (he took another large bite savoring it). They are *superb.*" He turned to the woman who was making a fresh batch. "Thank you! These really are delicious." Turning, Jim walked over into the side room where the bakery items- freshly baked chocolate-chip cookies, scones, cherry, apple, peach and blueberry pies, bagels, and banana bread were all laid out, their pungent aroma tantalizing each person who strolled by. After grabbing a coffee and bottled water, he paid for everything and went back into the dining area. Sitting down, he was ready to share his new idea. He looked at Natalie as she sipped her water.

"They'll bring everything over when it's ready. So, where do we go after this?"

Jim made a quick summary in his head before speaking. "O.K.- here's my thesis. I've been thinking about this area as it was back in the late 1700s. It wasn't very developed; people knew their neighbors, even those who lived miles away. Humphry Marshall, Indian Hannah, James Fitzpatrick, Benjamin West and even Thomas McKean- they all lived in this general area at roughly the same time."

"Wait a minute- *Thomas McKean?*" Natalie's eyebrows rose as she heard him speak. "Where is his place in all this?"

"Thomas McKean was one of the best-known politicians in colonial era Pennsylvania. He was born in New London- southern Chester County, not that far from where we live- became Chief Justice of the Supreme Court of Pennsylvania and was also, at various times, Governor of *BOTH* Pennsylvania and Delaware. Add in the fact that he was a signer of the *Declaration of Independence* and you can see how important he was in our heritage."

"… but how does he fit in *here…??*" Natalie remained unconvinced.

"Thomas McKean was the ***presiding Judge*** for the trial of James Fitzpatrick- 'Sandy Flash'- the man who sentenced him to death by hanging in September 1778."

Natalie grinned with approval. "Interesting. That's important, but what about Benjamin West? How does *he* factor in?"

"Fascinating you ask. The very first biography written of West, titled *The Life, Works and Studies of Benjamin West* by John Galt, based on West's own recollections mentions that he was taught about using natural pigments for colors made by the *local Lenape* from various clays they found along riverbanks. It's quite possible some of them were from Hannah's own tribe. West was very interested in the Lenape- they inspired his painting *Penn's Treaty with the Indians.* Could he have come across Indian Hannah in his younger days, his travels? Perhaps…"

Natalie's face showed tacit agreement. "Well, that's worth considering. From your comments, linking all these people together seems at least *plausible.*"

"I've also been thinking about the layout of this region back in the 1770s. There weren't anywhere near as many roads through Chester County back then and the population of the entire county was about 15,000- *only 2.5%* of what it is today. These characters lived and traveled fairly close to each other, likely on the same roads around the same time. Remember- people weren't flying by each other at 60 miles an hour- they were going relatively slowly, about 10 miles an hour by horse or coach, a 'crawl' to us. They saw other residents daily, ***up close***- and probably even stopped to talk. The slower pace of life and travel at the time made interactions between people much more likely.  It's a good bet that many, perhaps most of them met up with each other. Think about it- Humphry Marshall was one of the best-known botanists in America, Indian Hannah was a local fixture on the scene, offering her wares and working odd jobs all around here, Thomas McKean was one of the best-known politicians in Pennsylvania, Fitzpatrick was recognized all around for his robberies… and Benjamin West's family ran a very popular tavern. No one has ever written about this, but I think I'll be able to connect them… in some way."

"Well, if you could show they actually came into contact with each other, maybe exchanged letters, that would prove some kind of a link, but *where do you want to take this?*" Natalie looked up as the bearded man placed their lunches on the table in front of them.

"Just showing how they likely all interacted in some way would be interesting." He took a bite of his Backwoods wrap, then a sip of coffee before looking at the wall above their heads. "I love this place. Where else can you hear great bluegrass music- *and* have lunch with a Jackalope?"

Natalie couldn't contain her laugh. "It is… rustic. I'll give it that." She was enjoying her Shepherd sandwich as she thought about what they might do next. "Do you have a list of places you want to check out?"

"You're right on target, madam. I want to visit Humphry Marshall's home, the house where Fitzpatrick lived with his mother and the Longwood Gardens archives for information on Indian Hannah. I visited the house where Benjamin West was born on the campus of Swarthmore College a while back, took several photos and notes. Those should all be interesting- and may give me some clues."

"What about Thomas McKean? You forgot him." Natalie was enjoying her lamb and waited for him to speak.

"Remember a few years ago, I was doing some research at the Delaware County Historical Society? I got a private tour of the 1724 Chester Court House- where Fitzpatrick was convicted by McKean. I went and walked around inside- probably right where Fitzpatrick stood. Even went up to the attic and rang the bell. I have some great photos of that place, so I'll revisit my notes. Fitzpatrick was hung not too far from there." Jim crunched his way through several Uncle Harold's Barn Good Chips, washing them down with coffee.

"A lot to explore. I'd love to see Marshall's house. Speaking of houses, Bayard Taylor fits in here as well. He 'invented' Sandy Flash and his house Cedarcroft is just outside of downtown Kennett. We should stop over there, too."

"Great idea. Even better if we could get inside. It's on the National Register of Historic Places." He started thinking about 'trails'… "You know, I think there's a Bayard Taylor connection here. If I could somehow tie his background to what happened around in the area-specifically with Fitzpatrick- that would be interesting."

She nodded as she finished her sandwich. "How, exactly? He lived *well after* most of these people. Wasn't he born around the 1820s or 1830s?"

"Taylor was born in 1825. Taylor's father wanted him to work on the farm, but Bayard had more interest in books. That led to him working as an apprentice in a printing shop. He started writing on his own and yearned to become a great poet. Just a guess, but I think he was fascinated reading stories about Fitzpatrick in the local newspapers and he created Flash as a romantic, *larger-than-life* person to captivate people in the region, as all good novelists try to do. Did you know his name was actually *James* Bayard Taylor?"

Natalie wiped her lips. "No, I thought it was just Bayard Taylor. Isn't that the way he portrayed himself?"

"Yes, but his parents named him after Delaware Congressman and Senator James Bayard. Bayard was very well regarded as a politician. Although he was a Federalist who opposed Thomas Jefferson in his bid to become President in 1800, Aaron Burr was Jefferson's main opponent. They both had more Electoral Votes than John Adams, who was trying to get reelected. The Federalists weren't thrilled with Jefferson *OR* Adams, but they knew after much prodding from people like Alexander Hamilton that Burr would be a horrific choice for President. So, Bayard helped persuade other Federalists to abstain from voting, *allowing Jefferson to win the vote* in one of the most contentious Presidential elections in American history. Bayard was later appointed as the only Federalist to help negotiate the Treaty of Ghent, which ended the War of 1812. Taylor's parents must have really liked Bayard, naming their son after him." Jim finished his lunch and waited for Natalie's decision.

"Interesting. I'm sure most people don't know that about him. Ready?" Natalie got up out of the booth- and glanced up at the Jackalope. "*That* little guy is why we eat here, right?"

"I like him. They're very rare."

"Next week, we'll head back out onto the trail. First- I think we should hunt down the haunts and hiding places of Sandy Flash. That may lead us to other sites. I never thought I'd say this again, but… ***ROAD TRIP!***" Natalie took Jim's hand as they walked through to the parking lot.

"You and me, doing some exploring- like the old days. Now… I want to find a way to get *into Cedarcroft*. That house is a gem."

"Jim! We're not getting in trouble trying to break into his home. If we can get an invitation from the current owners, fine. Otherwise, no shenanigans."

Jim opened the car door for her. "Wouldn't think of it…"

Indian Hannah plaque behind the former
Longwood Progressive Friends Meeting House

Dedication of Indian Hannah marker 1925 with Beulah
H. Webb, a Boy Scout bugler and Chief Strong Wolf
courtesy of Hagley Museum and Library

Indian Hannah burial marker on the grounds of the
former Chester County Alms House

Indian Hannah historical marker on Route 162
in front of the grounds of the former Chester
County Alms House

Historical marker identifying Indian Hannah home site, located on Indian Hannah Rd., Newlin Township

Historical marker for the Lenape burial ground, located on Brandywine Drive, Newlin Township

Historical marker identifying 'Indian Rock' and the claim of the Lenape for land up to the source of the Brandywine, located on Brandywine Drive, West Bradford Township

*Examination of Indian Hannah* by artist Adrian Martinez

1798
3rd mo. the 1st

## Kindness extended.

Hannah Freeman Commonly Called Indian Hannah an Antient woman of the Delaware Tribe and the only Person of that Description left amongst us being afflicted with Rheumatism and unable to Support herself accustomed to Travel from house to House which is some times attended with Great difficulty and Inconvenience it is thought her Situation Claims the Sympathy of the humane in order that she may be more Regularly and Permanently Provided for in a manner Suited to her usual way of living. —— Therefore Be it Remembered that We the Subscribers do severally agree to Contribute towards her maintainance (if Providence Should favour us with ability) Yearly and every year during her natural Life in Money or otherwise agreeable to what we Subscribe Subject to the Disposal of two Guardians or Trustees and a Treasurer annually appointed at a Meeting of the Subscribers on the first 2nd day in the Eleventh month at one o' Clock on said day at the House of Richard Barnard at which time said Trustees are to Produce full accounts of what they have Received and expended on the occasion which Service is Submitted to the Care of Mordecai and Jacob Peirce for the Present year and Joseph Barnard named for Treasurer who is not to pay any thing out of the stock without Written orders from one of the Trustees, and after her decease her funeral Expences being discharged if there should be an overplus the Trustees and Treasurer are to Return it to the Subscribers in Proportion to what they have advanced —

| Subscribers to keep her and the time per Year — | Weeks | Days |
| --- | --- | --- |
| Richard Barnard | 2 | - |
| Joseph Barnard | 1 | |
| Samuel Marshall | 1 | 2 |
| William Allan | 2 | |
| Richard Bernard Jr | 1 | |
| Isaac Baily Jr | 1 | |

| Subscribers to pay money and the yearly Sum | £ | s | d |
| --- | --- | --- | --- |
| Richard Jones | 2 | 5 | 6 |
| Thos. Sugar | | 2 | 6 |
| Joshua Buffington | | 7 | 6½ |
| George Speakman | | 5 | 7½ |
| James Smith | | 5 | 6 |
| Enoch Taylor | | 7 | 6 |
| Charles Wilson | - | 7 | 6 |

**Kindness Extended document signed by local citizens in 1798 supporting Indian Hannah courtesy of Chester County History Center**

**Northbrook Marketplace on Route 842 in Pocopson Township**

# Chapter 11

*"Ground arms!" he cried, "or you are a dead man." He was obeyed, although slowly and with grinding teeth. "Stand aside!" he then commanded. "You have pluck, and I should hate to shoot you. Make way, the rest o' ye!... Whoever puts finger to trigger, falls."*
-Sandy Flash in Bayard Taylor's *The Story of Kennett*

*The prisoner stood in his assigned spot inside the courthouse, its stone walls erected 54 years earlier to hold criminals and other rogues accountable to the community. Chief Justice McKean stared directly at the barrister. "What are the charges against this man?" The attorney representing the state looked at the long list in front of him. "Robbery, abduction, assault, torture, kidnapping and deserting from the Continental Army, Sir." McKean looked over at the man, who mumbled to himself that the rebels would not come close to delivering an equitable verdict.*

*"… and how do you plead, sir?!" Fitzpatrick refused to answer, instead looking down at the floor beneath his shackled feet. "Sir!! How do you plead?! Answer me now!" After several seconds elapsed, the prisoner said "Not guilty…."*

****************************************************************************

Jim jotted down several lines of notes sitting at the glass table as Natalie did chores around the inside and outside of the house. The notes pointed him in a direction and nudged him to lay out a plan for the next few days as she came back into the kitchen. "O.K., here's the deal. The Delaware County Historical Society has a huge amount on Sandy Flash; the Chester County History Center and Longwood Gardens have extensive information on Humphry Marshall, Benjamin West, William Darlington and Indian Hannah. Lightning speed research- with digitized archives. You identify the exact files you want to see without physically handling the entire collection. They're all open this week. I want to start at the Delco site, then work my way through the others. I should be able to get it done fairly quickly. I already know what I want to see."

"Want some company?" Natalie sipped her iced tea as she waited for confirmation.

"Sure. Let's start in Chester at the Delaware County Historical Society archives and afterwards, have lunch nearby. Then we'll go over to the old Courthouse where they put Fitzpatrick on trial. Afterwards we'll do some exploring on the streets and try to find the spot where they hung him. I think it's near the intersection of Edgmont and Providence Avenues." Jim looked around the room quickly, lights flickering several times. "What the Hell *was that?!* Did we lose power for a minute?"

Natalie put down her drink. "We did. Maybe somebody's trying to shake us up- as if we haven't had enough shaking up already."

"Some spirits, giving us messages?"

Natalie laughed. "To do what- *pay our electric bill- which just got stolen?*"

"Let's finish here, then head over to the Delco Historical Society. They open soon."

The displays inside the stately Delaware County Historical Society building invite the viewer to delve into more than three centuries of the people, places and events which helped create our nation. Jim and Natalie walked through the front door expecting to find extensive information on the infamous Sandy Flash.

"Welcome. You folks members?" A svelte middle-aged woman with short, dark brown wavy hair, wearing earrings, a form-fitting dress and a friendly smile approached them from the rear room, which held file cabinets and stacks of books along the walls.

"We are. I'm Jim Peterson."

"Oh yes, our Director Paul told me you might be coming. Our records and artifacts go back to the late 17th century. We've pulled several files for you on James Fitzpatrick. I've laid the boxes here on this cart; feel free to sit anywhere and review them." The woman led them to the back room, motioning where the files for them were waiting.

"That's great. Thanks so much." Jim strode over to the table and pulled out a chair for Natalie. "There's *a lot* here, sweetie. You could build a room divider with these boxes. Choose which files you want. I'll take second pick."

Natalie promptly sat down, then pulled over one large grey box, flipping open the lid and seeing several Manilla folders stuffed with documents and newspaper clippings. "We've got a ton to go through. Here's several old newspaper accounts of him. They have photographs of the house he was captured in." She paged through each small folder, then found something that seemed to jump out at her. "Look: an article on Fitzpatrick from the *Village Record*, May 19, 1824, discussing his exploits and capture. Check this out- there have been dozens of articles written about this guy, from the 1800s to recent years."

Jim looked intently at each page in the folder in front of him. "Here's one of the earliest accounts of Fitzgerald, from *The Pennsylvania Packet*, July 13, 1778:

*"James Fitzpatrick… doth… in Chester County, infest the highway from this city to Lancaster, committing robbery on the good subjects of this State… a reward of ONE THOUSAND DOLLARS be paid to the person who shall secure the said James Fitzpatrick, so that he be convicted of the said offence* (sic). *Extract from the Minutes, T. Matlack, Secretary."*

He glanced over at Natalie. "Do you know who T. Matlack was?"

"No, but I'm sure you do." Natalie kept paging through the files.

"Timothy Matlack was Clerk to the Secretary of the Continental Congress. He helped keep notes of the proceedings during the Revolution and penned the official version of the

*Declaration of Independence.*" Jim kept the folder right in front of him. "The reward to capture him was *huge*. A thousand dollars was a *LOT* of money in those days."

Natalie had several documents laid out on the table in front of her. "O.K., here's a synopsis. Fitzpatrick was born in 1748 in the Doe Run area, about 7 miles northwest of Kennett Square as you go on Route 82. We don't have his exact date of birth. He was trained as a blacksmith- a tradesman, like *Marshall*- and was an apprentice to a man named John Passmore in that area. He is reported to have been a large, muscular man, about 6-foot 4 inches tall (a 'giant' at the time) with broad shoulders and sandy reddish hair. After his apprenticeship was complete around age 21, which would be about 1769, he started plying his trade around southern Chester County. Sometime in 1776, he joined the Patriot cause and enlisted in the Chester County militia, accompanied the 'Flying Camp' and served with Washington's forces in the Battle of Long Island in August of that year. Unfortunately, the battle was a disaster for our side. Several sources mention that he was disciplined for some reason- possibly disobeying an order- and felt he was severely mistreated in the Army. This enraged him and he went AWOL, sometime either in late 1776 or early 1777; no clear date is given. Here's where the story gets 'questionable.' Some accounts claim he swam across the Hudson River and made it back down the coast to the Philadelphia area. His 'swimming the Hudson' seems a tad unbelievable: the narrowest extent of the Hudson on the western side of Long Island (today's Brooklyn) is over a mile wide and it empties into the Bay which is well over *five* miles wide. He likely stole a boat or somehow got a ride across. Either way, he wanted to get back home to Chester County and be *out* of the Army. He didn't want anything to do with the Patriots because they had punished him."

"O.K. so… he made it back to the area. Wasn't he quickly captured?" Jim's raised eyebrows showed his attention.

"Yes. An excellent narrative by Rosemary Warden of Penn State University titled '*The Infamous Fitch: The Tory Bandit, James Fitzpatrick of Chester County*' is one of the most detailed analyses I've seen and describes his exploits. Some soldiers recognized him in Philadelphia and apprehended him, sending him to the Walnut Street Prison. He told his captors that he was willing to rejoin the Army *if they let him free*- and they did. *Wrong move.* Fitzpatrick deserted **AGAIN** and went back home to Doe Run in Chester County, working on Passmore's farm to earn a living. In the Summer of 1777 militia apprehended him, but he somehow persuaded them to allow him to go back to his mother's house to get some belongings, which they did. Another bad move- Fitzpatrick grabbed a gun and threatened to kill them if they ever approached him again. So, they let him go. Seems that he could escape at any time, any place."

Jim couldn't help but chuckle. "This guy was a regular Houdini. Then what happened?"

"By late Summer of 1777, the British had landed at the Head of Elk and were marching toward the Philadelphia area, ending up in Chadds Ford west of the city. Fitzpatrick apparently learned of their presence and joined up with them, some sources stating that he was present at the Battle of the Brandywine in support of General Howe's Army fighting against Washington. It is estimated that he used his knowledge of local terrain and farms to steal horses and supplies for the British. No proof has been found listing his service in *their* Army, but he started calling himself 'Captain Fitz' (sometimes 'Fitch'), which became his nickname. Howe's forces finally left the Philadelphia area in June 1778. By that time, apparently Fitz was robbing people all around Chester County to get back at the Patriots and their sympathizers who he felt had treated him badly. His main targets were tax collectors and military recruiters, although he apparently attacked anyone he felt was a Whig sympathizer in support of the rebels. For about nine months- some sources say a year or more- he terrorized the region, going all the way from Lancaster toward Philadelphia, a large swath of territory, accosting people, often kidnapping them, tying them to trees and flogging them severely. There are reports that state he threatened to blow their brains out and often left some people tied up in a forest, abandoned out in the elements to die, but there are no mentions of him actually killing anyone. Apparently he was huge, far bigger than the average male at the time, often with two pistols in his hands. So, you can see why he was feared by most of the population."

"I'm not surprised he got away with his nefarious deeds. Many of the residents in the area were Quakers, who were very hesitant to help anyone associated with Washington's Army. Some of them may have secretly *sympathized with* Fitz opposing those they associated with war- or at least a few of them may have just looked the other way." Jim noticed many articles from decades past in the folder in front of him, including a copy of the same Darden source Natalie had mentioned.

"Darden mentions evidence for that in her narrative:

*'East Marlborough Township, a predominantly Quaker Township... refused to organize a militia unit or to elect officers... General Anthony Wayne wrote to Council President Thomas Wharton in the spring of 1778, to suggest that he stop recruiting troops in Chester County, a wasted effort, and concentrate on raising men in Berks, Lancaster, York or Cumberland Counties.'*

"She states that a loyalist bandit like Fitzpatrick would find support and even friendly places to hide in the area." Natalie looked over at Jim and noticed the table completely covered with references.

"Well, his exploits got enough attention over the years. I've gone through several articles which give him almost superhuman powers, corroborating that he escaped capture numerous times from large groups of armed men out to get him. The article from the *Village Record* in 1824 mentions:

*'On one occasion fifty or more persons assembled well armed and resolved to take him if possible dead or alive…. but becoming weary of the chase, they called at a tavern to rest… every one of them expressing his wish to meet with Fitch, suddenly to their great astonishment he presented himself before them with his rifle in hand… declaring that he would shoot the first man that moved. Then having called for a small glass of rum and drank it off, he walked backwards… and took to his heels, leaving the stupefied company in silent amazement.'*

Jim shook his head. "Think about it- *50 well armed men* couldn't capture **one** man? It really smacks of sensationalism. They romanticize him, some even making him out to be a hero on the order of Robin Hood- stealing only from the rich and giving to the poor. My estimate is that he was a ruthless opportunist, a common thief, out to get money any way he could. He was a deserter during the war; many deserters got the *death penalty*, so he was a desperate man. He did have an accomplice- a guy named Mordecai Dougherty, who likely helped him escape at times. Nonetheless, many of these accounts just seem 'larger than life.'"

"Guess what? That sells newspapers." Natalie held the articles written in the mid-late 1800s in front of her. "From these here- and in several on-line searches I did before- I am certain there are **no mentions of a man with the nickname 'Sandy Flash' before 1866**- the year Bayard Taylor's *The Story of Kennett* came out. Before that, Sandy Flash did **not exist**. He was a creation of the author, based very loosely on the real man Fitzpatrick. Taylor's book also has him in the wrong time period- the mid-1790s, almost 18 years after he passed from the scene. Many of these later articles written in the 20th century even mention a treasure he supposedly accumulated, amazingly 'worth more than the wealth of Chester County'- hidden in the boulder-strewn hills of Castle Rock, near Newtown Square. It's never been found. As the years went on, the legend grew… as they often do… and took on a life of its own."

"I agree. Fitzpatrick *morphed* into Sandy Flash through Taylor's book, which was quite popular, until finally **there was no Fitzpatrick, only Sandy Flash**. I have a theory on how Taylor created him: he reminded Taylor of *his own* experiences. In his book '*Eldorado, Or Adventures in the Path of Empire*', Taylor wrote about going out to California during the Gold Rush days of 1849- 1850. He toured all around the area, but on the way back East, he decided to go through Mexico, even though he was sharply warned by many people that the area was highly dangerous and filled with bandits. Being the adventurer who loved to visit wild, exotic places, Taylor ignored all their advice and went back through remote, uninhabited areas. You know what happened? *He got accosted by bandits, was robbed, tied up and left for dead in the sweltering desert.* He was penniless, with only the shirt on his back and almost died- but somehow made it to a nearby town and was rescued. It's a good bet he incorporated some of his personal experiences in the character of Sandy Flash."

Natalie's face widened to a grin hearing the details about Taylor's book. "I didn't know that. It's a good theory for how Taylor invented Flash, helped by somewhat sensationalized local newspaper reports of the mid-1800s which it's likely he read. I've gone through all these files- and made good notes. Want to get lunch?"

"Sure- I've jotted down quite a bit from what I've seen here- and… I'm hungry." Jim looked up at the woman attendant there. "This is wonderful information. I'll certainly check back with you and Paul if I have other questions."

"We're glad you found it helpful and appreciate you maintaining your membership. We rely on people like you to keep the lights on and the coffee going."

Jim and Natalie strolled out the door and turned to look both ways down the street for a diner or coffee shop. "There's a place just down the road which looks… a bit funky, but it's open. Let's try there." He took her hand and walked to the front door of 'The Lunch Basket.' "Well, guess this is as good as we're going to do around here. Can't be too bad- it seems to be packed with people." They entered and stood about 20 feet in front of a large wooden counter with memorabilia which came from another era. A young attendant was standing there, waiting to serve them.

"*Funky is right.*" Natalie kept her voice low, as she spoke in Jim's ear. "Check out the person over there, ready to take our order. Is that a man… *or a woman?*"

Jim eyed the person intensely for several seconds, then leaned over to Natalie and whispered: *"It's a coin toss."*

She cracked up, but turned away to hide her face from the attendant.

He stared again at the server, then spoke in a low voice to Natalie. "I guess to get a job today, a nose ring and neck tattoos are mandatory."

"Don't forget the pink hair. *Very important.*" She couldn't contain her laugh. "Actually… they don't have a bad menu. A lot of sandwiches, soups and salads. I think I know what I want. What do you say- give this place a try?"

"Life all comes down to a few moments. Order me the chicken salad melt, with a side Caesar. I need to use the restroom. I'll be back in a little bit. Let's take that booth over there."

Natalie moved toward the counter. "This'll be together: I'll have the Harvest salad with vinaigrette dressing and the corn chowder soup. My husband will have the chicken salad melt with a side Caesar. How much is that?"

"That'll be… \$37.24 with tax."

Even hearing the voice, Natalie still couldn't determine male or female, but shrugged it off and paid, then took her seat at the booth. Looking all around, she determined it was likely that a group of aging hippies ran the place, stocking it with old posters from the 1960s- 1970s and photographs from the period. "This place is funky, but… it is… *interesting*…" Her eyes wandered all around the room, taking in every memento and oddity. Several minutes passed as she was enraptured by an environment she wasn't familiar with, but the sound of two trays placed on the table broke her reverie. "Oh! *That was fast!*" She looked up to see a very voluptuous woman in a low-cut, V-neck top with a smirk across her face, shaking her head.

"What, you don't *WANT* your food served quick?" She walked back toward the kitchen without even waiting for a response.

Natalie was not impressed. "I'm sure *she* gets a lot of attention from the customers. Now… *where is Jim?* He's been in the restroom for… over 10 minutes."

Just then, his footsteps signaled his approach. "I'm back. Ready to eat?"

"Yes- but why did it *take you so long?*"

"I was checking out the bathroom; it's even funkier than out here, like time travel back to 1968. Did you ever figure out who- or *what*- the front attendant was?"

"No, but the waitress who brought our orders is… a piece of work…"

"How's that?"

"Blonde with an attitude… big boobs. Your basic nightmare." Natalie tried the soup and was pleasantly surprised. "Actually, the food here is *quite good.*"

Jim took a large bite out of his sandwich and then tried the salad. "Yes, sometimes funky is… *good.*"

After lunch they wandered down the street to the 1724 Courthouse, the grey stone structure still standing firm after three centuries. "The private tour I got here was great. Fitzpatrick was tried and convicted here on September 15, 1778. Sentenced to hang on September 26th- your Birthday, babe."

"*Not* something I'll add to our calendar." Natalie scanned the walls of the structure. "The building is in good shape. That historical marker tells an interesting story:

*'Georgian Colonial design. Built in 1724, restored in 1920. In use for Chester County till 1786, for Delaware County 1789-1851. Later used as City Hall. Oldest public building in continuous use in U.S.'*

Natalie's eyes wandered all around the site. "Wish we could go inside- I guess you have to arrange for a tour now. A while back I read they had scheduled a complete renovation to celebrate 300 years in use."

"From what I recall in my visit, the inside's still in excellent condition. An article I saw at the Society mentioned they did a reenactment of the trial back here in 1924 for the 200th anniversary of the Courthouse and also another one in the early 1990s. Would love to have seen that. I recently contacted the Pennsylvania State Archives and got a copy of the verdict given in this case where McKean was the Chief Justice. It reads: *'Therefore it is considered by the said Justices that the said James Fitzpatrick be hanged by the neck till he be dead.'* They executed him not too far away. Do you know much about McKean?"

Natalie shook her head. "You know far more about local history. Give me just the highlights?"

"McKean was educated at Francis Alison's New London Academy, one of the first schools in the colonies. Alison's other students included George Read and James Smith. All three were signers of the *Declaration of Independence*. New London Academy later moved and became the Newark Academy- forerunner of the University of Delaware. McKean's moment in the spotlight came when Delaware's delegates were about to vote regarding independence. When his colleague George Read indicated he was *against* the motion, 'cancelling' McKean's vote, he was <u>not</u> happy. On July 1, 1776, McKean urgently requested that Caesar Rodney attend the meeting to break the tie and put Delaware in the 'YES' camp. Rodney rode all night through a rainstorm, arriving the next day, casting his vote *FOR* independence."

Jim knew she might be on 'overload' and said "Just a few more facts about this guy. McKean died June 24, 1817 in Philadelphia. He's memorialized in many places. McKean County, Pennsylvania was created in his honor. There's a Thomas McKean High School in Delaware and a dormitory at the University of Delaware named after him. A simple blue and gold historical marker stands at his former property near New London, not too far from our house. We've driven by it."

Natalie was impressed. "Kudos. I didn't want a Doctoral Dissertation. I was just wondering if we could see where Fitzpatrick was hung."

"Want to venture down there?"

"Sure." They proceeded back to the car and drove to the intersection of 12th and Edgmont Streets. She looked around and saw the roadway of I-95 in the distance. "Now this is completely changed since they put the Interstate here. An article I read in the *Philadelphia Times* from January 3, 1886 stated that apparently many people were hung and buried around this spot, including a woman named Elizabeth Wilson, who was tried and convicted of murder. After she was taken to be hung at the gallows, her brother *found the people* she was accused of killing. They were *still alive*- so he frantically rode his horse at breakneck speed to try and stop her execution. He was a bit late- she'd already been hanged. In 1868 a row of townhouses were built on the east side of Edgmont Street- and in the digging, found human bones. Natalie pulled out a small pad that held her notes. "The article claimed:

***'These were doubtless the mortal relics of Elizabeth Wilson, James Fitzpatrick, the 'Sandy Flash' of Bayard Taylor's 'Story of Kennett' and less conspicuous criminals, who were… strangled to death on 'Hangman's Lot…'***

"The townhouses are gone now, but we're standing right around where they reported the bones were found." She put the notepad back in her purse.

Jim traipsed around the edge of the roadway, noticing the rough-hewn embankment rimmed by a low wall with dozens of stones, twigs, bits of trash and other debris sticking out from the soil. After kicking the dirt in numerous spots, he noticed something a bit… *different* protruding from the crusty soil. Bending down, he picked up what appeared to be a greyish-white rock and examined it closely. "As a former geologist, I'll say- this is *NOT* a rock." He looked at it up close in the sunlight. "Can't tell for sure, but I'd guess this is a piece of… *bone?*"

Natalie strode right up to him. "Let me see it." Her eyes widened as she flipped it over and closer to her face. "I think… you're right. It *DOES* look like a bone."

"It doesn't appear to be an *animal* bone- and from my biology courses, I'd say this is human. In college, I loved biology and chemistry. They were my favorite courses."

"Congratulations. What about this thing you're holding in front of your nose?"

"I recall from my studies- this is what human bones look like. Even though it's just a section, it's pretty thick, maybe part of an upper arm bone- the *humerus*? A man's bones would be thicker than a woman's; this is *thick*. Could it be part of the remains of… *James Fitzpatrick?*"

Natalie took it from his hands. "We'll never know for sure but… *it just might be.* You may be holding the last remnants of… the Highwayman of Castle Rock."

**Spot where James Fitzpatrick is believed to have been hanged near 12th and Edgmont Streets Chester, Pa**

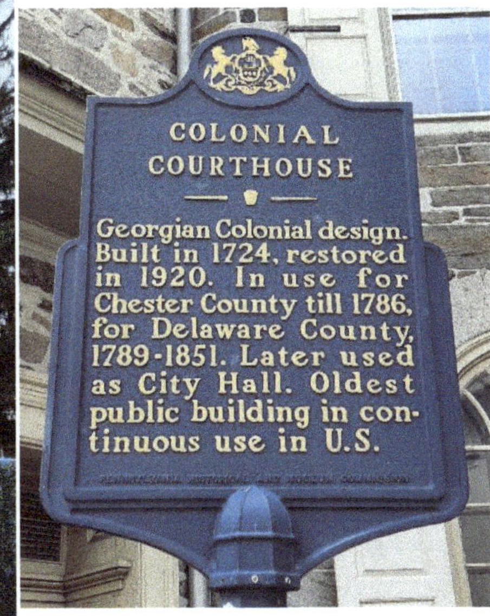

Interior of the 1724 Chester County Courthouse

Mock trial held in 1924 courtesy
*The Philadelphia Inquirer*
September 20, 1992

**A re-enactment of the trial** of James Fitzpatrick, or Sandy Flash, was held in 1924 in Chester. The actual trial, which resulted in a death sentence, took place in 1778.

McAfee home where James Fitzpatrick was arrested

Portrait of Thomas McKean
by Charles Willson Peale

Thomas McKean historical marker
New London Township, Pa.

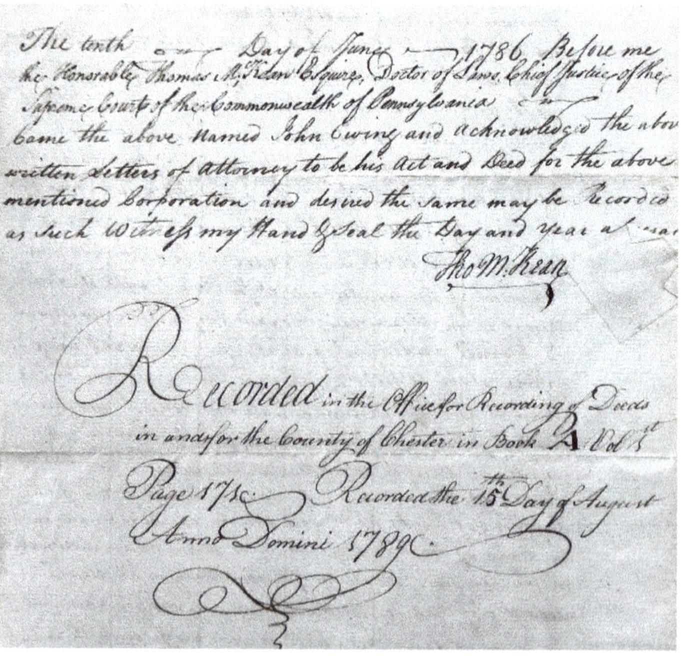

State document signed by Pennsylvania Chief Justice
Thomas McKean August 15, 1789
courtesy Chester County History Center

# Chapter 12

*"My deeds are dust in air… My words are ghosts of thought… I ride through the night alone, detached from the life that seemed… And the best I have felt or known… Is less than the least I dreamed."*      -Bayard Taylor, "The Ghosts of Night"

*Gazing at the heavy oak bookcase in his library which held the many books he had written, the world traveler and poet dwelled upon his next project: a novel, telling the story of his hometown of Kennett Square, taking the reader all around the rolling, verdant hillsides of Chester County, its rustic back roads and farms with rural charm the setting for a series of adventures involving faces familiar to many in the community, giving new life to the tale of a notorious bandit from decades ago. "Write what you know… that's the best source of inspiration." He thought of the life-threatening experience he had traveling the back roads in Mexico after his tour out West and that 'connected' with numerous stories he'd read of a Revolutionary War outlaw who terrorized Chester County…*

********************************************************************

Jim stepped out onto the terrace in the early morning light, surrounded by all the 'friends' Natalie had planted for them: the maroon and lime-green pointed coleus leaves reveling in the cool, crisp air, the tawny, furry ends of the spiking purple fountain grasses standing tall near the vibrant basil plants and nearby climbing Morning Glory vines with their deep violet and fuchsia flowers doing their best to wrap around the black metal banister all the way to the top step. "Love this time of day… no phone ringing, no car horns- just the chirps of the robins, wrens and yellow finches as they play their morning symphony." As he turned to go back through the tall, heavy glass sliding doors into the Breakfast Room, he distinctly felt something gently rubbing up against his leg. He looked down- but there was *nothing there*. No Frankie. He thought for a few seconds… then knew instantly who it was and smiled. "Thank you, Francis for coming to see me." Jim walked back inside, then glanced over at their 12-year old parakeet. "Hi Patty! I love you, my girl." Peppermint Patty chirped repeatedly and hopped toward him in her cage by the window.

He went over to the teapot which was singing loudly. The chamomile teabag already in the cup, he filled it and dunked it up and down several times, then heard Natalie's footsteps coming down the back stairs. "Good morning."

"Hi hon. Good morning." She kissed him and grabbed her cup, which he'd already filled with coffee. "O.K.- what's the plan for today? More archives to visit?"

"Yes. Going over to the Chester County History Center; they have a huge number of documents and images on Marshall, Hannah, William Darlington and Bayard Taylor. A lot of ground to cover, but I've already noted which files I want to see. Then I'm heading over to

Longwood Gardens to see their archives, too. I'm curious to see if they have any material indicating the spot where Indian Hannah was born."

"We know where her cross is, there on the hillside, back away from the trail. You'll be there all day, I guess?" Her voice turned a bit sad in its tone, but then perked up.

"Pretty much, but I'll try to be back home by around 4:00 p.m."

"You know, that's alright. I have a lot of weeding and pruning in the garden to do- and also around the house, where that Rose of Sharon bush is hanging way over the path. Just weeding will take me a few hours. I'll be ready for a break by the time you get back." She sipped her coffee and welcomed Frankie into her lap. "Stay here with us for a while." Then her tone turned somber. "*I think of all our kitties…*"

"I do, every day. Francis, Momcat and Dadcat- they're all here with us- and always will be."  His thoughts were on them, but also racing across several topics. "I'm eager to delve into the lives of these people- where they lived, worked, people they knew, things they accomplished."

Natalie noticed he was almost finished his tea. "That's a lot of ground to cover." She took another sip. "Stick around for a bit?" Natalie finished her coffee and handed the cup over to him for a refill.

"Just a bit. I'll give you more coffee first. Then I'll be off." He wandered back to the kitchen, filled her cup and returned to the Conservatory, walking through their 'Southwest Wing' with its ornately carved and painted wooden Indian figures they'd gotten at the historic El Tovar Hotel at the Grand Canyon, as well as a bull's skull and horns, tomahawks, a rattlesnake skin and dozens of other artifacts from their many trips out West. "I'm glad we preserved these beautiful pieces of the past." He came up to Natalie, sitting down. "Here you go." After a few minutes, he rose. "Going now. You and Frankie hold down the fort- and tell Frank to catch that mouse."

"Don't wade too deep. You may get swamped with information."

Jim laughed as he headed out to the car. "O.K., first stop- the Chester County History Center (CCHC). Sent their lead Librarian a note with all the files I'd like to view. Should be quick." As the Forester weaved onto Route 52 North, he noticed lighter traffic than usual. "A nice change- not too many cars crowding the roads." Turning right onto Price Street, rolling past the well-kept lawns and turn-of-the-century houses in pristine condition, the lush tree-lined road provided cover from the late Summer sunlight, the dappled rays filtering through the white oak, maple and American elm trees stationed on both sides of the street. It was a dazzling light show of nature, breaking open to direct sunshine at the STOP sign at High Street.

"I always love this drive." Parking out in front of the CCHC, he fed the meter and was quickly inside the front doors. "Hello, William. How are you?"

"Great, Jim- good to see you. I pulled those files for you- they're on the table."

"Many thanks!" Jim seated himself before the three vertical grey boxes and started taking out folders. "A lot here on Humphry Marshall. Now, this is interesting. Marshall built his house *by hand* in 1773- must've been a pretty good stone mason. The Historical Society was given the Marshall house in 1982 in a bequest from Campbell Weir. It was sold ten years later to the Thomas family. Another couple lives there now." He noticed a very old copy of *Arbustum Americanum* and immediately opened it, paging gingerly through for descriptions of local medicinal plants- and right off, he found several.

*'... we may gain by tedious experience... many useful discoveries respecting the uses and medicinal virtues of plants... Xanthoxylum- The Tooth-Ach (sic) Tree... the bark and capsules are of a hot acrid taste, and are used for easing the tooth-ach (sic)... a tincture of them are also much commended for the cure of Rheumatism... Tilia caroliniana... An infusion of the flowers... has been used with success in an Epilepsy... Spiraea tomentofa alba... This is called Indian Pipe Shank, from the pithy stems used by the natives for that purpose... Viburnum dentatum... the young shoots of this tree are generally used by the natives for arrows... Sambucus nigra. American Black-berried Elder... An infusion of the inner bark is purgative. From the berries may be prepared a spirit, a wine and an oil, which promote urine, perspiration and sweat.'*

His head was flooded with ideas. "Marshall's book established him as one of the preeminent and most respected botanists in America. The information he documented about the characteristics and uses of hundreds of trees, plants and shrubs was a landmark in American science. His words 'used by the natives' is clear evidence that he got information about local plants and their usage from- *who else?* The Lenape who'd used them for centuries. It's highly likely he discussed these concepts *with one that lived on his property who spoke English-* **Indian Hannah.**

Jim opened the next box and found more agricultural information: a first edition printing of William Darlington's *Florula Cestrica* in 1826... a handwritten manuscript by Darlington of *Agricultural Botany*... 'Indian Names of Streams and Places: Manaiunk... Cosohockin, Susquehannah, Neshaminy, Apalachia from Colonial Records'... "Quite a lot here to digest."

He looked through the other boxes and found a gem: a letter from William Darlington to Bayard Taylor dated September 7, 1861 discussing the flag that flew at Fort McHenry during the Battle of Baltimore in the War of 1812. "Clearly *they* knew each other... One patriot deserved the title 'Renaissance Man.' The first citizen of Chester County to earn a medical degree from the University of Pennsylvania, he proved himself in many pursuits. That man was William Darlington." He kept reading from the notes he'd brought, now laying in front of him.

Darlington was born into a Quaker family on April 28, 1782 near the village of Dilworthtown. He got his medical education and after graduation, returned to Chester County and was appointed physician at the Chester County Almshouse, the same place where Indian Hannah lived her final years. Darlington was one of the most accomplished statesmen, industrialists and entrepreneurs of his era. Darlington served three terms in the U.S. House of Representatives. In 1828, he and some colleagues created the Medical Society of Chester County. He was its first President. Darlington served the Society for the next 24 years. During this time, he and some associates created the West Chester Railroad, where he was President and superintendent of construction. In 1830, he was elected President of the Bank of Chester County, where he served for the rest of his life. Jim dwelled on all he was reading. *"Did this guy ever sleep?"* Somehow Darlington found time for botany, publishing his second major botanical treatise *Flora Cestrica* in 1837, describing plants of the region.

Although Darlington was only 19 when Humphry Marshall died, he revered Marshall's botanical accomplishments. He published *Memorials of John Bartram and Humphry Marshall; with notices of the Botanical Contemporaries* in 1849. It was Marshall who inspired Darlington to study local flora and later publish his own research. "What a life of accomplishment; something we could all aspire to. William Darlington died on April 23, 1863, accomplishing more in his nearly 81 years than most people could ever dream about."

Next he saw 'Memorial to Bayard Taylor and Thomas Buchanan Read, September 28, 1912, Cedarcroft Kennett Square' indicating that Taylor was a true nature lover. "All of these men cherished our landscapes, plants and trees. Marshall, Darlington and Taylor were on the same page." He looked up and over at William. "This is excellent- and quite helpful. Thanks so much for all this information."

"You're very welcome, Jim. Let us know if we can be of further assistance."

Getting back into the car, Jim drove back down High Street and headed toward Kennett Square. On the way, he couldn't help but notice all the signs honoring one of the men: 'Darlington Road'… 'Darlington Estates'… Turning right onto Route 1, he came up the back way to Longwood Gardens.

"Hello. Looking for Colleen. I'm Jim, here to do some research."

"Hi! *I'm* Colleen! Good to meet you. We have some things pulled for you on the table upstairs."

He followed her past several desks to the Library, where Library Manager Audrey had set out a large cart which held several boxes. "Thanks so much. I do appreciate this."

"My pleasure. Let me know if you have any questions."

As he sat down, he went through each box. "Now this is interesting: Humphry Marshall's niece Hannah Greaves Peirce was the mother of Joshua and Samuel Peirce, who established the arboretum which became Peirce's Park, and in the 20<sup>th</sup> century, Longwood Gardens. The family's name at one time or another was spelled *three different ways-* Peirce (correctly), but also Pierce and Pearce. One family- three names; that must have driven them a bit crazy. Humphry and his nephew Moses Marshall were neighbors of the Peirce family. William Darlington knew Joshua and Samuel Peirce and credits them in his book *Flora Cestrica*. The Peirce brothers also knew industrialist and *plant lover… E. I. du Pont.*"

On the cart he saw what looked like one of his own Master's Theses. "Well, look at this. *'Humphry Marshall's Botanic Garden: Living Collections 1773- 1813'* by Robert R. Gutowski, Master's Thesis, University of Delaware, December 1988. He paged through the red leather-bound tome, searching for key words. *'Humphry befriended… Indian Hannah, who often was welcome to his Marshallton home, and was said to share her knowledge of useful plants with him.'* He looked over at Audrey and couldn't help but yell out. ***"This is EXACTLY what I've been saying!!"***

Audrey's head perked up- and she smiled as she saw him there: "That's good. I'm glad you've found some useful information."

He read further: *'Medicinal plants were of special interest, as were plants which might prove useful resources in promoting independence for the developing New World economy.'* Jim's thoughts were on fire. "This is *important.* Not only did Indian Hannah share her understanding of medicinal plants with Marshall- this knowledge appears to have been somewhat of a *catalyst* over the years in people studying the medicinal values of hundreds of different plants, the value from which was realized in the medical world decades later." He noted Gutowski's Thesis referenced Marshall's book: *'Marshall published the first botanical description of Acer saccharum, the Sugar Maple… and noted the back inhabitants make a pretty good sugar, and in considerable quantity, of the sap of this and the Silver-leafed Maple…'* "It's clear to me- at *least one* of those 'back inhabitants' was likely… *Indian Hannah,* who lived on his property. This knowledge was subsequently further developed as the medical world synthesized important medicines like aspirin (made from willow bark, which the Lenape used), digitalis (made from the foxglove plant), quinine (made from the cinchona tree) and dozens of other treatments we now utilize today."

He couldn't control the torrent of ideas raging through his mind. "Here's just a short list of medicinal plants Indian Hannah and the Lenape studied and used for centuries, which I downloaded from a site focused on them: birch bark for coughs and colds, cattail to stop bleeding and reduce pain, sassafras to help lower blood pressure and bloodroot to treat stomach issues, cramps and vomiting. At that time, scientists were called 'natural philosophers' due to their intense interest in and study of nature. In a sense, you could consider Hannah and the other Lenape herbalists 'natural philosophers' and in some *small way-* early medical researchers."

Jim was thrilled. "A lot here. There also appears to be a 'special' link between the Quakers and the Lenape. Quakers believed that knowledge of nature was one way to *know and understand God*. The Lenape- and most Indians- quite similarly believe that nature is a *sacred gift* from God which they revere and that *all* living things- even plants and trees- have a soul or spirit. Well- I totally agree with that. Quaker farmer Jacob Peirce (uncle of Joshua and Samuel) is listed as one of Hannah's supporters on *'Kindness Extended.'* They likely were *fascinated* by these people who lived off the land and Peirce's descendant George Washington Peirce wanted to keep Hannah's memory alive."

Just then, Jim had an epiphany. "Many of the people whose lives we're delving into were… Quakers- or at least from Quaker families. Quakers believed in an *'inner light'-* a spirit which dwelled in every human being, a direct connection to the Divine. The Lenape believe a spirit dwells within all things, connected to our Creator. These two groups- Quakers and the Lenape- shared this same *'connection'* to God, revered it as the foundation of their 'world view.' That was probably why so many Quakers felt a special bond with Hannah- and supported her in her final years. Lenape also believe life has four phases: birth, growth, death and… *rebirth*. I absolutely agree with that."

Jim thought further about the local Quakers. "I know that *Kindness Extended* also listed Richard Barnard as one of her supporters. I believe… he was- Eusebius Barnard's grandfather! *YES!!* Natalie would want to know this; she volunteers at and supports Barnard Station, Eusebius's former home which was once part of the Underground Railroad."

His face held a very wide grin as he looked over at Audrey, sitting at her desk. "Well, this is excellent. You've put together a lot of very helpful material. I really appreciate this." Jim grabbed his notebook and ambled toward the door. *"THANK YOU!"*

"You're welcome. Let us know if there is anything else we can assist you with."

On the drive home, he wondered where to start discussing it all with Natalie. "I think she's gonna' like this. *I like it.* Information which recognizes Indian Hannah as having at least *a minor role* in the development of plant-based medicine. Not bad for a poor, old Indian woman." He pulled into the garage and turned off the engine. "Perhaps she'll eventually get some recognition." He saw Frankie waiting for him in the kitchen. "Hi Frank!" He strode into the Conservatory and couldn't wait to share it with Natalie.

"How did your research go?"

"Couldn't have gone better… not only for me… but… for Indian Hannah."

"What do you mean?" Natalie's wide-eyed expression revealed positive expectations.

"I mean Hannah and the other Lenape had extensive plant-based knowledge which decades later, in some small way aided in the development of modern medicines. Maybe someday… she'll get some credit."

"Sounds good."

*************************************************************

Samuel Martin Dougherty sat in the library of his home in Downingtown, viewing the small, solid silver tea set he'd recently inherited from his grandmother. He lifted up the teapot, turned it over and saw *'T. McKean'* imprinted on the bottom. "T. McKean- who was that? Why did grandmom have this? She wasn't a McKean…" Intrigued, he went onto the Ancestry.com website where he'd already done some genealogical work weeks before hoping to explore his family tree. "O.K.- let's dig a bit deeper… maybe back into the late 1700s, if there are records." He saw that his 4th maternal great-grandmother lived from 1768 to 1851. Further probing led him to a name he'd not seen before. "Mordecai Dougherty. Mordecai- that's a name you never hear nowadays… maybe it was popular back in the 18th century. Who was Mordecai Dougherty?"

His previous searches on various historical society websites had led him into a wealth of information on Revolutionary War-era people, places and events, but now he was focused on the strange name he'd just seen. "Mordecai… Oh my Lord, this guy was a bandit! A common thief… along with his cohort, James Fitzpatrick. I guess no one in the family ever wanted to mention him to me- and I'm not surprised!" He glanced again at the lovely silver teapot and turned it over again, seeing another imprint on its bottom. *"'Joseph Richardson, Jr.'* I have no idea who that guy was- but I'm hungry. A stop over at The Whip is long overdue…"

*************************************************************

The Whip Tavern on North Chatham Road outside Coatesville is the closest thing you'll find to an old English pub in Chester County- and Jim and Natalie were ready for a visit to jolly old England to enjoy some of their signature roast beef dishes. Driving north up PA Route 82 from Kennett Square gives visitors the full view of the emerging early Fall foliage and rustic back-country roads that people cherish when trying to escape the hustle and bustle of city life. Turning onto Route 841 South in West Marlborough Township, Jim steered the Forester up to the white-stucco walled tavern on the side of the road where he pulled off and came to a stop.

"We haven't been here in a while; it'll be a nice change of pace."

Natalie nodded as she closed her door and strolled up to take his hand. "I like their sandwiches; we can sit at the bar if you like, just for something different."

"Sure." He led the way through the front door where a waitress quickly greeted them.

The 25-ish girl said "There's only a few tables left inside, but you can sit outside on the patio, which is nice. You can also eat at the bar, if you prefer. There's plenty of seats there."

"Thank you. We'll sit at the bar." Jim moved quickly up to the two nearest open stools and grabbed them. "Right here, sweetie."

Sitting next to him at the rustic heavy oak bar, she noticed the bartender promptly placing menus before them. "First glance, the menu looks good, but I have no idea what some of it means. *'Bubble and Squeak'… 'Weck Spring Rolls'…?"*

"Beef on Weck is their signature dish- that's their famous roast beef served on a Kummelweck roll with horseradish, au jus and chips… 'Bubble and Squeak' is a browned potato cake filled with leeks and cabbage, topped with a dill-type dressing. Actually, that sounds good, along with their English Onion Soup and Beef on Weck for me. I might even order a beer on tap."

"That's fine, but remember- we rarely drink at lunch. You always fall asleep by mid-afternoon if you've had a beer."

"Well, we can *split* a beer. How's that sound?" Jim waited for approval before he motioned to the bartender.

"O.K. You choose one- preferably a lighter beer, not heavy like Guiness. I know that's their favorite drink here, but I prefer the ones less… overpowering…"

Jim motioned to the bartender. "Can we get two half-pints of the Morland Old Speckled Hen English Pale Ale? We'll be ready to order lunch in a minute."

The handsome blonde-haired bartender nodded. "Coming right over, mate."

"This'll be a first."

"How's that?" Natalie moved into a more comfortable position on her stool at the bar.

"Never drank a Speckled Hen before."

"You're goofy- and you haven't even had a drink yet."

"I like this bartender already. Reminds me of my English buddy Allen from graduate school. Still had an accent even though he'd lived in the U.S. for several years. We were best friends."

"Still are, aren't you?"

"Yes, but we don't connect that often… I'll make it a point to contact him sometime and let him know we dined at an English pub near us."

The bartender came up to where they sat with a smile for him and Natalie. "Here you go. Folks ready to order?"

Natalie was. "Sure- I'll have The Black Mack with a Tavern Salad, please."

"You, sir?"

"I'd like the Bubble and Squeak, English Onion Soup and the Beef on Weck."

"Very good. I'll put in your order." He turned to move back toward the kitchen as the crowd grew larger along the bar.

"I really enjoy this place- it gives you the sense of walking back in time to the late 1700s… and many of the people we've been researching would have loved a place like this, if it were around then. Maybe even Fitzpatrick and his pal Mordecai Dougherty would have dined here."

Samuel Martin Dougherty couldn't help overhear Jim speaking. "Mordecai Dougherty, you said?"

Jim's attention shifted to his left and he saw the late 30s gentleman a few feet from him on a stool at the bar. "Yes, I said Mordecai Dougherty. Do you know of him?"

"Well, I'm a Dougherty myself. Sam Dougherty." He offered his hand out to Jim.

"Shaking his hand, Jim said "Peterson here- I'm Jim; this is Natalie."

Natalie's curiosity was peaked. "Are you saying you might be related to Mordecai Dougherty?"

"I think so. I did a search on Ancestry and his name came up. It's a strange name; you never hear that name today. No one in my family ever told me I was related to a Mordecai."

Jim's eyebrows peaked. "You're related to Mordecai Dougherty- the Rev War outlaw?"

"Apparently… not that I'm proud to admit it!" He motioned to the bartender. "I'll have a Guinness, please. A full pint."

Jim glanced over at Natalie and grinned. "Well, this is interesting. We've been chasing down the exploits of James Fitzpatrick- 'Fitz' to many, Dougherty's partner in crime- but found very little on Dougherty. All we've come up with is that he joined Fitzpatrick on his highwayman exploits robbing people around 1777-1778, but basically disappeared from the scene after Fitz was hanged in September 1778. Some newspaper accounts state he went over to Lancaster County, others speculate that he escaped to Canada- but we believe he was never brought to trial for his deeds."

"I haven't found much either. All this started when I was examining a silver tea set I inherited from my grandmother. It prompted me to do some searching. I did find a name, though- on the bottom of the teapot: T. McKean."

Natalie perked up immediately. "Jim, is that the Judge you've been talking about- Thomas McKean?"

Jim's eyes widened as he sported a huge grin. "Your silver tea set says *'T. McKean'*?"

"Yes. Is that someone famous, too? I didn't get a chance to check…"

"Oh, my God. ***This is fascinating.*** You say the tea set was passed down to you in your family- the Dougherty family- and it says *'T. McKean'* on the bottom…" The analytical gears started moving quickly in Jim's head. "I'm wondering if you might have a piece of the booty plundered by the outlaws Dougherty and Fitzpatrick back in the late 1770s. I'd like to see the teapot to get a better idea."

"Well, you're in luck. I have the tea set in my car. I brought it with me, as I was planning to go into West Chester to visit some antique dealers, get their appraisal and opinion on it. Want me to bring it in?"

*"Hell, yes!* Bring it in here. I'd love to see it!"

Sam left his stool at the bar, quickly exiting the tavern. Within a few minutes, he was back, standing next to Jim, with the tea pot. "See, the bottom shows 'T. McKean'… and over here it says 'Joseph Richardson, Jr.- silversmith.'"

Jim's face was ecstatic. "Wow. You hit the jackpot here. Joseph Richardson was a very successful silversmith in Colonial-era Philadelphia. The Richardson family had a line of famous silversmiths. Joseph was one of them. He was so well regarded, George Washington appointed him as the Assayer of the Philadelphia Mint!"

Natalie couldn't believe what she was hearing. *"Now that is remarkable…"*

"I had no idea. That's interesting." Sam sipped his Guiness and waited for any more information Jim might offer.

Jim's eyes widened again as he thought of the implications of what he was looking at. "My Lord- this really *is* extraordinary. It just occurred to me. Your family appears to have Thomas McKean's silver tea set. It could have been stolen by Dougherty himself, but *may* have been taken when he and James Fitzpatrick were plundering *together* around the area. We'll never know for sure. McKean was the trial judge who *convicted* Fitzpatrick for *his* crimes- one of which theoretically may have been linked to the theft of ***this tea set from McKean!!***"

"Now that adds a lot of depth to this story. So, Fitzpatrick got hung… and Dougherty got the silver! I think it deserves a toast. Cheers!" Sam raised his glass to Jim's and then to Natalie's.

Jim stared directly at Sam. "We've been chasing down the trail of these guys for the last several weeks. Now I can say we have 'connected' with Fitzpatrick *and* Dougherty through a piece of stolen contraband. *Cheers!!* By the way, the house where Fitzpatrick lived is just about

50 yards away. Just cross the parking lot and it's the second house you'll see on this side of the road. We've driven right by it a hundred times, but never stopped in. We plan to check it out soon." Jim nodded to Sam as he raised his glass again- and saw him sporting a huge grin.

Chair owned by the family of Humphry Marshall
courtesy Chester County History Center

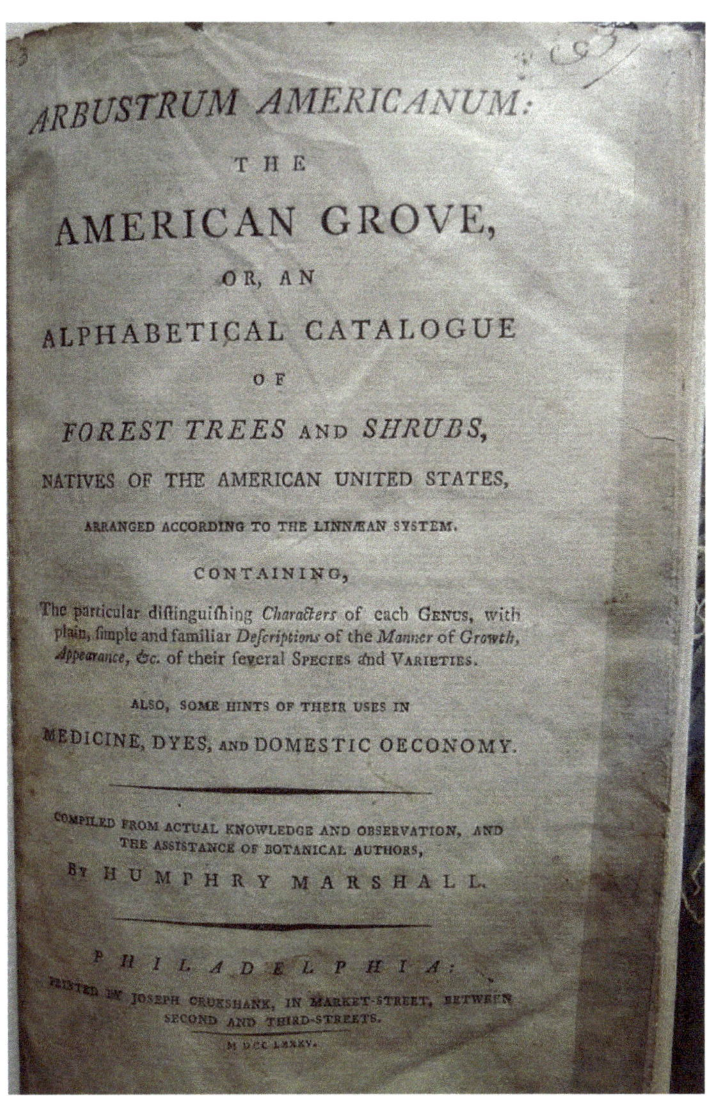

*Arbustum Americanum* by Humphry Marshall

Ancient microscope and housing owned by Humphry
Marshall courtesy Chester County History Center

*William Darlington* by John Neagle

Gravesite of William Darlington in Oaklands
Cemetery, West Chester, Pa.

William Darlington letter to Bayard Taylor September 7, 1861 regarding
the flag that flew at Fort McHenry during the War of 1812
courtesy Chester County History Center

Bloodroot used by the Lenape

Sassafras used by the Lenape

Interior bar area of The Whip Tavern

The author and his wife Phyllis raising a toast at The Whip Tavern

# Chapter 13

"Despite our research, we haven't done an in-depth Sandy Flash tour yet. Let's drive back up to Doe Run, see the house where he lived and survey the area. What do you think?" Natalie sipped her ice water as she walked toward the terrace to water the outside plants.

"I'm up for it. On the way back, we can stop over at Cedarcroft to see Bayard Taylor's home and catch lunch afterwards." Jim followed her outside and stopped at the banister overlooking the back yard. "The cleomes are the stars of the show this year- best ever. That Hibiscus bush also looks amazing, thanks to you. The pumpkins you put around the patio and terrace announce we're ready for Fall."

"I appreciate it. My backaches are proof of all the work I've done. I deliberately kept fewer potted plants this year- they take so much care. Glad we gave away over half the pots so we won't be spending dozens of hours on the garden every week. Whenever you're ready to do the tour, let me know."

"Let me take my notes; I want to bring them with us." He grabbed a pad and car keys and headed into the garage as Natalie followed. As the vehicle headed onto Route 82 North, Jim recalled his earlier readings. "I didn't know until now that Doe Run was a National Historic District, listed in 1985. This County has a lot of them, way more than most. Did you know that it spans two Townships- West Marlborough and East Fallowfield?"

"I knew you'd have that nailed down. All I know is the small building with the 'Doe Run' sign we pass whenever we're going to The Whip."

"Well, the Historic District has 26 structures and another site in Doe Run Village. The buildings include the old Doe Run Garage, a general store and some homes. They also had a cotton mill, but it was torn down and replaced with the Town Hall in 1898. The Town Hall later had a dairy. There was also a paper mill, a grist mill, the Doe Run School and a Presbyterian Church." The Forester cruised its way towards the intersection with Route 841, passing the Doe Run General Store building. "This is the heart of Sandy Flash country. He was born here, became a blacksmith here and went off to war from here."

"That white stucco house on the left is where he lived with his mother. Pull up right over here and we can try to go onto the property." Natalie saw the front porch and noticed a large plaque on the wall outside. "Let's go up. Worst thing they can do is chase us off."

Jim stopped the car and they both got out at the edge of The Whip parking lot. Approaching the house, it became apparent that someone was currently living there, as numerous personal items were outside on the porch. He cautiously walked up the stairs and the plaque came into view. "This is a long narrative, so I'll just cover the highlights:

*'The History of the House of Springdell built in 1750. Purchased by Graham and Leona Heath in 1929 and still owned by the Heath family today... The house's design is essentially unaltered from the original 'Penn Plan'... a vernacular design advocated by William Penn about 1700 as an economic house adapted to his new proprietary colony... During the American Revolution the house was used as a tenant house for the Passmore farm, and was reportedly occupied by the mother of James Fitzpatrick. James was a deserter from the Continental Army who was nearly captured at his mother's house. He later joined with the British Army under General Howe and fought in the nearby Battle of Brandywine. He then helped the British pillage the area. In September, 1778 he was captured and hung by the Continental Army.'*

Jim thought as he stared at the brass marker. "Well, they got *most* of it right. Fitzpatrick did live here with his mother, but our information indicates he was with the *militia in support* of the Continental Army. To my knowledge, there's no evidence that he actually *joined* the British Army under Howe- he apparently scouted the area and got them supplies. He may have been at the Battle of the Brandywine, the timing is correct. He *was* caught by a Continental Army soldier named McAfee, whose house was over near Edgmont, later torn down. Fitzpatrick was put on trial by the state of Pennsylvania and hung by state authorities in Chester, *not* by the Army. At least they got the big points right."

Natalie moved around the small, white-painted wooden porch. "The interesting part is what *some* narratives say he did *after* the British left the area- which was *start* his robbing spree around Chester County that various accounts say lasted for about a year. Yet, the Brits didn't leave Philadelphia until June 18, 1778, so if he **started** his spree then and he was hung in September, it would have lasted *only a few months- not* a year or more as many accounts state."

Jim's attention was piqued. "Nice catch! If Fitch was terrorizing the area as a highwayman for a year or more, he would have had to start around the time of the Battle in early September 1777, or even *before then*, perhaps the Spring or Summer of that year. He was probably stealing supplies from farms around the area to help General Howe, but it's not at all clear that he was robbing people at gunpoint that early. More evidence of contradictory stories- which are what create 'legends'."

Natalie nodded. "... and some narratives we already read make pretty unbelievable statements, like the total of all the money he stole was *'worth more than all of Chester County.'* Clearly that's wrong. He would have had to steal hundreds of thousands of dollars, which is absurd. How much could he get from robbing people on the road- maybe 50- 100 British pounds *at the very most?* Not much more. He would have had to rob literally thousands of people to accumulate such a huge amount. Even if he was on a robbing spree for a full year, to accumulate that kind of money, he would have had to hold up 3-4 people a day, every day for 12 months in a row. As the years went by, newspaper accounts from the 1800s up through the 1990s romanticized this guy and his exploits, exaggerating them to the point of disbelief."

*"You are CORRECT, Madam!* Add in superhuman attributes: escaping from dozens of armed men. If true, today he'd be able to hold off the 82nd Airborne and the First Armored Division. You'd mentioned the 'hidden treasure,' which some accounts say he kept in the Edgmont area inside a cave amongst the boulders. I agree with what you said a few days ago. As he was on the run and needed to survive, he would've just *spent* the stolen money. *Why hide most of it somewhere?* Maybe he paid some to local Tory sympathizers who were happy to put him up in their home for a few nights and feed him. Why put it in a cave that's hard to access? Read most of these sources with a grain of salt."

"More like a *BLOCK*." Natalie laughed out loud as she walked along the porch.

"You can only believe about half of what's printed in the newspapers." Jim glanced all around the porch and into the front windows, with no one in sight.

Natalie started to head toward the steps, then said *"… and the other half…?"*

"Use it to line your bird cage."

"Exactly. Want to go over to the Edgmont area to see where his hideout was?"

"Sure, but it's a shopping center now. Can't see much of anything. Even the big granite boulders nearby where he supposedly hid out for periods of time are mostly gone, courtesy of economic development. We can see what's there. Some other important spots he frequented and some say, robbed- are the Unicorn Tavern in Kennett and the Square Tavern- which we already visited. Too bad the Unicorn's no longer with us. Wonder if he robbed the Anvil Tavern. That's gone, too."

"Yes, but we did see a remnant. There's that anvil just off the side of Baltimore Pike heading South past Longwood Gardens. That's where the Anvil Tavern used to be." Natalie recalled flipping through the various narratives on the area. "There are artist drawings of some of those places."

"Right, I remember we walked over there a while back and saw the anvil. Barclay Rubincam did a painting of British troops marching past the Unicorn Tavern. I'd like to see the original." As the Forester weaved its way down Route 841, Jim noticed a street sign on the right. "Hey, check it out: *'This area under surveillance for Neighborhood Watch.'* What do you make of that?"

"Captain Fitz on the prowl."

He chuckled as he steered over toward West Chester Pike, then turned right. "O.K., up there is the Edgmont Shopping Center. I don't think there's anything left of the original landscape, but we can get out and check. One thing that's changed is the way some people insist on spelling it 'Edgemont' with an "e" instead of the *correct* spelling, 'Edgmont.'"

"Don't overestimate the intelligence of strip mall developers. They want one thing: people coming there to spend money, regardless of how they spell the name." Both got out of the car at the front of the shopping center. "I recall someone saying there's a house nearby which might be original, dating back to the 1800s, but I don't see it from this vantage point."

Jim hiked the length of the parking lot. "Not much here. Let's head over to Marshallton and see if we can get a glimpse of Humphry Marshall's house. Unfortunately, it's surrounded by fencing with a lot of overgrowth, but we can at least try." Back in the car, they headed East.

He tried to avoid taking his eyes off the winding road. "Speaking of Marshall, Adrian's portrait of him inside his home, with his microscope is quite good. I love his style. Adrian really is a superb artist."

"That's one of the reasons his paintings are hanging inside the White House and collections around the U.S. and Europe." Natalie raised her hand to point ahead. "Well, we're coming into Marshallton… it's on the left… over there… but where can we park?"

Jim glanced down the road. "No cops in sight. My rule: park at any open spot, just don't get a ticket. Right here works." They both walked down toward the blue and gold historical marker, which read:

*'Humphry Marshall (1722-1801)*

*One of the first nurserymen in the nation and the author of the first book on North American trees and shrubs. Arbustum Americanum: The American Grove. Marshall is known as the Father of American Dendrology. He regularly supplied native American plants to prominent Europeans eager to learn about species new to them. His plants graced the gardens of England's King George III and King Louis XVI of France. He built and lived in this house. Erected 2014 by Pennsylvania Historical and Museum Commission.'*

"So, two citizens of Chester County gave England's King George III something he liked."

"What do you mean?" Natalie's face revealed she had no idea what he was talking about.

"Humphry Marshall sent the King some of his prized plants; Benjamin West gave him some great paintings."

*"Whatever…"*

As they strolled along the side of West Strasburg Road, Jim watched for approaching traffic, usually heavy at this time of day.

"Let's make this quick. I don't want to get flattened."

"Too bad it's hard to see through this fence and underbrush to view the house. Marshall's one of the unsung heroes of Chester County history. He was a self-taught botanist and also an amateur astronomer. He made observations of sunspot activities with a crude telescope and sent his comments to Benjamin Franklin, who presented them to the Royal Society in London, where they were very well received. One thing most people don't know- the title of his monumental book, published by Joseph Crukshank in Philadelphia in 1785- was actually a *misprint*. The correct title is '*Arbust<u>um</u> Americanum: The American Grove*', not '*Arbust<u>rum</u>*' with an 'r.'"

"Thank you for that riveting editorial clarification. Now… where are we going?" Natalie had her eyes alternating to both sides of the road.

"There's supposed to be another historical marker up around here, on the side of a big boulder." Just then, a blasting cacophony of ***"ARF, ARF, ARF!!...ARF, ARF!!... ARF, ARF, ARF, ARF!!!"*** enveloped them in terror. Jim turned around and saw a huge animal about to leap onto his right shoulder. ***"What the Hell??!!"*** The enormous creature was being held back, just barely, on a leash gripped by a 35-ish, very athletically-built, ruby-haired woman who tried to prevent the dog from biting him. Jim sprinted about ten feet away, grabbing Natalie's hand with him, just in time to avoid a calamity.

"I am *SO* sorry!! My dog gets excited sometimes- he didn't mean to hurt you, I promise! Can I do something for you?"

Jim looked directly at her. "Yeah- get a *smaller* dog."

She giggled, then put her arms around the animal.

"He almost took my arm off." Jim was still a bit rattled standing there within the dog's possible jumping distance. "What breed is he?"

"He's an Irish Wolfhound, one of the *largest* types of dogs in the world."

"Yes- I can see that. What does he weigh?" Jim stood back as the hound tried again to lunge forward, the heavy leash holding him away from them both.

"He tilts in at just under 200 pounds. He really *IS* a good dog, though. He wouldn't hurt you- he's just very… *rambunctious*. I'm sorry if he scared you guys, I really am."

Jim thought he might as well get to know the most enormous dog he'd ever seen on Earth. "What's his name?"

"Tiny."

"*Tiny? You're kidding me, right?*" Jim started to laugh, but could see the woman was serious.

"He was the runt of the litter when he was born and we felt sorry for him, so we adopted him and called him Tiny. For the first month or so, he didn't grow very much… but then, he just… took off."

Natalie still couldn't believe the dog's size. "Are you sure he's not a *Buffalo?*"

"He's a big guy- but he's only nine months old, so he'll get a bit larger."

"To do what, *pull locomotives?*" Natalie couldn't help but burst out laughing.

"These dogs can grow to be roughly 42 inches at the shoulder and stand 7 feet tall on their hind legs. We love him, even though he does knock things around in our house. We live just up the road. What are you folks doing here today?"

Jim kept his eyes on Tiny, making sure he didn't try to jump up on him again. "We're exploring Humphry Marshall's legacy. There's supposed to be another historical marker around here somewhere."

"I know where it is, just around the corner. I can take you. My name's Vanessa. My husband and I live less than a mile from here. We love this historic little village- it's so charming."

"I'm Natalie. Nice to meet you."

"I'm Jim. We'd love to see the marker and maybe even get a glimpse of the house. Marshall was a fascinating man, aside from being one of the most famous botanists in America. He was a County Assessor and the County Treasurer. He exchanged plant information with scientists and collectors in England, Germany, Ireland, Sweden and Holland. It's estimated that he constructed the first greenhouse in Chester County and also had an astronomical observatory in his home. He started the nation's second botanical garden, following his cousin John Bartram, studying and identifying hundreds of species of plants, along with analyzing and preserving them for future study. Ben Franklin sent him a telescope with which he made interesting observations and Marshall dedicated his now famous book to Franklin and others at the American Philosophical Society in Philadelphia, where he was made a member due to his achievements. Indian Hannah lived on his property- and *I believe*- exchanged information with him about medicinal plants."

"Oh, yes we know about Indian Hannah. She deserves some credit for helping to further the fledgling science of botany and that of useful plants as well. My husband and I have read quite a bit about her. He was a biology major in college and I've been gardening most of my life. There's the other historical marker."

Jim approached the large boulder and noticed the plaque:

*'The Home and Arboretum of Humphry Marshall Early American Botanist 1722- 1801 marked by Chester County Historical Society 1913 Erected 1913 by The Chester County Historical Society'*

"A bit of trivia about him is that his first name is sometimes misspelled as 'Humphrey' instead of the correct 'Humphry', which is an uncommon spelling. Bogart preferred the *'e'* being in there. Just like Marshall's book title was misspelled, so was that of the Marshalton Inn, even today spelled with just one 'l' due to a typographical error on an old deed." Jim touched the huge rock, which reminded him of the one that Indian Hannah's plaque was set upon. "At least they both merited a big boulder. Is it possible to see the house any better?"

Vanessa grabbed the leash more tightly. "Yes, follow me around here. Up there you can look through the forested area and see the house." She held Tiny very close to her as Jim and Natalie looked on.

"It's a beautiful old stone house. Would love to get inside." Jim glanced back at Vanessa, hoping for some encouragement.

"No- can't do that. The family who lives there is very private and rarely allow visitors… but at least you saw the structure, an important part of Chester County history. I agree with you; I feel Marshall is one of the most significant scientists in America. His book still stands as a notable accomplishment."

"Marshall recommended to Thomas Jefferson the idea of an expedition to explore the unmapped areas of the West- *decades before* Lewis and Clark went there. You don't hear too much about it, but some of the most accomplished people in Pennsylvania history were Quakers or from Quaker families. Aside from founder William Penn who helped form the framework for an emerging republic- there were Marshall, Benjamin West- one of the most accomplished artists in American history and William Darlington- a noted botanist in his own right, with several books to his credit. Indian Hannah is reported to have been more comfortable around *Quaker colonists* than her own Lenape people- so much so that it is reported she almost forgot her native tongue. You might consider Hannah- no pun intended- an important *'Friend of the Quakers.'"*

Vanessa nodded. "Couldn't agree more. That designation is certainly appropriate."

Jim continued: "Bayard Taylor- the most famous citizen of Kennett Square- was born into a Quaker family, members of the local Kennett Friends Meeting. Even though he wasn't considered an actively practicing Quaker, he spoke like a Quaker and used the typical Quaker words 'thee' and 'thou' quite often, as shown in letters he wrote to his fiancé Mary Agnew. Quakers were the first group here in the United States to officially oppose slavery, decades before it was outlawed. In general, I'd say Quakers are overdue for more recognition of their contributions to this country."

Vanessa nodded. "Points well taken. Hopefully more people will recognize that in the future- and *I'm not even a Quaker!*"

"Thank you, Vanessa. We do appreciate the tour. You and Tiny have… a pleasant day… just make sure he doesn't *tackle anyone.*" Jim took Natalie's hand as they walked around the dog.

She chuckled. "You're welcome. You guys enjoy your visit." Vanessa kept Tiny within just a few feet of her as she rounded the corner and went out of sight.

Doe Run General Store

House where James Fitzpatrick and his mother lived
West Marlborough Township, Pa.

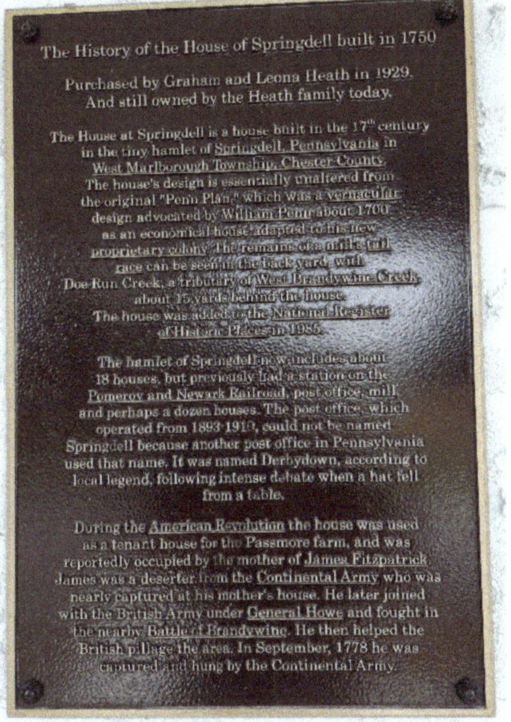


Bronze historical plaque at the house where
James Fitzpatrick once lived
West Marlborough Township, Pa.

Humphry Marshall historical marker
Marshallton, Pa.

Humphry Marshall House
Marshallton, Pa.

Plaque identifying home and arboretum of
Humphry Marshall

Humphry Marshall
historical marker

Malcolm Johnstone as Humphry Marshall at the 300
year celebration event in Marshallton, Pa

Sign denoting Humphry Marshall Historical Park

Sketch of the Unicorn Inn by Dr. Isaac D. Johnson

# Chapter 14

*William Darlington stared at the large collection of seeds, leaves, plants and bark he had assembled, spread out on the wide table before him. "I am honored to follow in the tradition of such a great man, Mr. Marshall... and his cousin, Mr. Bartram. I only hope that my work merits a fraction of the acclaim theirs has generated from diligent pursuits and study over so many years." His notes, all written by quill and ink were scattered before him- and he knew the pamphlet he planned to write required further examination and extensive analysis. "I shall call it: Flora Cestrica..."*

**************************************************************************

Jim awoke and looked next to him to see Natalie still asleep. His thoughts raced inside his head. "I just had a strange dream... or... *was* it a dream? Not sure... what it was about." Strolling to the closet to put on his robe, he quietly walked past the bed to the mahogany night table to grab his watch and the drinking glass always there and went downstairs to the foyer. Dim early morning light was just beginning to shine through the leaded glass sections of the front door.

"O.K: 1) I know I saw an image, that's a start, 2) it's hazy, but I believe it was... *a map?* and 3) it appeared to be quite old... that's all I can come up with."

*"What are you coming up with?"* Natalie's voice startled him, making his head turn.

"I'll pour you some coffee and then I have something to talk about."

"Nothing too serious at this hour. Keep it light." She followed him into the Conservatory.

"Well, you know I rarely remember what I think about when I sleep, but last night something came to me that was a bit... *odd*. All I saw was... a map. *That's it.* It wasn't a dream, per se... just... a map."

"A map *of what?*" She took her first sip to augment her analytical abilities.

"That's the thing. I'm not really sure. It was old, very old, like on parchment or velum, in a very crude frame. I've never woken up thinking about a map, so I don't know what to make of it. No people, no action- just the map."

"Did it look familiar? Did you recognize anything at all?"

"Not... really... it was just an ancient map." Jim shook his head, bewildered.

*"I know what it was.* That map you bought at the Blacksmith Shop in Marshallton." Natalie's third sip had kicked in her full mental powers.

He thought for several seconds. *"YES!! That's it!* I thought it looked vaguely familiar. Now I'm thinking back… it had what looked like the Brandywine, leading down into northern Delaware from Chester County. Just wondering: why did I dwell on a map?"

"I've done a lot of reading on this. Our subconscious minds often bring us thoughts or images symbolic of something occurring or having recently occurred in our lives. Other than symbols, your mind points you to concentrate on something specific: a person, a place, in this case- a map. For some reason, your mind is pointing you toward focusing on this map. Did you ever take it over to Strodes Mill Gallery to be framed?" Natalie finished her cup and held it out for Jim to refill.

"No, but I'm going to do that today. I'll have Donna put it in a really nice, rustic wooden frame. After a cup of Earl Grey I'm heading over there. They open early."

"Don't go anywhere until you refill this!" She smiled as he took the cup and proceeded back to the kitchen. "You're planning to come right back, correct? We were thinking about going over to Longwood to see the Webb House and find Hannah's cross."

He yelled back from the kitchen. "Do not fear- I will return from the Gallery promptly." As he strolled back into the Conservatory, he handed the cup to her and sat down. "This thing about a map has gotta' be more than a coincidence. I'm thinking back…to my trip to Pennsbury Manor: *'… thee will be rewarded with something of great value.'* Maybe I'm about to get an interesting piece to a puzzle…"

"Who knows? Maybe the map is valuable. You got it for $20, but if there's a copy of the *Declaration of Independence* on the back, we can retire early."

"Hey, I'm done my tea. Bringing this over to Strodes Mill Gallery. I'll be back soon."

"Come *RIGHT back,* no shopping excursions where you get enough groceries to feed the Navy."

"I promise- nothing for the Navy." He traipsed into the garage after grabbing the framed old map, opened the car door and started the engine. Just then, he was filled with the same soothing feeling he'd felt before. As he drove up Route 52, he saw the Strodes Mill Gallery sign ahead. Walking through the door, Jim noticed Donna's friendly face, who always beamed because she knew he'd be giving her some much-needed business.

"Good to see you. How are you, Jim?"

"Doing well. I hope business is good."

"It could always be better- lately people are trimming their spending on 'unnecessary' items, so it's been a bit slow. What can I help you with?"

"Here's an old map I got at the Blacksmith Shop in Marshallton. I think it's centuries, maybe even 300 years old. The frame is very crude and the paper appears quite fragile. I think it's a map of the Brandywine and nearby region."

Donna stared at the map and the frame for several seconds. "I've seen many of these over the years. You're probably right; frames like this are quite dated, could easily be two centuries old… and from my experience, the map itself looks like what they used back in the 1700s or that era."

"Well, I'd like it re-framed- and that rustic dark brown frame there on the wall looks like a good fit. I also like that tan matting for the inside, just like we did for the last few items I brought."

Donna measured the map, took the sample frame and matting down and laid them out for Jim to approve. "How's that look?"

"Very nice- that'll do. About how much?" Jim took out his wallet, with a VISA card ready for pre-payment.

"This is one of our finest frames… and the matting- which will make it look wonderful- brings the charge to… $285.24. Is that O.K.?" Donna waited for a reply before she put the materials aside.

"That's fine, you do great work. This map deserves a beautiful home. Here's my card." As she handed him back his VISA, he looked around at all the fine art work in the Gallery. "I love this place! You must be exposed to some great paintings every week- all inside an historic building."

"Oh- it *IS* a feast for the eyes. Meeting the artists is always so interesting. Now let's hope business picks up a bit more- that'll be appreciated." She smiled as he meandered toward the front door. "It should be done in about two weeks or so, but I'll call you if anything changes."

"Sounds good. Take care." As he left, he looked across the street to the remains of the centuries old Strodes Mill structure, which stood as Washington's troops fought nearby, now repainted and ready for a complete restoration. "We have to keep these places alive." The car cruised southward and turned right into moderately heavy traffic on Baltimore Pike, quickly making it back to the cul-de-sac leading to their garage. Strolling into their kitchen, Jim felt a sense of having *'saved'* something worthwhile. He yelled out to Natalie: "Hey- I'm home! You ready to dash over to Longwood? The weather's perfect- 70 degrees, mostly sunny with light cloud cover."

"On my way."

The turn going into Longwood Gardens prepares the visitor for a feast of floral delights. Every section of the property is expertly tailored with alternating rows of white, pink, yellow, orange, red and blue flowers flanked by neatly trimmed bushes and trees greeting each pair of visiting eyes. George Peirce purchased 402 acres of land from William Penn's commissioners in 1700; his son Joshua cleared the land and in 1730 built a solid red brick house which still stands today. In 1798 Joshua's grandsons who had inherited the property began planting a 15-acre arboretum which later held numerous species of trees and plants which they had collected and purchased from regional botanists, including Humphry Marshall. Peirce's Park became a popular place for people to gather and enjoy the outdoors amidst the beauty of nature. By the turn of the 20th century, the property had started to deteriorate and the family descendants lost interest in preserving it. A lumber mill operator was about to cut down all the trees, but industrialist Pierre S. du Pont learned of this and on July 20, 1906 he purchased the property to preserve the trees. Isabel Darlington- the first female attorney in Chester County and a relation of William Darlington- managed the transaction. The property was later renamed Longwood Gardens. Today it consists of over 1,100 acres of spectacular woodlands, meadows and gardens as well as gazebos, fountains and hiking trails, one of the premier botanical sites in the United States.

As their car cruised into an open parking spot, Jim noted Natalie's eager expression as she readied to get out. "We can tour the Peirce-du Pont House first, which has Pierre's office preserved and as I recall, an excellent exhibit on the history of the site. Then we'll walk over toward the Italian Water Garden area; I think Hannah's marker is up on the hillside there. Later we can hike up the hillside to the Webb House and see the displays inside. How's that sound?"

"Ready, willing and able."

Every visitor to the House and Gardens is surrounded by a cornucopia of flowers, each one kept near the peak of health by a dedicated team of employees and volunteers who love what they do. Jim noticed a patch of scarlet begonias beaming in the sunlight, not far from an extensive line of rose, amber, peach and copper-colored zinnias trimmed to perfection. Approaching the 18th century structure, Jim noticed a feline wandering about. *Beautiful cat! Hey, hon- look at this kitty.*

Natalie gazed over to the side of the house. "Oh, yes. What a gorgeous cat!"

An elderly man in khaki pants and a light blue shirt stood nearby. "That's Oscar. He hangs around here a lot. Oscar's very popular- and friendly."

"I love cats. Some people say men should love dogs, which I do enjoy, but I've always loved and felt very close to cats. Hemingway loved cats; had dozens of them. My wife and I took in a mother and her two kittens 17 years ago who were living in the forest in back of our house. They became our beloved family, our very best friends, our soulmates…" He thought about each of them for several seconds and… a tear came to his eyes. "Oscar is an *absolutely beautiful* cat." Jim walked right up to him, kneeled down and gently petted his fur; Oscar licked his hand for several seconds. "Lovely greyish-brown, striped tabby. *Look at his incredible markings!* You are a wonderful kitty, Oscar. God bless you, my furry friend. *May you have a very long, healthy and happy life…"*

As Jim and Natalie entered the old house, he saw two women standing there with friendly smiles, chatting together. He eyed a name tag on one of them, a 55-ish woman with light brown, wavy hair.

"Burgundy Sage. That's an interesting name. You here as part of a touring group?"

"Thank you. Yes, I'm in the Horticulturalists of America. My 5th maternal great-grandmother was named Sage- a full-blooded Lenape. Loved the color burgundy. She married an English settler and somehow persuaded him to change his last name to Sage. Apparently she was a gorgeous woman, with hazel-green eyes, a slender aquiline nose and stunning jet-black, waist-length hair. A real 'looker'. I've seen drawings of her."

Jim smiled as he heard the description. "So, she was a Lenape. When did she live?"

"She was born in 1742; passed away in 1811."

"That would be roughly the same time period as Indian Hannah." Natalie waited for her to offer more information on the ancestor.

"Yes, approximately the same time. It's possible they crossed paths. That sparked my interest in Hannah years ago. I've been studying her ever since." The woman noticed that Jim and Natalie's interest was primed. "The fact that she had hazel eyes also intrigued me. That's extremely rare for Native Americans. So, I started studying one of Hannah's hobbies- medicinal plants. The last name- sage- is the same as a plant used quite often by the Lenape. Sage was known by them to have anti-inflammatory, antioxidant and beneficial cognitive properties. I've studied them and their plant usage for a long time."

Natalie was impressed. "Just curious- what percentage Lenape bloodline are you?"

Burgundy smiled. "Oh, less than one per cent, but I'm one hundred per cent Lenape *in spirit.*"

Jim's grin became wider. "I can sense their 'presence' in you. How long have you been studying medicinal plants?"

"More than 30 years. It's become my major hobby. Did you know that sage also helps with controlling blood sugar levels- and aids indigestion?"

"Did not know that, but I've read up a bit on the general topic. I believe Hannah and the Lenape were ahead of the curve in identifying and using medicinal plants."

"Oh, yes. They led the way… modern study of drugs came a bit later, following the trail they explored…"

"Wonderful talking with you! Thanks so much." Jim felt better about his theory being corroborated as he took Natalie's hand and went into Pierre du Pont's office, where dozens of photographs of the property dating back well over a century hung alongside familiar names: George Peirce, Humphry Marshall, William Darlington and others. "Pierre's office is so well preserved, it looks like he just left for lunch." They navigated the pathway out toward the water garden and he held Natalie's hand as they got closer to the area where Hannah was memorialized. "I think it's up that way." Jim pointed over to the left side of the pathway fringed by ferns, small trees and wildflowers.

"It's right over there. See the cross?" Natalie nodded toward the spot about 20 feet off the trail.

"Yes… but… it's *on the ground!* That's not right."

"Go over and stand it back up. No one'll complain." Natalie watched as Jim approached the tan wooden cross with black lettering on its posts.

"It'd be nice if I had something to hammer it in."

"Look- to your left- there's a decent sized rock. Use that."

"Good thinking. I like rocks." Jim stood the cross to vertical, then grabbed the stone and started pounding. The wording on the cross read:

**'INDIAN HANNAH: *In memory of the last of the Lenapes Died 1802.'***

Natalie watched him fight against the dry, hardened soil. "You're gonna' have to hit it *HARD* several times to get it in. It hasn't rained in two weeks."

"The ground is like reinforced concrete!" He pounded the rock down onto the top of the cross, but it barely moved. After many strikes downward, it hit a solid object. "Hey- I just struck something hard- probably another rock. Let me get this out so I can see what's down there." He pulled the cross from its temporary hole and used the rock to dig down to the obstruction, clearing almost eight inches of dirt. Then he saw the cause of the blockage. "Hey, it's not a rock… it's… something kind of… *rectangular…?*" Jim kept digging and saw it clearly. "Looks like… maybe… a *box?*"

Natalie came up and stood right next to him. "I can't really see it. Can you dig it out?"

"I think so- but it'll take some effort." He kept digging with the sharp edge of the rock and got his hands under the object, pulling it out of the ground. "Look at this-… an old wooden box. Something from the last century- maybe older."

"I say more than 200 years. Look at the intricate carving on the surface. They don't make 'em like that anymore." Natalie kneeled down to get her face closer.

"This is interesting. It's got a solid latch. Should I open it?"

"*Of course!* What else would we do- *throw it in the trash bin over there?*"

Jim placed the box beside him on the ground, unlatching the highly tarnished brass clasp from the wooden peg holding the box closed, then lifted its cover. Inside he saw a few heavily moss-and-fungus-covered items. "What is this?" He started brushing layers of grime and dirt off a circular object and after several swipes, it started to shine in the sunlight. "My Lord- this is an old pocket watch, like they used back in the 1700s and 1800s. You rarely see these today. Looks like silver- it's badly weathered, but it's definitely a watch. I can see its glass face." He flipped it over and cleaned the back side. "I can make out… a *'J'* and… an *'F'* and… the year… *1776*. Nice design on the back, too."

"That is *beautiful!*" Natalie couldn't help leaning onto his side to be closer to the action. "What are those other things?"

Jim put the watch aside and saw what appeared to be a highly weathered sack, with a cord tightly tied at the top. "Looks like an old leather pouch, it's badly cracked, but still in one piece." He unraveled the rawhide string and pulled the material open to see what was inside. "Now, this is interesting… I can't believe it survived the decades. It looks like… a letter of some sort, but the paper is so damaged, it's hard to tell…" He held it gingerly in his hands and put his face within two inches of the page. "Natalie- look at this! I can barely make out the words. *It's so hard to read…* but I think it says… *'Hannah, I thank you… for… saving my health… Yours, Jas. Fitzpatrick…'*" Jim stared at the letter, his hands *shaking nervously*, his eyes not believing what was in front of him. Then he looked over at the initials *'J'* and *'F'* on back of the watch- and couldn't contain his excitement.

"*OH, MY GOD!!*" Natalie grabbed the letter and scrutinized it for several seconds. "***Do you know what this is?*** It's a note from the outlaw James Fitzpatrick… to Indian Hannah, thanking her for healing him!"

Jim took the letter and insisted on examining it and the watch again, as he couldn't fully fathom what was happening. "*YES!!* The *'J'* and the *'F'*- James Fitzpatrick- it's *got* to be him! This is *remarkable*- a letter from 'Captain' Fitz- to Hannah. The watch is the right time period: 1776 is the year Fitzpatrick left to join the militia. His mother probably gave it to him as a memento before he left home! The initials *'J'* and *'F'* corroborate the letter. I'm guessing those stories of Sandy Flash running into an old woman and refusing to rob her *are* accurate. He was probably really sick when he tried to rob her- and she knew it from his voice- so she agreed to heal him with one of her medicines. He likely gave her his watch in payment- and wrote this brief note to thank her. How the letter came to be in this box is anyone's guess." He peered over at Natalie, hoping for some ideas.

"George Washington Peirce was determined to maintain a memorial to Hannah, so he placed the cross here. He probably saved these personal items of Hannah's they'd collected over the years and included them here in this box to be part of the memorial. What's over there? Looks circular."

Jim noticed the object and started cleaning it of debris. "Looks like… *a coin?* Yes, it *is* a coin. Let me see if I can clear it off enough to read." He scratched the surface with his thumbnail and it started coming to life. "**My Lord!** This is an English coin, dated… 1778. It looks like… gold. I've seen pictures of these. I think it's what's called a gold Half Guinea, which they issued to honor *King George III of England*. Look! On the other side it's an engraving of… what looks like… *a King*."

Natalie held the coin close to her eyes. "Somehow we stumbled onto a package dedicated to Hannah from Fitzpatrick- all courtesy of George Washington Peirce- who was determined to preserve her legacy. Thank God he did. ***THIS IS INCREDIBLE!!***"

"*We really lucked out here!* I'm putting the cross back in the ground… but I'm bringing these items to Colleen and the people at the Archives. They likely have no idea this is here. I'm sure they'll appreciate them- and add these artifacts to their archives. Fitzpatrick and Hannah *DID* interact… and somehow, helped each other."

"Wait a minute. A point of clarification, sir. If Fitzgerald gave her money- since she was so poor- wouldn't she have just *spent* it all?"

Jim thought for a few seconds. "Maybe he gave her *several* gold coins- she spent most of them, but kept this one to remember his generosity. He had enough gold to *buy Chester County*- so what's a few coins to help an old Indian woman?"

Natalie laughed out loud. "Let's not go there. He just had some money and paid Hannah for healing him."

"It was a joke, hon."

"Not funny."

"It was a little funny."

Her eyes studied all the items in front of her. "This is a great find! *Who would have guessed it was here?!*"

"I'm just glad it was *us* who found it- and not some thief who'd steal everything!" Jim put each item back in the box and closed it. Pounding the rock several more times onto the top of the cross, it went securely into the dirt. "There. At least her cross is intact for everyone to see. Now we'll make sure this part of her story gets recognized." He stood up and grabbed Natalie's hand, helping her to stand beside him. "*I'd say this is the best visit we've ever had to Longwood Gardens. Seeing the gardens is nice, but this is way beyond…*"

"Definitely."

"Let's walk over to the Webb House; later we can bring the box to the personnel in the Archives here." They ambled along the path leading to the meadow, then advanced along the edge of the hillside toward the tan and grey stone house with maroon-painted shutters on the windows. "Their website mentions that the land here was purchased by James Wallis from William Penn. William Webb purchased 203 acres of the original 1,000-acre tract from George Harlan in 1713 and 301 acres from Samuel Pyle in 1725. The house was built around 1734-1735; the Pyle tract formed the majority of what's called the Meadow Garden today. Isn't it beautiful?"

"I love it. I always enjoy walking here; it's so calming- and gorgeous in the Fall. This is the area where Hannah spent a lot of time; some reports say she was born right around here." They stepped up the slope and entered the house. "The displays are interesting; they've done an excellent job restoring and maintaining the place. Look at the oversized fireplace."

Jim gazed all around. "Absolutely first-rate job. The panels highlighting the agricultural history of the area are nicely done. John Milner Architects were hired to restore the home and they get an A+." After roaming into the adjacent rooms, he glanced at the Eddie Bauer watch given to him by his sister, who he'd mailed the Birthday card to. "We should head over to their offices at the rear entrance, where the Archives are. I'll bring these to Colleen and the Team there." He took her hand as they walked back down the Meadow Garden, then up the slope to the parking area.

"This has been an absolutely *wonderful* day. Finding something of historical value makes it even more memorable." Her grasp showed Jim how proud she was of him as he started the engine.

The car cruised around to the side road which led to the alternate entrance, where Jim stopped in the closest parking spot. "Want to come in with me?"

"**YES!** This is *way too exciting*." She took his hand as they entered the building.

"Hi, I'm Jim Peterson. I did research here recently. Is Colleen here today?"

The 45-ish woman in a lovely turquoise linen top with shoulder-length, wavy blonde hair answered right away in a melodious voice. "You're in luck- she is. Take the elevator to the second floor, then go through the double glass doors. She should be there. I'll buzz her and let her know you're coming."

As they went through the double-doors, Colleen came right up to greet them. "Good to see you, Jim. Did you need to do more research?"

"Actually, no. Today we have something *for you*. This is my wife Natalie. We were walking through the Gardens and saw Hannah's cross had fallen over, so I walked up to it and started to pound it into the ground so people could see it. As I was trying to pound it back in,

I sensed something very hard stopping it from going further, so I pulled her cross out and started digging. This box is what we found." He walked with Colleen over to the nearest table and laid it down. "Open it. I think you'll be very interested to see what's inside."

Colleen was intrigued. "Only occasionally do we have people bring *US* things to examine." She opened the box and saw the pocket watch, examining it closely. "Very nice old watch. Looks like… *'J'*… and *'F'*… and… 1776 on the back." She picked up the weathered leather pouch, opening it and taking out the fragile paper. "What is… *this…?*" She held the letter close to her face and started reading. Suddenly the initials on the watch and the words in front of her came together in one message. "Could this be a note from… the outlaw James Fitzpatrick… *to Hannah?*" She held it for several seconds. "You found this today, underneath Hannah's cross?"

"We did and I wanted to bring it right over to you, to be part of your archives. We can't say for sure, but we believe this looks authentic- and is proof that Hannah interacted with Fitzpatrick, probably healed him with some herbal medicine she had. Look at the watch: it's got his initials. Examine the coin; it's the right time period- 1778. By the way, Fitz turned against the local rebels and *supported the British* in 1778 when they were here fighting Washington's troops. Having a coin honoring King George III makes perfect sense. Check it out- it's pure gold." Jim watched as she stared at the coin.

"I'm not an expert on these items; our Curator is. I'll give her all these things to examine- but I *think*… tentatively… your conclusion seems to be correct. These items appear to be linked to both Fitzpatrick and… Indian Hannah. If genuine, these are superb finds, Jim. ***Thank you so much for bringing them to me!!***"

"My pleasure. We wouldn't consider doing anything else but preserving them- and Longwood is the place to do that. Assuming you folks authenticate these, maybe you can make Hannah's little memorial area a bit more inviting- perhaps even place a small sculpture or monument there for her. Just a thought." Jim glanced over at Natalie, who was nodding with her approval.

"Absolutely. That's a wonderful idea. Thank you, Jim- for coming today. This looks like a great find! I'll get back with you."

As Jim shook her hand, he could feel her excitement. "Wonderful. Let's keep in touch."

**Strodes Mill Gallery sign courtesy of**
**Strodes Mill Gallery**

**Longwood Gardens - Kennett Square, Pa.**

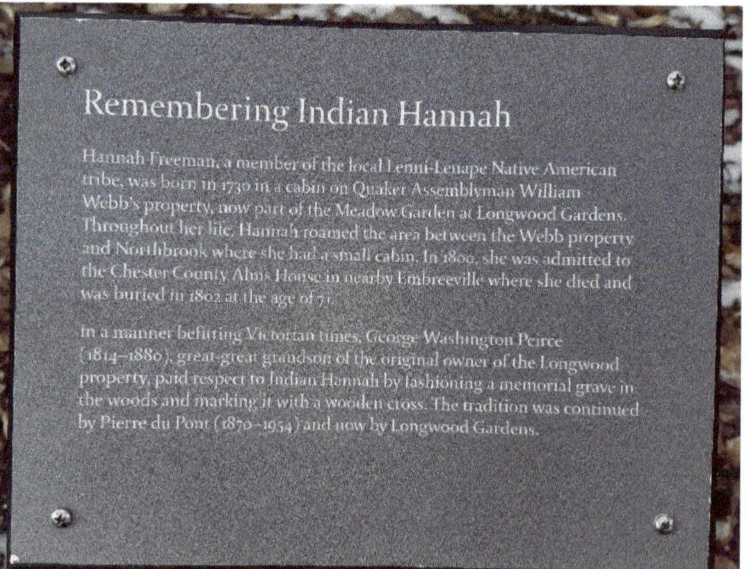



**Historical plaque honoring Indian Hannah
inside Longwood Gardens**

**Indian Hannah historical marker inside
Longwood Gardens**

**William Webb House, now owned by Longwood Gardens; Indian Hannah once lived on the property**

**Historical land use display inside the William Webb House**

**Interior of William Webb House, Longwood Gardens**

# Chapter 15

*"... the house is built, and likely to stand for two or three centuries, when, in all probability, the inscribed stone over its portal will be the only memorial of the name of its builder... While I live, I trust I shall have my trees, my peaceful, idyllic landscape, my free country life..."*     -Bayard Taylor, Letter to R. H. Stoddard, May 10, 1860

*********************************************************************

Jim examined the mass of files in front of him on the table, then noticed the clock: 10:21 a.m. He slowly paged through folder after folder. His eyes got heavy... *and his mind drifted off...*

Bayard Taylor was born in Kennett Square, Pennsylvania on January 11, 1825. James Monroe was President; it was the 'Era of Good Feelings.' The nation had been victorious in a second war against England and rebounded with a decade of peace and prosperity. Two major issues would hold the country's attention over the next 40 years: western expansion... and slavery. The first one contributed to its greatness and economic strength, the other to its near collapse. The former topic captivated Taylor starting in his early years, leading him to explore foreign lands, become a poet, a lecturer and the best-known travel writer of his era.

Taylor's life from the very start seemed inextricably linked to important places and events in our heritage. The house he was born in was across the street from the historic Unicorn Tavern and just a few steps from where British and Hessian troops camped before the Battle of the Brandywine. Six months after Taylor came into the world, the Marquis de Lafayette visited nearby Chadds Ford, strolling terrain he'd defended decades before as part of General Washington's army. That site would later be the subject of one of Taylor's first commercial writing efforts, *To the Brandywine*, a poem describing his trek exploring the grounds where the battle occurred.

Although his father was a successful Quaker farmer, Bayard displayed little inclination toward agrarian pursuits. Early on he was attracted to books, reading at age four, writing poetry by seven. In 1837, the family moved to West Chester. This gave him an opportunity to attend the region's best schools- Bolmer's Academy and subsequently the Unionville Academy. The latter institution spawned notable talent: future historian J. Smith Futhey, co-author of *History of Chester County* and sculptor William Marshall Swayne, who would go on to create acclaimed busts of Taylor and Abraham Lincoln. Taylor did not pursue a college education, but he was a voracious reader and gained an almost encyclopedic knowledge of countries around the globe, as well as art and literature while learning Latin, French and Spanish.

Bayard Taylor possessed writing ability *and* artistic talent. As a young man, he produced sketches and paintings of local landscapes. This combination of skills served him well in the years ahead as he depicted in words and images the numerous sites he explored in his travels. The first step on his momentous journey was into the offices of the West Chester *Village Record*, the newspaper where Bayard became an apprentice. He later corresponded with Rufus W. Griswold, editor of *Graham's Magazine*, who encouraged Taylor to publish his poems, some of which had already appeared in the *Saturday Evening Post*. This resulted in Taylor's *Ximena, or, the Battle of the Sierra Morena, and Other Poems* in 1844. He was just 19 years old. The book provided his first income as a published author.

A book titled *The Tourist in Europe* by George P. Putnam captured Taylor's attention and fanned the flames of his desire to see other countries. Bayard's cousin Franklin Taylor encouraged him to accompany Franklin and Barclay Pennock on a trip to Europe. Bayard persuaded personnel at the *Saturday Evening Post*, the *United States Gazette* and *Graham's Magazine* to fund his adventure in exchange for accounts of his travels. As he was about to leave New York, he met someone who would help his rise to fame: Horace Greeley, editor of the *New York Tribune*.

An exciting trip through England, France, Germany, Switzerland and Italy ended up changing the course of Taylor's life. His letters to the editors were printed and gained wide popularity with a public eager to learn of other cultures. After he returned to the U.S., Taylor published his writings in 1846 in *Views A-foot, or Europe Seen with Knapsack and Staff*. The book went through twenty-four editions in the first thirteen years.

In 1847 Taylor started work as an editor for both *Union Magazine* and the *New York Tribune*. At the *Tribune*, Horace Greeley asked him to review a submission by an unknown writer. "Now you must do something for this young man. His name is Thoreau. He lives in a shanty at Walden Pond… and he must be encouraged." Taylor later toured New England, where he met James Russell Lowell, Henry Wadsworth Longfellow and John Greenleaf Whittier.

The collaboration with Greeley took Taylor to the next level of his career. When gold nuggets were discovered at Sutter's mill outside of Sacramento, the nation was changed forever. Tens of thousands ventured out West to join the California gold rush. Greeley directed Taylor to cover the event; in June 1849, he sailed to California. Over the next five months, he visited several gold mining operations. His return trip through Mexico brought *terror.* He nearly perished, alone in the wilderness of a foreign country and detailed his harrowing experiences in *Eldorado, or Adventures in the Path of Empire* (1850). With his travel books, Taylor gained invaluable experience as a chronicler of fascinating places and diverse cultures. He gave presentations in states from Maine to Wisconsin sharing his knowledge of foreign lands.

Taylor's novel *The Story of Kennett* returned the author to his roots. In the Prologue, he states: "To my friends and neighbors in Kennett: I… dedicate this story to you…" The book chronicles life in Chester County following the American Revolution; the interactions of local families form its framework. Chadds Ford 'village historian' Chris Sanderson made notes within his copy of the book identifying the actual people depicted in the novel.

After serving briefly as Minister to Germany, Bayard Taylor died on December 19, 1878. The next day, the *Wilmington News Journal* printed the announcement. "The Poet, Novelist, Traveler and Diplomatist Dies Quietly at his Post of Duty… It is as an author and a poet that he will be remembered with ever increasing admiration and respect…" Newspapers across America mourned his passing. The *New York Times* posted his obituary on the front page, noting him as "a great traveler, both on land and paper." His body was returned to the U.S., the casket displayed in New York's City Hall. On March 15, 1879, Taylor was honored lying in state at Cedarcroft before he was laid to rest at Longwood Cemetery. Above his grave is a cylinder of Indiana limestone, on its side a bronze bas-relief of the poet. His brother Charles, hero at the Battle of Gettysburg, lies next to him.

In his 53 years, Bayard Taylor experienced more than most people could see in five lifetimes. Yet his poetry is simple and elegant, yearnings of a soul constantly seeking new insights. A beautiful bust of Bayard Taylor is prominently displayed at the Kennett Library in the Bayard Taylor Room, next to a plaque and framed articles honoring his many achievements…

*"Wow!!"* Jim shook his head backwards, which had been drooped forward over the glass Breakfast Room table. He thought of all the images that had flashed in front of his eyes. "Was I… *out*…?" He glanced up at the clock: 10:23 a.m. "That *can't be*. Just ***two minutes?*** Did I drift off? It felt like I was thinking… daydreaming for hours…"

Natalie strolled into the kitchen, Frankie following close behind her. "I've been in the Conservatory reading. What have you been up to? Didn't you say you wanted to visit Cedarcroft?"

"*Yes!* I just had a vivid, shall we say- '*experience.*' I was reading and I got drowsy, closed my eyes, I guess. Seemed like I was out for several hours- but it was just a couple of minutes. I wasn't asleep, I don't think. It was *not* a dream… more like *a 'visitation'*…?"

"O.K.- who'd you meet this time?" She had a smirk on her face as she waited for him to respond.

"I was reviewing the information about Bayard Taylor in these folders- there are more than a dozen here and I must have dozed off while reading. A *'presence'* came over me... I know what you're probably thinking, so don't get cute. Somehow, it seems... I was *actually talking with* Bayard Taylor. He was telling me about his life- *which was fascinating!!* I swear- **he was right here with me**... not two feet away. We were chatting over a cup of coffee. I felt a strong bond with him, like we'd known each other for years. Right before the end he was asking me... to... *'keep his memory alive.'* **I'm telling you- this wasn't a dream. He was here.**" Jim's eyes were wide open as he stared at Natalie, almost in shock.

"Look, I've had some *incredibly vivid* dreams where *I would swear on a Bible* that it really happened. Those are special messages. Some analysts say that they're *'connection'* dreams- where that person's spirit *IS* reaching out to you. Maybe that's what you had."

Jim nodded. "Yes, whatever it was- it touched me in a way I've *never experienced before...*"

"You seem to have an ability to 'connect' with people from history..." Natalie touched his hand and held it as he searched for an answer.

"Maybe it's some kind of a gift? Not easy to explain... *Perhaps I'm 'hard wired' to... intercept signals like these?*"

Natalie looked at the brown-rimmed clock and noticed it was almost 10:45 a.m. "Do you want to go to Cedarcroft, walk around and get some photos, then have lunch?"

"Yes- let's head over. I don't know if we'll be able to walk all around the property, but at least we can see the house. Then, maybe... eat at Hood's?"

"That's a plan. I'm craving their barbecue pork platter. Let's go- my treat."

The charcoal grey Mercedes SUV left the cul-de-sac turning right onto Rosedale heading into Kennett Square. "One thing- *don't* walk right up to the windows of the place and try to look in. You might get us in trouble."

"I won't. Scout's honor."

"You weren't a Boy Scout, *were you?*"

"Not exactly, but I do respect their discipline. My brother was a Scout. I remember my father took me to one of his Scout meetings where the parents wanted their *other* children to get involved- so they pushed me up on stage with a few totally confused kids and tried to make us all sing a song I'd never heard of. I literally had *no idea* what we were doing. The adults in the audience thought it was hilarious. Now *THAT* was a strange experience- weirder than the one I just had." Jim's mind shifted from the memory to the present. "I'd like to stroll around the edge of the property there at Cedarcroft, see some of the trees and landscaping and get some photos of the house." As the car cruised onto Route 82 going towards Unionville, it passed by the Union Hill Cemetery (1869) on the left and St. Patrick's Cemetery (1904) on the right. He said a silent prayer for all the souls interred on each side of the road. "Ever think about all the fascinating people who passed through here over the centuries?"

Natalie started to speak, but *jammed on the brakes*, narrowly avoiding a young kid sprinting recklessly across the street directly in front of the car. "**My God!** He was inches from my bumper! What *kind of a person* would *do* that?!"

Jim glanced over at her. "Nut case?"

*"Affirmative."*

He chuckled. "So far, so good. No tickets, no accidents, we're all in one piece. Bayard Taylor describes scenes in *Views A-Foot* where he was climbing across a HUGE chasm and nearly died… and also hiking in a lightning thunderstorm with nowhere to hide for cover, getting completely drenched."

Natalie stared over at him. *"… and your point would be…?"*

"Just saying we're quite a bit luckier than Taylor. He walked thousands of miles all around Europe- out in the elements- and was almost *killed*. We're relatively safe in our car."

*"Key word is RELATIVELY."*

Jim's eyes were alert. "O.K.- we passed Cedarcroft Road… so up there is Gatehouse Drive- turn left. It circles around and leads into Taylor Lane, named in his honor."

"I know. We came up here one time. It's a winding back road."

"Hey! I just realized this- some of the streets are named after people in *The Story of Kennett*: Fairthorn Drive, Potter Drive… There it is- can't miss it. Still beautiful after 165 years." The Mercedes stopped and they both advanced toward the stately home where Bayard Taylor wrote his best-known novel, *The Story of Kennett,* in his library. The solid burgundy brick, white trim structure seems to lean out towards the visitor, saying *'Welcome. Walk around. This is my home, which I love.'* Jim hiked toward the 4 ½ story tower which dominates the property. "Look at that- a magnificent design by the author. Did you know Taylor was also a botanical enthusiast? He planted a variety of flowers, shrubs and trees all throughout the property- originally about 200 acres, which must have been a treat to stroll around back then. Now it's under 5 acres- and in private hands. There's the plaque:"

**'Cedarcroft has been designated a Registered National Historic Landmark… 1972'**

Natalie had her cell phone raised, taking photos. "I didn't know he was such a fan of arboretums, but it makes sense, due to his descriptions of nature you've mentioned in many of his travel books."

"Another American writer had a house with a tower, where he sometimes wrote: Ernest Hemingway. His home, the Finca Vigia just outside downtown Havana has a three-story tower. His wife Mary had it constructed so he could write there, but he actually preferred writing in the main house." Jim marched further ahead, around the side of the stately mansion, hoping no one was inside to chase them off. "If you lived around here in 1866 and read *The Story of Kennett*, it's been said you would have recognized all the characters in it. Chris Sanderson enjoyed the book so much, he decided to live in the area. His descriptions of each character in notes in his copy of the book are fascinating: Gilbert Potter, Old Man Barton, Martha Deane, Betsy Lavender, Sally Fairthorn. He identified each of them as people living at the time."

"Yes, but remember you said in the book, they describe Sandy Flash as 'short, thickset, with a red face, jet-black hair and heavy whiskers?' Most narratives we've read describes Flash-Fitzpatrick in reality- as a very tall, 6 foot, four-inch muscular man, with sandy red hair and no beard- almost the *opposite* of Taylor's Sandy Flash. Why is that?"

"One scene in the book does describe him with black hair- that was apparently a *disguise*. Yet, other sections of the book describe him as 'short, broad-shouldered'- nowhere near a 6 foot-four inch man. REALITY CHECK: Talk to any police officer about someone committing a crime. They speak with five witnesses- and get five different descriptions: 'short, medium height, light hair, dark hair.' Remember my theory? It's a good bet that he was partially describing one of the thieves who robbed him in Mexico, who were likely 'short, thickset.' He blended his real-life experience to create an entirely new character. His book has a link with an outlaw today in *The Story of Kennett*, one character complains about the authorities not being able to catch Sandy Flash."

***"What's the sheriff and constables good for?... It's a burnin' shame that the whole country has been plundered so long, and the fellow still runnin' at large."***

Natalie looked up as he spoke. "You mean that murderer, Danelo Cavalcante? He escaped from the Chester County Prison in 2023, somehow 'crab-walking' up the wall without anyone noticing him- and was on the loose for two weeks, even though there were up to 500 State Police and other officers looking for him. He even made his way *through Longwood Gardens*, got filmed on their 'night-camera'- and the cops *weren't able to find him!*"

Jim nodded. "I remember: we got 'reverse-911' calls alerting us to the fact that he was likely *within a mile* of our house. Think about it: they had *500 police* looking for this dude- and they *still couldn't catch him!* Finally- after two weeks of his terrorizing the citizens, they managed to get him. A modern-day Sandy Flash. Some of the comments from law enforcement justifying the long manhunt were a tad hard to believe, saying it was such *difficult terrain* here, with sticker bushes and creek beds to crawl around in. *Get real!* Southern Chester County is mostly meadows and rolling hills- not exactly the mountains of Afghanistan. If Taylor were here today, he'd be writing about this in his fifth novel- *Murderer On the Loose*. There's also one interesting connection here- with Indian Hannah."

Natalie strolled toward the front of the house where they were parked. "What's that?"

"C. A. Weslager in his book *Red Men on the Brandywine* mentions that:

***'Hannah's skill as an herbalist was such that many consulted her for cures, and she is supposed to have prescribed for Joseph Taylor, the father of the writer, Bayard Taylor.'***

"If that's accurate, then Indian Hannah could have had a more profound influence on local society than previously revealed. Bayard Taylor may even have heard stories about her from his family." Jim kept walking the perimeter, then ventured a bit closer and tried from a distance to peer inside the windows. "I've heard the house was quite elegant in its day."

"I read an article a while back in *The Hunt Magazine* which mentioned that they had a beautiful Grand Staircase inside, a lovely cut-glass chandelier and an oversized mirror atop the fireplace: late 19th century Gilded Age opulence. Too bad you can't see those things from out here. I think we've pretty much seen the house- head back?" She waited for Jim's response.

"Sure. They laid the cornerstone with one of Taylor's books and personal items inside. Speaking of personal items- *guess who was very impressed with Bayard Taylor.*"

Natalie thought for several seconds and came up blank. "You're the only guy who would know this. *Who?*"

"The creator of Longwood Gardens- *Pierre S. du Pont!!* I did a search and found an article in their archives. One of their staff mentioned that du Pont *owned at least 21 books* by Taylor. He also had a framed portrait of him and a cyanotype of Cedarcroft. Apparently he was a *HUGE* Taylor fan. These two nature lovers had very similar tastes and interests. They even did a production of *The Story of Kennett* at the Longwood Gardens Open-Air Theatre in 1940."

"Now that's interesting. Never knew that…"

"They also shared a 'travel' connection: Bayard Taylor went to Europe to explore when he *was just 19*; Pierre did the same thing, visiting Europe when *he was 19*. Taylor created some of the best-written travel books of the 19th century and a beautiful home which ended up on the National Register; du Pont created a wondrous garden filled with thousands of beautiful plants, trees and shrubs which ranks among the most outstanding in the United States. Thinking about this place… I would love to have been here for the Housewarming Party in 1860: Ralph Waldo Emerson, John Greenleaf Whittier, Horace Greeley all showed up. I'm sure libations were extensively consumed. Taylor knew Alfred Lord Tennyson, Henry David Thoreau, Mark Twain- some of the best known 'Men of Letters' of the era. The Taylor display over at the Sanderson Museum is quite good; they have several first editions of his books, old period photographs, some of Chris's notes about the characters in *The Story of Kennett*. Now if they had a lock of Fitzpatrick's hair, his pants and boots, we could probably prove he really *was* 6-foot four with sandy red hair- not a short, dark-haired Mexican dude."

Natalie chuckled as she stood at the car door. "It's been a great day. You said you somehow got in touch with the guy who owns this place?"

"Not the owner, the owner's father. Chatted with him for a while- a retired Penn doctor- nice gentleman. He said his son was doing a lot of refurbishment here and although I asked, he said his son wasn't likely to give tours. Maybe with some luck, someday he will… and people can get inside the house to know Kennett Square's most famous son a bit better. Did you know there's a school named in his honor?"

"No. Where's that?"

"Sadly, nowhere near Kennett. The Bayard Taylor School is a Colonial Revival style building in the Hunting Park neighborhood of Philadelphia. It was designed by famous architect Henry DeCourcy Richards and built in 1907-1908. The structure was listed on the National Register of Historic Places in 1988. So… Bayard Taylor's love of reading and exploring helps school kids today expand their knowledge of the world."

"That's quite interesting. I bet few people know that." Natalie smiled as she buckled her seat belt and put her hand on his shoulder.

"Maybe someday, his hometown of Kennett Square will name a school in his honor. That would be a fitting tribute to this underappreciated author, poet, lecturer, world traveler." As the car cruised slowly past the historic home, down Taylor Lane, out of the corner of the windshield Jim spotted a very faint rainbow in the distance over the edge of town. *Let's head over to Hood's… for some great barbecue…*

**Katsura tree in Fall splendor**

**Hood's Barbecue fireplace with buffalo**

Bayard Taylor lithograph from *History of Chester County* by Futhey and Cope 1881

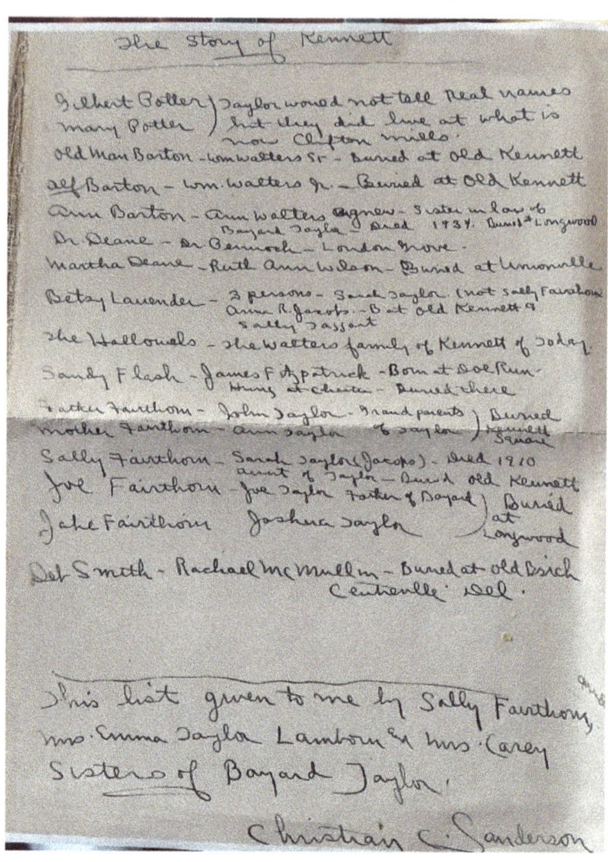

Chris Sanderson's notes on characters in *The Story of Kennett*

*Views A Foot* by Bayard Taylor
courtesy Kennett Library

*Eldorado* by Bayard Taylor
courtesy Kennett Library

Above: *Painting of Cedarcroft* by Bayard Taylor demonstrating Taylor's love of nature courtesy Chester County History Center

Left: Cedarcroft in 2015

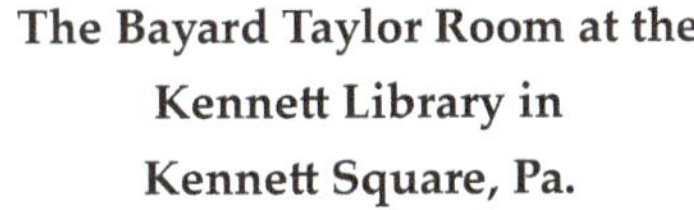

The Bayard Taylor Room at the Kennett Library in Kennett Square, Pa.

Bayard Taylor display at the Christian Sanderson
Museum in Chadds Ford, Pa.

Bayard Taylor gravesite monument at Longwood
Cemetery in Kennett Square, Pa.

Bayard Taylor School in the Hunting Park neighborhood Philadelphia

# Chapter 16

*'Sir,*

*It affords me ineffable pleasure to present to your Excellency the <u>Thanks</u> of the United States in Congress assembled, for the distinguished services you have rendered to your Country, and particularly for the conquest of Lord Cornwallis… Words fail me when I attempt to bestow my small tribute of thanks and praise to a Character so eminent for wisdom, courage and patriotism, & one who appears to be no less the Favorite of Heaven than of his Country…'* -Thomas McKean (1734-1817), Letter to George Washington October 31, 1781 after his decisive victory at the Battle of Yorktown

****************************************************************************

Jim's eyes opened as he lay in bed, then turned to see the digital clock on the night table: 5:02 a.m. "I'm wide awake, but she'll be asleep for well over an hour. Why not get up and go for an early morning hike?" He rose slowly, went over to the bench and got dressed. As he walked out the side door, Jim noticed the thermometer: 48 degrees. "Mornings are getting a bit cooler. Glad I wore my heavy red flannel shirt." Strolling up Woodview, then turning on Forest, he reached the community greenspace that sat on the edge of the original woodlands before the area was developed for housing.

Entering the forest in the early morning's dawn, a hint of fog transformed the scene into a dreamlike, N.C. Wyeth medieval landscape, hundreds of oak, maple, tulip poplar and beeches extending 60… 70… 80 feet upward into the misty cerulean sky. Just then, an exquisite, radiant crimson and amber maple leaf more than eight inches across fell right into his hands. "This… is ravishing, a real gem. You left the party a bit early, my friend. Your buddies are still on the trees. I'll take you home and keep you in a safe place."

His footsteps took him along the dusty, leaf-strewn deer path, trod for centuries by the Lenape as they hunted game and foraged for wild strawberries, nuts and other edibles along the forest floor. Jim's gaze took in the serenity of each tree, the smooth, silvery-slate colored bark of the beech trees, undulating, rope-like grey-brown trunks of the oaks and many others as he studied their treasure trove of leaves, twigs and seeds scattered along the ground by his feet. "Now I understand why Marshall and Darlington were fascinated by this… and why the Lenape called it all sacred."

As he returned and reached the side door of their home, he made a silent promise not to wake her, but as he entered, he could sense she was already up and about.

Natalie roamed around the edge of their garden, towards the woods fringing the property, looking up at the large Hibiscus off to the side with its fuchsia flowers in full bloom…

and she smiled. "Our yard was Indian land. I'm just glad we still have this forest surrounding us to give us some peace and quiet." She strolled over to the path- and the joyful memories of the kitties running with them into the woods brought her mind some peace. Natalie perused the canopy of trees giving her shade from the morning sun: cherry, London plane, locust and swamp maple, resplendent in their greenery. Circling back to the house, she saw Jim out on the Terrace, the large black ceramic planter with its pink overflowing petunias partly blocking him from view. "Hey up there! What's the cruising course today, Captain?"

Jim moved down the steps leading to the patio. He descended the stairs with their wall of lush Morning Glory vines, glanced over at them and his face beamed. Their deep violet flowers opened to greet the day, he gently brushed past the attached forest green, heart-shaped leaves. "Well, what about breakfast at the *new* Hank's Place? This time, it's *my* treat."

"O.K.- I'm officially starving. Let's eat."

The drive down the curving streets of their complex, fringed with old growth forest reminded Jim of stories he'd read over the years about the development of the area. "You know, we're just the latest caretakers of this property."

"I was just thinking about that. This was *Indian* domain for centuries, but sadly, history didn't work out in their favor. It's not something most people dwell on… but I do."

He leaned over in the car and gave her a kiss. "Me, too. I'm just wondering if there's a way we could give them some land back…"

"I'm generous, but- *let's keep the house.*" Natalie grinned as she saw the neatly lined scarlet begonias planted at the edge of the entrance to Bayard Estates.

"There's so much wide-open space around here, completely undeveloped… maybe at least a small piece of that could be given back. Just a thought." He pulled up in front of Hank's Place on Baltimore Pike in Chadds Ford, the parking lot always busy with cars pulling in and out every few seconds. As he drove slowly into a space, he thought of the sign that was there many years ago…

***"HANK'S PLACE- WHERE FRIENDLY PEOPLE MEET AND HUNGRY PEOPLE EAT"***

He nudged the car forward to a front-facing spot. "I always try to park face-forward so I don't have to back out."

"*… and you can avoid getting hit by someone flying through the parking lot at 30 miles an hour…*"

He took her hand as they came up the new walkway to the front door. Dark-haired, handsome Pablo, their long-time server greeted them with his always welcoming smile. Jim was ready with a question. "Two- for breakfast. Can we get a table by the window?"

"Sure, choose any one you want. I'll be right over."

As they strolled underneath the exotic, beautifully designed tree-branch lamp fixture which enlightened the high-ceilinged room, Jim noticed the counter was about twice the length of the 'old' Hank's, flanked by elegant black marble walls and an extension to the building- an exterior patio for diners to enjoy. After Pablo brought napkins and utensils to their table, a 35-ish, full-figured woman with a friendly face brought them two menus. "Anything to drink?"

"I'll have an orange juice and also ice water." Natalie perused the menu as Jim got comfortable on his side.

"I'll have coffee, with cream. An ice water, too, please." As the woman turned to go back to the kitchen, Jim held his menu up to read. "I already know what I want: corned beef hash and eggs. They make it fresh here; it's excellent. I used to love it when I was a kid."

"Sometimes I think you still *ARE* a kid…"

"In many respects, it's healthy to keep a *childlike* fascination with life." Jim looked up as the waitress returned with their drinks.

Natalie glanced at her. "I'll have the biscuits and gravy, with a side of bacon, please."

"For me, corned beef hash and eggs, with rye toast. I like the place! Anthony and Katie deserve a medal for their patience, waiting over two years for it to open."

The waitress couldn't help laughing. "Yes, they do. We're all just happy to be here."

As Jim sipped his coffee, his cell phone rang. "Don't get too many calls on my cell phone- especially this early in the morning, so it's either a telemarketer or… maybe something important. *Hello, this is Jim…*"

"Hi, Jim. It's Donna from Strodes Mill Gallery. Good news- we're starting to work on the map you brought us. Even though it's quite old, it looks like it'll hold together well, especially behind special museum quality glass with a solid backing and the frame you ordered. I wanted to let you know we found something *in back of* the map, in between its support panel and the frame itself- a written document of some sort. Whatever it is, it's very old- I think well over 200 years, maybe older. I wanted to have you come over and look at it before I did anything further."

"That sounds… *very interesting.*" He glanced at Natalie as her eyebrows raised with suspicion. "We're at breakfast now, but we'll be over in about an hour. See you then."

"Sounds good- I'll be here."

"What was that all about?" Natalie sipped her orange juice and saw the waitress coming back with their orders.

"It was Donna at Strodes Mill Gallery. They're about to frame the map I brought over- and found something in back of it. She said it looks pretty old. No idea what that could be, but it's got my analyst ears perked up. We'll find out when we go over there, after breakfast. Now… I get to savor two of my favorite things- fresh, hot coffee and… homemade corned beef hash."

"You drink *tea* most of the time at home. Why do you drink *coffee* when we go out?"

"I think of it as a special treat. I like tea- Earl Grey, green tea, chamomile… so having coffee is something a bit *different*."

Natalie shook her head and enjoyed the biscuits and gravy, then tried the bacon. "Actually, their bacon here is excellent."

"I love bacon, I just don't eat it. I love potato chips, too- but I can consume an entire bag in *less than two minutes*- so they're OUT. This is good, though. They always have tasty breakfasts here- even if this isn't exactly the most nutritious… but you know what chef Julia Child said."

Natalie looked up at him. "What?"

*"The only time to eat diet food is while you're waiting for the steak to cook."*

Natalie broke out laughing. "Sounds fair to me."

As he finished up, Jim raised his hand to get the waitress's attention for the check, which she brought right over. "Everything was great. We *love* the New Hank's! Thank you." He put down a bill with Ulysses S. Grant's face, leaving a more than generous tip as they both started to get up to leave. "Now I'm very curious to see what Donna has waiting for us."

The Gallery parking lot only had one car, so Jim pulled right up near the building. The rustic wooden sign with its gold lettering and maroon trim standing outside the old stone structure welcomes visitors with its rural charm. Jim strolled first into the shop, quickly followed by Natalie. "Hello. Donna?"

"Coming right out… Oh, hi Jim, Natalie. I have the materials back here. Come take a look." She strode over to a wide table blanketed with several prints in the process of being framed. "Here's what I found on back of the map. You tell me- but it looks like it might be some kind of an agreement with local Indian tribes, although the writing has faded significantly."

Jim leaned down very close to the table. "Do you have a magnifying glass?"

"Sure. Here's one you can use." Donna handed him the black-handled glass which had a battery-powered light switch on it for close reading.

Speaking very slowly, Jim said: "It's pretty faded, kind of difficult to read… but, if I squint, I can make out:

*'In this year of our Lord one-thousand six hundred and eighty three, in the fifth month, is made a memorandum of understanding, of peace and goodwill, between said William Penn and his Commissioners and Seketarius of the tribe called Lenape, whose members have inhabited the lands for many years within the said colony granted to William Penn by King Charles II of England. This agreement shall be held in effect and respected by all who lay claims, that the land through which said river Brandywine runs…'*

As he read the words, his hands couldn't control their shaking. *"If this is authentic, it would be amazing.* It's really hard to read the rest, but I'll give it another try…" Jim leaned even closer, his nose within two inches of the document, its surface illuminated by the magnifying glass with its small light.

*'… from the North in the river's source or beginning, in what is now recognized by William Penn and his Majesty's government as the hills called Welsh in the northern realm of the County of Chester, southward to the river's intersection with the east branch of said river Brandywine, then southward along the main branch of said Brandywine River, for one mile extent on both sides, shall be held and owned and forever used by the said Lenape, for their benefit and for all their peoples…'*

*His eyes bugged open wide. "DO YOU KNOW WHAT THIS IS?!"* Jim stared directly into Natalie's eyes. *"This is the lost agreement between the Lenape and William Penn!!" It was fought over for decades*, but never resolved. In Futhey and Cope's *History of Chester County* they mention the ongoing fight between Lenape leaders and the colonists over this swath of land one mile on each side. The Lenape went to court a few times for rulings- which they *did get in their favor*- but they were never adhered to by the local landowners, especially up in Newlin Township. The Lenape claimed their copy of the document was destroyed in a fire and apparently the early colonial government either lost or destroyed their copy, because it's *never been found, but this **HAS GOT TO BE IT!!"***

Natalie leaned inward, very close to the table, eyeing the document for over a minute without speaking. *"Oh, my God- I think you're right!* It's a very complicated story, though. The Lenape *did claim* that Penn had granted them this land for one mile on each side of the Brandywine, but in 1706, Commissioners purchased property from the Lenape for 100 British pounds, land that was positioned on either side, from the mouth of the Brandywine in the south, going northwards up to a rock which stood on Abraham Marshall's land along the west branch, in line with or intersecting property already owned by Nathaniel Newlin. Newlin started selling parcels of what he considered *his* land all along the west branch in the north, but the Lenape claimed they *still owned* the rights to land from the rock *all the way north to the source in the Welsh Mountains.* Their case was brought to court in 1725 by Lenape Chief Checochinican and in a later session in 1729, where Newlin claimed he would honor the Indians' claims, but he never did. Newlin died in 1729, yet by that time, many of the local Lenape had moved out of the area and the case was never resolved… This *would seem to support the Lenape claim* to land from the rock on Marshall's property up to the source in the Welsh Mountains. *If legitimate, it's the agreement which has been missing for over THREE CENTURIES!!"*

Donna nudged her way closer to the table. "That *IS* remarkable. You may have a tremendous find here. Did you want me to frame it?"

"Oh, I couldn't do that." Jim stepped back from the table. "Assuming this is real, it's a critical part of our history. First, I need to have it authenticated. Natalie- remember I was talking with that guy from the Historical Society of Pennsylvania a while back, their Curator of colonial-era materials? *What was his name?*" He thought for several seconds. "John- John Phillips. That's him! Nice man. He told me if I ever had any interesting documents- maps, whatever- that I wanted examined, he'd be happy to help me. We're members there- Patron level- so they'll be glad to help us. He knows this stuff, inside out. I'm taking it to him- today."

"Well, I'll have your map framed soon, probably later this week. I'll call you in a few days and have it ready for you."

Natalie continued to stare at the antiquated document, its tan, weathered surface lined with hairline cracks which seemed ready to break wide open. "Donna- do you have something secure we can carry this in, so it won't get destroyed? I'd hate for Jim to take it down there and then it falls apart."

"I do. Here- use this. It's a specially-lined document tube and it's very secure. Nothing will happen to it if you have it inside. You can bring it back when you pick up your map."

Jim took the tube from her and watched Donna roll up the fragile document very slowly. "Thanks so much. We appreciate all your help. Now I just need to contact Phillips- and tell him I'm coming downtown to show him something he'll be interested in." He looked at Natalie. "Want to come downtown with me?"

"Not a chance. With all the maniacs on I-95, that's way out of my comfort zone. You go- but you better call him right away so he'll know you're coming."

"Will do. Donna- thank you so much! I'm so happy that bringing an old, weathered map to you for framing has led to what might be a great discovery. We'll be in touch." Jim walked out the door with Natalie, on Cloud Nine. His feet barely seemed to touch the ground. "Ever feel like you've experienced something ***truly extraordinary?***"

"Yes. The day you offered to help me weed the garden. It was a miracle. I called the Vatican." As she got into the car, she added in a more serious tone: "This *IS* really important- we just don't know *how* important yet."

"What do you mean?" Jim started the engine and cruised down Route 52 towards Kennett Square, the centuries-old stone houses on either side a testament to the rich heritage they were driving through.

"When members of the Lenape become aware of this, it's likely to re-write colonial history, at least in their eyes. They'll probably insist on getting a copy for themselves, so their tribe can now legally state that their claims *were* valid."

"I'd be glad to have an archivist expert in colonial documents make a copy with their preferred printer. First, I need to have this authenticated. Historical Society of Pennsylvania, here I come! I just sent Phillips a text message saying I'm on my way with a special item he'll like to see. He responded, said stop on by." After he pulled the car into their garage, he kissed Natalie and said: "I understand you're not coming, even though I think you'd enjoy seeing him evaluate this for us. Traffic shouldn't be too bad right now- it's way off rush hour. I'll be home before five and hopefully we'll be celebrating."

As the blue Forester glided onto I-95 North, Jim thought about what they'd just experienced… his visit to Pennsbury Manor and the drive home, then it came to him. ***"This is Penn's message!*** *'Continue your search… thee will be rewarded with something of great value…'* Somehow he 'connected' with me and wanted us to *find this document*. Penn's deal with the Lenape about land along the Brandywine *was* legitimate- and this is proof!"

As he turned onto Locust Street, he saw the Society building up ahead, then almost jammed on the brakes. "My God, a parking spot! Now I just need a bunch of quarters." The red brick building at 1300 Locust with the stately columns out front is flanked by something most people just walk by without noticing, but Jim stopped to read the lovely blue and gold historical marker out front:

### 'HISTORICAL SOCIETY OF PENNSYLVANIA

***Among the oldest of its kind in the nation, the special collections library holds many of the nation's important founding documents. Founded by prominent citizens in 1824 and located here since 1884, it traces America's history from the 17th century to the present.'***

Jim stopped at the Reception Desk, where the attendant viewed him cautiously. "Here to see John Phillips- he's expecting me. I'm Jim Peterson."

"Oh yes, he told me you were coming. Take the elevator to the fourth floor. He's waiting there for you."

"Thank you." The elevator ride seemed to last *for hours* as he clutched the tube in his hands, eager to show it- and possibly make history for the Lenape.

"Jim- great to see you! Thank you for stopping by. So… what do you have for me?" Phillips noticed the tube and waited for him to place it on the table next to him.

"Thanks for seeing me on such short notice. I do have something which I think you'll… *appreciate*." Jim opened the tube and unrolled the document. "Here is what I *think* just may be the long-lost agreement between Penn and the Lenape Indians regarding land on either side of the Brandywine. Check it- and let me know if you feel it's… *authentic*."

Phillips held a very large magnifying glass in his right hand and scoured the entire document slowly… carefully… from top to bottom. "Well, it's old enough- that's for sure. You can tell by the material it's written on… We have numerous documents of this age. The style of writing and wording appear to be legitimate, in line with other agreements and treaties between Penn and the Indians. I'm familiar with the treaty you mentioned regarding land along the Brandywine, which it purports to reflect. There's one way I can tell you if this is real. I need to place this in our X-ray fluorescence (XRF) scanner which we use. It's right over there. It'll give us a read out in seconds." Phillips took the document and laid it out on the wide metal plate inside the machine, then closed the door and pushed 'SCAN.' "I'll tell you right up front- at first glance, it *does* look legitimate- which would be a great find. Where did you get it?"

"Believe it or not, it was on the back of an old map I was having framed. Got a call from the vendor and we looked at it today- and I knew you were the best person to bring it to. I've done a bit of research on the Lenape. You probably know that they were the very first Indian tribe to sign a treaty with the United States government."

John managed a grin. "Oh, yes. It's not widely known, but deserves much more attention in reviewing our nation's history and interactions with Native American tribes. The Lenape hold the distinction of being the first."

"Exactly. The Treaty of Fort Pitt, also known as the Treaty with the Delawares or the Delaware Treaty was truly groundbreaking, as it established formal, friendly relations between them and the fledgling U.S. government, specifically allowing Continental Army troops to travel freely through Lenape territory, have the Indians assist as guides and promised the Lenape (Delaware Indians) the possibility of forming a future 14th state if they joined with other tribes. Its most important aspect was formalizing a lasting friendship with the Lenape and recognizing their sovereignty."

John nodded in agreement. "You've done your homework. You don't hear too much about the Lenape these days, but the people in this area really should know more about their history."

Jim's grin widened to a full smile. "Add to that the Treaty was signed on September 17, 1778… and ***exactly nine years later to the day, on September 17, 1787***- 39 men met in Philadelphia to sign the *United States Constitution*- which recognized the existence and sovereignty of the Indian tribes. It even incorporated some of their ideas about a confederation of states working together in union for the benefit of all. One of those signers was Benjamin Franklin, who had extensive dealings with the Indians, admired the 'confederacy' of the Iroquois and other tribes as a possible model for our own government and served as Indian Commissioner in Pennsylvania."

"You really have done a bit of research. It's refreshing to hear someone talk about our local heritage with some degree of familiarity." John viewed the controls on the X-ray scanner and waited for well over a minute. "Well, here we go… All the readings for type of material, even type of ink used- all point to a document roughly 300 years, perhaps 350 years old. That would put it in the correct time frame for Penn's treaty, which I believe occurred around… *1683*… Now I'll put the edge of it into the Scanning Electron Microscope (SEM) for a visual confirmation." Phillips placed the document onto the small scanner and turned on the machine, focusing up to 2,800 times regular magnification. "Yes, that's quite old material- appears to be velum, which would be in line with the time period you mentioned, roughly late 1600s."

*"So- this IS REAL!"* Jim jumped up and down near the machine. *"YES!!"* I used the SEM when I was in graduate school analyzing rock samples and was always interested to see what it might show me. This is *way* more exciting than feldspar crystals."

"Your document looks legitimate, Jim. Congratulations! Just curious- would you consider donating it to the Society here?"

"John, thank you so much for all your help. I normally *WOULD* donate it to you, but I believe this belongs in the place where I found it- Chester County. I'm going to gift it to the Chester County History Center. They have an extensive collection of colonial-era documents and artifacts- and I think the appropriate home for this is over there."

"Understand completely. Well, if you change your mind, let me know. This *is* a significant find- probably the most important one I've seen in the last ten years. I wish you luck with this and please keep in touch."

"Thank you, John. Will do." They shook hands as Jim walked through the double-glass doors to the elevator. Going down to street level, he was trying to grasp the magnitude of what had happened. "Thank you, Lord. This is a great discovery and I'm going to make sure *this time* it gets permanently preserved."

On the drive home, traffic was unusually light on I-95 South. Taking the turn for Route 322 West, he was trying to gauge Natalie's excitement when he told her it was real. "She's gonna' love this almost as much as I do." Turning into their driveway, he couldn't wait to jump out of the car and go inside. "Hey, sweetie… I have some *very GOOD NEWS!!*"

"It's *real?*" She came up to Jim and wrapped her arms around him as he put the tube onto the counter.

*"YES!* This *is* the lost agreement between Penn and the Lenape. It deserves something special. I have a bottle of Dom Perignon on ice. We don't usually drink champagne, but this is a once in a lifetime find… Let's crack it open."

*"That is so exciting!"* She gave him a very long, passionate kiss.

Jim smiled as their lips parted. "Well, I should find *these* kinds of documents more often."

"Let's toast to a rare find, one which may reshape how we interpret the history between colonists and the Indians." Natalie's face was exuberant as she waited for the toast.

He slowly filled the elongated, cut crystal glasses with the bubbly liquid, then handed one glass to her. "It's long overdue… but finally, with this, we'll be able to tell the *full story* about the Lenape along the Brandywine. I just wish *Hannah* were here with us to celebrate."

Natalie held her glass high, then glanced over at the beautiful painting of the old Indian woman on the wall. *"Oh, she is… Cheers."*

********************************************************************

Jim wanted to check the outside of the house right after dinner. The light was fading, but he could still see clearly all around their home as he walked outside onto the driveway and approached the front walk. Just then, a small nondescript sedan pulled up to their mailbox, a 40-ish man jumped out, quickly opened the box and seeing nothing there, he jumped back into the car and it sped off down the cul-de-sac.

*"DAMN IT!! They're back!"* His anger was subdued as he thought for a few seconds. "Our camera set up out front here has got to have captured him and his car on film! We might get this guy!" Jim ran back inside and yelled out to Natalie. "Hey, hon- we just got an unwelcome visitor. Some jerk just tried- again- to steal from our mailbox. The 'trap' we set with the 'FLAG' up worked! Now I just hope we recorded it all. Let's check the camera footage- and I'll call Captain Wallingford." Natalie viewed the footage as Jim dialed. "Kennett Police? This is Jim Peterson; can I speak with Captain Wallingford? I have an attempted burglary to report."

"I'll put you right through, sir."

"This is Captain Wallingford. Who am I speaking with?"

"Captain, it's Jim Peterson. You came out to our home several weeks back when we reported two mailbox incidents. Well- tonight we had another one, but I think we got it on tape. Could you come over? Id' like to give the evidence to you."

"Sure thing. I'll be right over."

Within minutes, the patrol car was in their driveway. The knock on the front door was highly welcome.

"Captain, thanks so much for coming. I know this is small potatoes compared to other things you deal with…"

"Not at all. We want people to report all criminal activity, large and small. What do you have for me?"

"Well, some jerk just drove up within the last 30 minutes and tried to rob our mailbox-again. Strangely enough, I have no idea what kind of car it was. It looked… a *bit odd*… I couldn't make out if it was a Toyota… or a Chevrolet. Our front camera recorded it- and here's the file, which you can download for your records. With any luck, you can trace the car. They didn't get anything from our mailbox, but you said to report any suspicious activity."

"Absolutely. Can I borrow this USB drive? I promise I'll return it as soon as we have it in our records."

"Oh, sure. Take it. If it helps track down these thugs, it'll have been worth all our efforts setting up the cameras."

"Thank you, folks. I'll be back in touch."

As his car left the driveway, Jim and Natalie both felt the same sense of relief…

The famous sign at Hank's Place in 2011

Artist's conception of the new Hank's Place
courtesy of Hank's Place Chadds Ford, Pa.

**Historical Society of Pennsylvania**

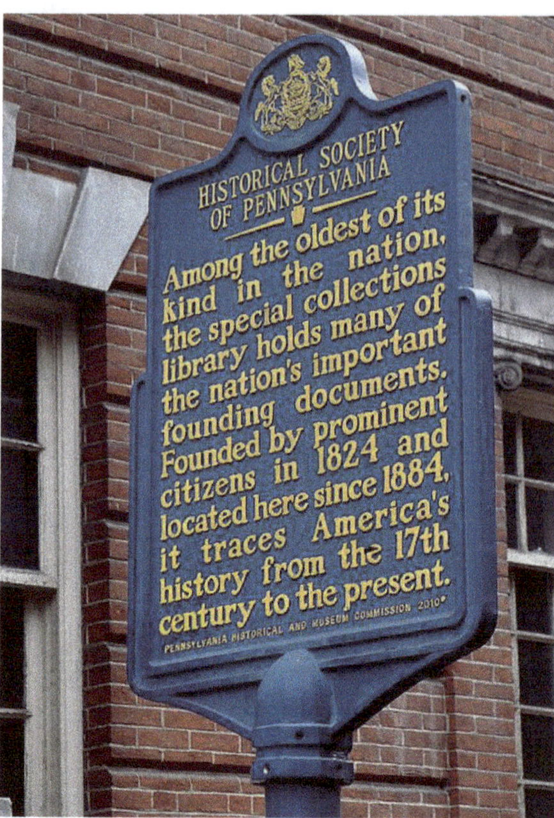

**Historical marker at Historical Society of Pennsylvania, Philadelphia**

**Historical Society of Pennsylvania reading room**

**Frieze of William Penn making the Treaty of Shackamaxon with the Lenape Indians by sculptor Constantino Brumidi in the United States Capitol Building**

# Chapter 17

*"Life is at all times uncertain… but the reputation of a man of honor … soars above all accidents, and remains an imperishable jewel…"*
-William Darlington (1782-1863), Doctor, sailor, statesman, scientist
*****************************************************************

The mid-September days were glorious… Jim looked outside and yearned for a hike. After purchasing a pair of sturdy Skechers hiking boots in June, he was ready to take on any trail. His camping days out West, hiking from Canada to Mexico and back had given him a love of the outdoors he knew would never die. As he scanned the edge of the forest behind their home, he thought what his suggestion to Natalie would be.

"Good morning! I see you and Frankie got down here before I did." Natalie walked over to the coffee maker, but Jim made it there first.

"I'll pour you some coffee if you make me a promise." As he grabbed the cup, he could see the smirk take shape on her face.

"O.K… as long as it's legal… and I'm *not* driving on I-95."

"A simple request: let's go for a hike at Nixon Park! It's early and still cool outside- and the bugs are not bad at all. We can have our first cup, then go over. How's that sound?"

"You enjoy hiking a lot more than I do. I'm barely awake. Let me have my coffee first and afterwards, I'll give you some form of a reasonable answer."

"I just love the outdoors. One nice thing about the Park is you can hike all around and be in the shade about 75% of the time. Besides, it's a great place to stretch your legs, enjoy nature and come up with new ideas." He sipped his Earl Grey and petted Frankie as she lay on Natalie's lap.

"I love the outdoors, too- just not every day like you. My idea of fun is this: relaxing here with Frankie… and playing games on my iPad."

"We're just a *tad* different. To you, 'roughing it' is a luxury bungalow with room service. To me, it's a bivouac under the stars by a roaring campfire. I'll put on my boots and grab my hat. We can go in… five minutes."

"Hold your horses. I may need half a refill."

"Will do." He took her cup and went into the kitchen directly over to the Cuisinart. Frankie followed him from the Conservatory and he noticed her standing right next to his leg. "Mom and I are going to take a hike for a while, so you guard the house. We'll be back in about an hour." He traipsed back to the couch and handed Natalie her refill. "I'll be geared up in a few minutes… Let me know." He strolled over to the closet, got out his boots and white hat, sat down on the steps and laced up.

"O.K. I'm ready. You drive." Coffee had changed Natalie's attitude from *'Don't even think about it'* to *'O.K.- if we have to….'* They were going on a hike: deal with it.

The trek into downtown Kennett Square was easier the back way along Rosedale, which turned into Birch Street as it approached town. Turning right before all the road construction blocked their passage, the Forester cruised all the way to State Street, then turned left. Going down the road to just before Blitz Automotive, it turned right onto North Walnut Street. Up the road which twists and turns, the vehicle reached the green and white sign, turned left and entered an oasis in a small town: the simple beauty of Anson B. Nixon Park.

"This'll be quick, right? About a half-hour?" Natalie shut her car door and decided she was ready- for *some* kind of an excursion.

"Well, roughly 35 minutes or so. Depends on whether we see any wildlife." As they joined hands and walked down the gravel trail, they passed the bandstand which held concerts in the Summer months. Going by the lake, they saw the few Canadian geese remaining for the season. "There used to be about 50 of these guys here just a few weeks back; now there's less than five. Maybe they headed *back North?"*

"Could be." They hiked around the paved macadam trail into the old growth forest.

"You know, the Chambers family owned this property beginning in 1817; they called it 'Bloomfield.' Chambers wrote a book titled *Bloomfield: Memories and Records* (1920) and reminisces about it: *'I love all the trees, the meadows and brooks and memories of Old Bloomfield.'"* Just as they passed the edge of the lake, they turned right and entered the Old Beech Grove. "Lovely time of year- all the leaves are changing! The maples are offering their range from scarlet and vermilion to honey and flaxen, alongside the lemon and golden beech leaves. There it is- the star of the show: the Kennett Beech!! I always stop here."

"Yes, we did this before. So… why are we pausing here today?"

"Look at the sign:

*'The large American Beech tree you see about forty feet beyond this sign is the largest and oldest tree in this woodland. It may have been a young tree at the time of William Penn 300 years ago.'*

"I've gone over to the tree and measured it: the diameter just above the base is well over five feet. *HUGE.* This tree was here when Penn made the treaty with the Lenape. It was here when Indian Hannah roamed the region giving people her medicinal remedies, it was here when Humphry Marshall, Benjamin West, James Fitzpatrick, William Darlington, Thomas

McKean and Bayard Taylor were all living nearby. Some of them probably came here and enjoyed its beauty."

"Possibly. I wouldn't be surprised if they knew this forest and strolled through it."

"Oh, look! It's Henry the Great Blue Heron- up there in the creek, on the left."

Natalie saw the elegant bird and smiled. "You said he's not always here; lucky we saw him today."

"… and over there- on the log dipping into the water- it's Terence the Turtle and his buddy. This Park gives my head a place to absorb new ideas… and speaking of new ideas, I have one: I want to give some land back to the Lenape, in honor of Indian Hannah."

*"… and exactly how would you do that…?"*

"I did some checking. You remember we heard that a private party had agreed to purchase the old Lenape Park? Well, they did… but apparently they gave it *back* to East Bradford Township, saying they were 'gifting' it to them because they couldn't do anything with the property. That's where we come in: I propose we buy the land from the Township and donate it to the Delaware Indians, in honor of the Lenape tribe and Indian Hannah. What do you think?" Jim glanced at her face and sensed she was rolling the idea over in her mind.

"Maybe- but what would it cost?"

"I'm way ahead of you. I contacted the Property and Recreation Manager for the Township, guy named Arnie Townsend, and asked the same question. He said it was interesting that I was calling because it's been sitting vacant for over two years. We chatted for a while; he's a nice guy. He mentioned that the Township might be very eager for someone to take it off their hands for a couple of reasons: 1) the annual maintenance costs are rising for clearing away debris and 2) expenditures for riverbank restoration after storm damage are becoming exorbitant. He told me there would be paperwork involved and Township approval necessary, but *he's* the person who generally approves such transfers, so he was quite open to the idea. I'm thinking we could offer them a nominal amount and they'd accept, because the land's already been abandoned as a flood zone! They won't be expecting a huge amount for it. Then we gift it back to the Delaware Indians, who owned it in the first place."

"Just how would you do that?" Natalie stepped carefully along the gravel portion of the trail.

"I contacted a representative for the Delaware Nation and they said they would gladly accept any donation in honor of Indian Hannah; he knew who she was. I mentioned the idea of a land grant to them- of a Park which used to have *their name* on it, the old **Lenape Park**- and he liked it even better." Jim held her hand in his as they strolled through the lush canopy of beech, white oak, umbrella magnolia and maple trees giving them shade. "Right there is the edge of a local resident's property- you can see his lawn ends at the side of the trail. They used to have a big, colorful 8-foot by 3-foot **'HARRIS- WALZ'** sign there."

"I know- you told me that last time we were here."

"They kept it up *for months* after the election, but they finally figured out she wasn't going to win. Nice sign, though."

Natalie chuckled, then focused intently on his suggestion. "I like the idea of gifting some land back to the Indians. Clearly it is way overdue, but *then what?* What are *they* going to do with it? It's in a flood zone; they can't build any housing or businesses there."

"Not a problem, my dear. That's my next idea: having Tom Weathersby create a sculpture of three of the most interesting local personalities, to be placed up on a large granite pedestal inside the Park. I nominate Indian Hannah, flanked by Humphry Marshall and Bayard Taylor. It'll be a wonderful monument. I don't think anyone would object to that."

Natalie rolled the idea over in her mind for several seconds. "Sounds interesting, but having a sculpture made- that's a big deal. It could take quite a while for him to make such a thing. How big would it be?"

"Big enough for everyone who was driving by on their way to and from West Chester along the Brandywine to see. I say a granite pedestal five feet wide and ten feet high and a bronze sculpture ten feet high of the three standing together on top. What do you think?" Jim waited for what he thought might be a very cautious response.

"Well, that does sound fascinating and it would be perfect set up right near the old Lenape Totem pole there, which is the one thing still standing after Hurricane Ida roared through the area. It would be a wonderful memorial to all of them, but it'd be a *huge* project and could take a long time to complete."

"I agree, but our Guardian Angels are with us. I already contacted Tom Weathersby and mentioned the idea to him. He *LOVED* it- and said *'The stars are in alignment!'* He already had a cast of Hannah and is currently close to completing one of Marshall. He'd only have to do Taylor- and of course we'd have to get a granite base excavated from somewhere in the area."

*"How much would all this cost?"*

"Maybe less than you think. We chatted about that and he said since he already had two of the three started, it would only cost in the $75,000 range. That's not too much for what would be a permanent sculpture honoring them all."

Natalie's face couldn't hide her smile. "We *can* afford that- and I really like the idea that we'll be putting something in place memorializing people important in our local history. Nice job! I have to say, you did your homework here." She gave Jim a quick kiss on his cheek.

"So, you want to go forward with it?" He kept her hand in his as they approached the water tower.

"I do. I think it would be a wonderful way to honor these people."

"… and here's the Kennett Water Tower: *'Mushroom Capital of the World.'* It was built in the early 1990s replacing a structure from around 1910. The tower holds hundreds of thousands of gallons of water; you can see it for miles around. I always stop here." Jim turned around and headed back down the trail. As he did, could feel from the friendly tug of her hand that she liked all his suggestions.

"You really *DO* get good ideas here. I'll have to hike with you at the Park more often."

"That would be splendid. I'm going to get back in touch the Township and mention we want to purchase the land. If they approve, I'm calling Weathersby back and telling him to move forward with the sculpture."

"Where are you going to find a HUGE granite boulder?"

"Hey, I'm a former geologist. We can detect granite a mile away…" He tried to contain his laugh as Natalie hugged him. "Brandywine Quarry has granite boulders- not a problem."

"I like it. You've got your bases covered. I know you'll get this done and it'll be something to cherish."

**The Water Tower at Anson B. Nixon Park**
**which dates to the 1990s**

A branch of Red Clay
Creek and the Lake at
Anson B. Nixon Park,
Kennett Square, Pa.

Above: Henry the Great
Blue Heron at Anson B.
Nixon Park October 2024

THE OLD BEECH GROVE

Nixon Park lies on the site of Bloomfield, the home of the Chambers Family. John T. Chambers, in his reminiscences about Bloomfield, talks about visiting the "Beech Grove" when he was a child in the 1840s.

Although small, this woodland is a remnant of the forests that covered this area when Europeans first settled here in the 17th century.

Despite regular timbering over the years, this woodland still contains some trees that may be 300 years old as well as much of the species diversity of the original woodland including a mix of native trees rarely found elsewhere in the area.

THE KENNETT BEECH

The large American Beech tree
you see about forty feet beyond
this sign is the largest and
oldest tree in this woodland.
It may have been a young tree
at the time of William Penn,
300 years ago.

# Chapter 18

*"When the Purchase was agreed, great Promises past* (sic) *between us of Kindness and good Neighbourhood, and that the Indians and English must live in Love, as long as the Sun gave light..."*
-William Penn, *William Penn's Own Account of the Lenni Lenape or Delaware Indians*
*****************************************************************

Jim's footsteps led him fleetingly out onto the stone terrace, the new day's first gleamings over the horizon enlightening his favorite local landscape. "Katsura, my friend- you're starting to show your best colors. *Fall is finally in full bloom.*" The tree's smooth, grey boughs were draped more than 30-feet across with dabs of apricot and lime-green hues shining amidst hundreds of flecks of beige, peach and coral beginning their Autumnal kaleidoscope of color. "October- my favorite month of the year." He turned back toward the glass double-sliding doors as he heard Natalie in the kitchen.

"We've got a few places to visit today. First stop is the Township office, where we meet with Mr. Townsend and make them an offer for the Park. Second is in Newtown Square to see Tom Weathersby and give him specific instructions for the sculpture. Third is Brandywine Quarry to pick out a large piece of granite. Afterwards we can get lunch at Sovana Bistro on the way back. How's that sound?" Jim sipped his tumbler of ice water as he watched Natalie come up to him in the Breakfast Room.

"Wait a minute. Have you made arrangements to *meet with* each of these people?"

"Done. I sent each of them an e-mail mentioning we would like to stop by today to discuss exactly what you and I have been talking about. I heard back from every party; they're all ready to meet with us. *You drive?*"

"O.K., but *you* buy lunch, since I'll probably be writing some big checks."

"Deal. You fly, I'll buy, at least the food."

Turning left onto Bayard Road, Natalie quickly glanced at the gauges on the dashboard. "I need to get gasoline. Let's stop at the Wawa and then we'll be on our way." She pulled the car past the stoplight at Baltimore Pike and into the first bay by the pumps. "I'll get this; it'll just be a few minutes."

Natalie got out, opened the gasoline tank, then placed her credit card into the reader. *'ERROR'* flashed in front of her at the pump. *"What's going on?"* She tried the card again. *'ERROR.'* "I *know* my card is good- I just used it last night. I'm going in to the attendant." She shook her head as she put the nozzle back in its housing.

Jim rolled down his window. "Having trouble?"

"Yes. This pump is malfunctioning. I'll be right back." She strode quickly into the WaWa where, amazingly, there were no people in line. "Hi! I'm at pump #7 and it doesn't seem to be working. Can you help?"

The 19-year old with a crew-cut in front of a foot-long ponytail down his back stared blankly at her. "Oh… I'll try… There you go. It should work now."

Natalie rushed back to the pump, put her AMEX card back into the reader… and got the same response. *'ERROR.'* She could barely hold her anger, but she counted to ten to hold it back. As she looked around, all the other gasoline pumps had cars at them, so she leaned into the open window to talk with Jim. "This is plain stupid. All the pumps are being used and I need to fill up. It's not working- *again*. I'm going back inside to get this taken care of once and for all." Nearly running back inside, she saw a *different* teenager this time at the check-out counter. "You work here, right?"

"Well, I *guess so*…" The boy with rainbow-colored braids and two nose rings along with a pierced left cheek stared blankly at her. "What do you need?"

Flustered, Natalie tried to hold back her irritation. "Pump #7 is acting up. It won't accept my card, but I *know* it's usable. Can you please *re-set the pump?* I'm kind of in a hurry."

"Uhhh… *It should be O.K.….*"

Natalie turned and rushed through the glass doors *again* out to the pump. "If this doesn't work, I'm going to *scream!!*" She placed her AMEX card in again. *'ERROR.'* Then she stared over at Jim and yelled ***"Oh my God!! These guys are…"***

"Real men of genius." Jim got out of the car and marched over to her side. "There's a 'CALL' button here. I'm using it. Hey, folks!! Get your act together. ***Pump #7 isn't working!!***" Just then, they both heard the computer on the pump elicit high-pitched sounds and the words *"RE-TRY CARD"* appear on the screen. "O.K., hon, give it one last try."

Natalie pushed the AMEX card into the slot- and it registered. "Some things about the electronic age are *not* good. I liked it back when you paid the attendant in cash and they washed your windshield while filling your tank." She shook her head while glancing over at Jim.

*"… and asked to check the oil and radiator, too- no charge. Those were the days."*

She filled the tank and hopped back into the Mercedes. "O.K., NOW we can get going!"

Jim's face couldn't camouflage his grin, which he did his best to hide as he looked out the passenger side window.

"You think that was funny." Natalie shook her head, then stared at him.

"It was a little funny."

"No it *wasn't!* These people are incompetent. How they can get a job at a respectable place of business is beyond me."

"Don't look now- but those are the people who are going to be *running the country* someday."

"*God help us…* I think the Township Building is right up there, on the left." She pulled into an open parking spot under a shady maple tree.

"Yes- that's it. We're looking to meet with Arnie Townsend. He's expecting us."  He put her hand in his as they stepped through the double-doors into the Lobby. "Hello. I'm Jim and this is my wife Natalie. We're here to see Arnie; he knows we're coming."

The receptionist reminded Jim of his 9th grade typewriting class teacher. The woman's wavy blonde hair was coiffed into a style frozen in the late 1950s, her cats-eye glasses a good companion. "He's back in Room 2, down the hall on the right." She turned her attention to a memo she was composing on the computer in front of her as they proceeded down the hallway.

"Arnie? Jim Peterson. I chatted with you about Lenape Park." Jim put out his hand and gave a firm handshake. "This is Natalie."

"Oh, yes! Good to meet you. I have the file right over here." After returning Jim's handshake, he opened the folder in front of him on the desk. "You found the right person- sometimes it can be a bit nebulous as to who handles certain Township operations. Let's see… yes- Lenape Park. It was gifted back to the Township over two years ago; vacant ever since. You said you were interested in purchasing it?"

"Yes. We'd like to make a grant of the land back to the Delaware Nation, the Lenape tribe who lived here for centuries. We also want to put up a statue there honoring Indian Hannah and two other people well known in local history: Humphry Marshall and Bayard Taylor." He waited with hopefulness as Arnie flipped through several pages in the folder.

"I can't see any reason why you shouldn't be able to do that. I'm looking at the land transfer documents and the previous owner actually stated his *desire* that the land be put to 'some public use honoring our local heritage' in the future. Of course, we couldn't guarantee that to him… but *your* offer fits the bill pretty well. Did you have a monetary amount in mind?"

Jim knew from years in business that you never offer a dollar amount without getting a sense of what the other party was willing to accept. "Did *you* have a dollar amount you were expecting for it?" He waited as Arnie read through the paperwork again.

"In light of this having been a no-cost gift to the Township and the likelihood that you'll be able to fulfill the donor's wishes- along with the fact that the Township will be saving *substantial sums of money* in the future by *not* having responsibility for ongoing maintenance,

I'm sure that a nominal amount- say $1,000- would be acceptable. How does that sound to you folks?" He looked at Natalie, from whose face suddenly emerged a big smile.

Natalie leaned closer to his desk. "That sounds completely fair. I can write you a check now. I understand this will need official approval, so it'll take some time- but I'm willing to give you a good-faith deposit, so to speak, to secure the property. Is that O.K.?"

Arnie grinned. "I *am* the 'official approval', but I do very much appreciate your offer and will accept your check to at least hold the property for you. Yes, this will need approval of the Board and some paperwork will have to be filed, but I can't see any reason why they wouldn't accept it. They've been complaining about all the river maintenance expenses every few months- and you know, residents are always wary of so-called 'unnecessary government spending,' so your offer really solves two problems at once. I'll give you an official RECEIPT which you should keep as proof of payment. I'll file the necessary paperwork today. You should hear back from us in about two weeks. I expect you'll be approved. Anything else I can help you with? You people are history buffs?"

Jim started to rise from his seat, then sat back down. "Yes, we both love preserving historic sites. We've been doing a lot of research about people like Indian Hannah, Humphry Marshall, Bayard Taylor, William Darlington..."

Arnie's eyes perked up. "I'm actually a distant relative of Bayard Taylor. I've even read a couple of his books."

Jim's smile grew larger as Arnie spoke. "I loved *Eldorado* and also *Colorado: A Summer Trip*. His narratives of the bustling young San Francisco and the western landscapes are really superb. *Views Afoot, or Europe Seen with Knapsack and Staff* is also very good. You know, he really wanted to be remembered as a poet- but I think his finest works are his travel books, which still read quite well today."

"I agree. I'm so glad to meet local people who are both *interested* in history- and dedicated to *preserving it*. Thank you, folks for stopping by. We'll be in touch." He reached out and shook Natalie's hand, then Jim's.

"Thanks, Arnie."

As they went through the door out to the parking lot, Natalie gave Jim's hand the 'I really like that' squeeze. "That went well."

"About as well as could be expected. Trust me- local governments *love* getting money- it happens so rarely. Next stop- Tom's house. He lives not far from The Square Tavern, so we'll be going into familiar territory."

"No meanderings on unknown back roads..."

"Nope. Turn right up there and that… should be his house up on the left, just one from the corner."

She pulled the charcoal grey Mercedes up to the curb and stopped. "He's got a nice house."

"He's actually a very accomplished sculptor; he's done ones of Hemingway and several other famous people." They walked up to the front door and Jim rang the doorbell.

After a few seconds, the sculptor came to the door. "Jim, Natalie. Good to see you both! Last time we met was… at The Square Tavern?"

*"That is right!"* Natalie went into the house first and Jim followed, gazing at art work all around the room. "You've done quite a few sculptures, Tom. Nice work."

"Over 200. So, you're interested in doing a three-person sculpture with Indian Hannah, Humphry Marshall and Bayard Taylor, right?"

"Yes. We'd like Hannah to be in the middle, with Marshall on her right and Taylor on her left. You said you already had molds for Hannah and Marshall?" Jim couldn't help staring at all the art objects surrounding them.

"Yes, pretty much. Hannah's done; Marshall's almost done and will be soon. I'll just have to make one for Taylor. It's interesting that you include Taylor- I've long had an interest in portraying him. This gives me the chance." He pulled out sketches of all three persons for them to view, with dimensions and materials listed. He smiled at Natalie first, then looked directly at Jim. "I mentioned that since I already had the molds for two of them, the price wouldn't be too high. You also said they would be placed on some kind of a pedestal? Granite?"

Jim held the sketches in front of himself and Natalie. "Yes. I'm purchasing the base separately. You just need to do the sculptures, which will go on top. The granite pedestal will be roughly five feet wide and ten feet high. The three bronze figures you sketched will be perfect size- right on top. You'd mentioned it would be roughly… $75,000 for all three together?" Jim waited anxiously as he noticed Natalie opening her pocketbook.

"I ran the numbers. It's gonna' be about $75,000… *maybe $80,000 tops-* but only if I have problems with the molds. How does that sound?"

Jim's smile emerged just as Natalie gave his hand another loving grasp. "That's just about what we expected- and totally fine. Let's do it. When do you think you might have this all completed?"

Tom stood up and scratched the back of his head. "I'm gonna' say… at least a month or so. I'll call my foundry today and give them the word. They're pretty good with turnaround, so I feel comfortable with that as an estimate."

Natalie already had her checkbook out. "Can I write you a check as a deposit, or do you need the full amount?"

"I always like it when people offer payment up front- so yes, a check for $75,000 would be very much appreciated." He took the check as she entered the amount in her ledger.

"Tom, thanks so much for taking on this project. We realize you're busy with other things. By the way, we really enjoy your work. We have your sculpture of Joshua Chamberlain at Gettysburg. I love it!"

"Oh, thank you. That's one of my personal favorites… and thank you for this check. I'll try to begin work right away."

"We'll let you get started on this. Give me a call with any updates or if you have any questions." Jim shook his hand and Natalie quickly followed suit as they headed toward the front door. As they approached the car, Jim beamed with joy. "Well, that's two down, one more to go."

"He's a very nice man. I'm glad we have an accomplished sculptor nearby to do this. Now… how do we get to Brandywine Quarry?"

"Let's head back and get on Route 82 North. It'll take us to Strasburg Road, where we turn and it takes us right there." The Mercedes cruised its way back and entered the lane onto Route 82, going northwest through Chester County toward Parkesburg.

"I like the fact that he accepted the job right away. That's a good sign."

"Yes, turn left up there onto Strasburg Road. Next turn is RIGHT onto North Church Street. See it? They're at 151 Church Street."

"I see it." She pulled into the parking lot and they both got out and walked briskly inside.

"Hello. I'm Jim Peterson. I called previously about a large granite boulder."

The man at the front desk. "Oh yes, I talked with you. I'm Ralph Johnson." He put his hand out and shook Jim's vigorously. "You'd mentioned that you wanted a granite base five feet wide and ten feet high, two feet in depth. We don't have a 10-foot high block available, but we can do *two* 5-foot high granite blocks, stacked one on top of the other. Is that O.K.? Here are the samples- I think you'd picked the pink granite, which is our most popular item."

Jim looked at the stone. "That's fine- two five-foot high blocks will work. I assume they can be placed easily and sturdily on top of each other, aligned vertically, right? It'll all be stable?"

"Absolutely. Not a problem. What's your due date?"

Natalie spoke up first. "Well, we'll need it in the next few weeks. We're hoping to have a sculpture completed and placed on top of the granite within a month. You deliver, correct?"

"Yes, of course. Where will this be going?" Ralph looked at both Natalie and Jim.

"The old Lenape Park in East Bradford Township, just outside of West Chester, along the Brandywine. In their parking lot, within a few feet of the Totem Pole that's still standing. Do you know where that is?"

"Oh, yes! I grew up not far from there; went to Lenape Park when I was a kid. I remember that Totem Pole! I know exactly where it is. I heard the park was devastated in the flood on September 2021, but then someone purchased the property, I believe…?"

"Yes, that's right. The owner apparently had a change of heart, because he gifted it back to the Township. It's been vacant for a couple of years. We're planning to take possession of the land, donate it to the local Indians and honor them with a monument, which is what you'll be helping us to make with the granite blocks. A sculpture of three figures will be placed on top."

Ralph grinned. "I majored in history at West Chester University. That sounds like an interesting monument. Who are the figures?"

"Indian Hannah in the middle, Humphry Marshall on her right and Bayard Taylor on her left."

"Nice. The price for the two blocks, plus delivery is going to be… $5,300 total. I prefer a check up front, if possible."

"Not a problem." Natalie had her checkbook open and filled out the amount, handing Ralph the check as he shook her hand in thanks.

"That's great; here's your receipt. I have your number and e-mail; I'll send you an update in the coming days, to be delivered in the next couple of weeks after the blocks are cut and ready. Is that O.K.?"

"Ralph, that's fine. We appreciate your attention to this and look forward to hearing from you." Jim gave him a brisk handshake and started walking back toward the door with Natalie.

"Great, folks. I'll be in touch soon. Many thanks."

As they got into the car, Natalie's grin was widening. "Everything seems to be working out well. What a nice change from dealing with other contractors- he was polite, professional and up-front with all the details. I'm hungry… ready for lunch at Sovana Bistro?"

"I am and I'm ordering their delicious Grain Bowl- beans, squash, quinoa, onions- kind of like what *the natives around here used to eat…*"

******************************************************************

Natalie held the latest edition of *The Chester County Press* in her hands as she stood in the Conservatory- and couldn't believe her eyes. 'Local Mailbox Crime Ring Leaders Captured; Police Say More Arrests are Imminent.' "Hey, Jim!! Come over here! I have some good news."

He strolled past the Western Wing of their home and saw Natalie's face beaming. "What's up?"

"Check this out. They caught some of the people stealing from mailboxes around the area… maybe not the guys who we saw, but some of them. Isn't that great?" She handed the newspaper to him.

"It sure is." He quickly read the three-column story and smiled. 'Coatesville Police arrested three men: Francis Robinson, Anthony DiAngelo and Salvatore Esposito who were charged with multiple counts of burglary around the Chester County area.' "Looks like it was pretty widespread. This is a welcome development. It does mention Captain Wallingford, so crimes *around this area* were likely involved. Just a guess- maybe the file we gave him helped? I was hoping somebody would finally get these jerks behind bars."

"Whatever helped, it's wonderful. Looks like they're on to the other rings in the region, so with any luck, this 'roadside robbery' will be over soon." She put her arms around him, ready for a kiss.

"Hey, I'm just glad we played a small part in bringing some of these 'highwaymen' to justice." Their arms wrapped tightly around each other in a very long embrace...

**Brandywine Quarry sign courtesy**
**Brandywine Quarry**

**East Bradford Township Municipal**
**Building**

**WaWa store on Baltimore Pike, Kennett Square, Pa.**

# Chapter 19

*"We are the indigenous people of this land. We have always been here."*
-Lenape Chief Quiet Thunder (1934-2020)
*The turtle moved slowly across the edge of the riverbank, dipping its mouth into the water, always looking around for predators which might cause harm. The native people who inhabited the region all seemed to revere him, treating him with kindness whenever they were near. For centuries the Lenape passed the tale from generation to generation of how the world began- the Earth coming to life on the back of one of its kind millennia ago... and thus the turtle took on a sacred quality, representing the beginning of existence and the foundation of their society, the giver of life to their clan...*
******************************************************************

Jim reviewed the many pages of notes he put together over months of searching for the history of the Lenape- and found some bits of trivia he'd almost forgotten. "The Lenape called themselves the Lenapehokink and considered themselves the caretakers of southern New York, New Jersey, eastern Pennsylvania, northern Delaware and the nearby Delaware River, which they called *'The River of Human Beings.'* Interesting- their website mentions that the Lenape thought very highly of Penn, almost like a 'brother.' I seem to remember that and also they were the first tribe to be granted land in 'the Jerseys.' They were here for 10,000 years, but in the course of just 200, pushed out. Their 'spirit' still remains… and now we can give them a monument which recognizes them in perpetuity."

Having contacted the Lenape Nation of Pennsylvania almost a month back, he'd alerted them to the ceremony planned for next week in Lenape Park. Tom had completed the sculptures; he and Natalie saw the monument just yesterday and it was magnificent, its bronze figures standing tall, with Indian Hannah in the center, her arms wrapped around both Humphry Marshall and Bayard Taylor. Tom arranged for delivery in a few days, following the placement of the two huge granite blocks there as the base for the sculpture. Jim had also ordered the historic marker which would be placed at their feet.

As he was deep in thought, he heard Natalie's footsteps. He turned to see her coming into the foyer.

"I saw the framed map you picked up yesterday from Strodes Mill Gallery. It looks really good!"

"Yes, Donna did a great job. I'm going to hang it in the Family Room, near Hannah."

"Sounds fine. Planning some things?"

"Just going over what we'll be doing- and seeing- next week at Lenape Park. I'm so glad we got the paperwork from the Township, so that's all resolved. I'd like to go over to the Park today to see how the granite blocks are sitting on the macadam surface there after last night's heavy thunderstorm. They laid them out in the right spot in front of the Totem Pole as we watched them lower them to the ground last week. I'm just wondering how stable they are in very high winds. The weather report said gusts were over 70 miles per hour last night."

"Jim, you of *all people* know those granite blocks weigh *a ton*. It'd take hurricane-force winds to make them budge half an inch."

"I guess, but I'd just like to be sure and there could easily be storm debris around them. Remember what happened after remnants of Hurricane Ida passed through? There were branches, logs and trash scattered everywhere. Want to take a quick ride over there now?"

Natalie hesitated for a few seconds. "O.K. You drive, then we can stop at Antica on the way back for lunch."

"Deal." He grabbed his keys and she followed him into the garage. "Be prepared to do a bit of clean-up. I brought my work gloves and the heavy rake, they're in the back." As the Forester made its way toward Route 52, Jim reminisced. "Just over there is where they had the Indian Hannah monument for years. Then they changed the road access to Longwood. I kind of liked it in its old place, where they had the ceremony back in 1925."

"Times change. At least now people can easily see it in back of what was the old Longwood Progressive Friends Meeting. Be careful. Yesterday I was coming back from West Chester and some guy ran the red light at the intersection with Route 926 and almost slammed right into me!"

"You didn't say anything about that. Why not?" Jim glanced over at her and shook his head.

"I didn't want you to get upset. Look, just being out on the roads today can be a life-changing event."

"I won't argue with that." As they wound their way up Route 52 past historic Baldwin's Book Barn, Jim couldn't help but make a comment. "My favorite bookstore in the country- the building dates back to 1822. I love that place!"

"O.K., no Tour Guide while you're driving."

"I know; it's just an important part of our heritage. Wish I could have met William Baldwin, the founder when he started the establishment in the old barn back in 1946. His son Tom was a nice gentleman. So sad that he passed away a few years back."

"*JIM!! Look out!!* That car up ahead… looks like it's… ***ON FIRE!!***"

He immediately swerved to avoid the vehicle, which had small flames lapping around its sides as it stood right in the middle of his lane. "Oh, my God! There's someone inside there and… it looks like they're trapped!!" He jammed on the brakes, skidded to a halt on the narrow shoulder and jumped out of the car. Running up to the burning blue Dodge Durango, he saw an elderly female inside, screaming.

"*HELP ME!! HELP ME!!!*" A white-haired woman in her early 80s was panicking in the driver's seat.

Jim ran right up to her car and tried to open the door, but it was jammed. Sprinting over to the passenger side, he felt it was jammed as well. "Natalie! She can't get out! Grab the rake from our car- I'll have to break the window to get her out. *QUICK!!!*"

Natalie jumped into action, pulling the rake from the rear storage area of their car, coming over to him near the other car as it began to be enveloped in smoke. "*HERE!! GO AHEAD!!*"

Jim yelled to the woman: "*Close your eyes- and lean down, away from the window!! NOW!!*" He saw her bend forward with her eyes closed, then he pounded the heavy metal end of the rake against the window. "*Damn it!! It won't break!!*" He stepped back, then leaped forward with the rake and hit the driver's window, breaking the glass, the shattered fragments spraying all over the woman's lap and into the street. He dropped the rake and leaned in through the jagged window and felt for the door latch. "*Where the Hell is it…? O.K.- I got it!!*" He tugged on it hard, but the door would *not budge*. Then he tensed his shoulders and arms and yanked the latch with one, huge pull… and the door finally opened. He saw the lady shaking violently. "*I got you!! You're O.K.!!*" He put both his arms into the car and grabbed the woman, pulling her out onto the street, where several cars had already slowed down to see the commotion. "*Natalie- call 9-1-1!!* They're gonna' need Police and a tow truck here."

The elderly woman was shaken, but not burned and seemingly all right. Standing with Jim, she hugged him for several seconds. "You… *SAVED MY LIFE!!* Thank you so much!!" She started hugging him again.

"I'm just glad you're O.K. Stand over here; there's a lot of cars going by." She continued with her arms wrapped tightly around his waist for well over a minute. "You can let go of me now."

She smiled and burst into a laugh. "Oh, I'm sorry!"

"No problem. So, what happened, Ma'am?" As the flames died down, Jim gazed inside the car and didn't see anything burnt.

"I don't know. All of a sudden, my car slowed down- like the engine was stalling… then it came to a complete stop. I didn't put on the breaks. It stopped all on its own… and I saw smoke coming from under the hood. I put the car in "PARK" and then there were tiny flames coming from the engine. I tried to get out right away, but the door was jammed. I guess I panicked."

"Unfortunately, cars today are nearly 90% electronic. All you need is one thing to short circuit and the whole car can shut down. I bet your electrical panel has a flaw which caused the engine fire- and your doors to jam, but thank God you're O.K."

"I know- all these electronic things are nuts and these crazy *'Apps'* I never heard of- like I'll accidentally touch a part of the screen on the dashboard- and find out the next day I just bought life insurance."

He looked at her face and saw she was crying. *"No… no reason to cry.* You're gonna' be fine, Ma'am."

Her face was streaked with tears as she sobbed and wrapped her arms around him again, nearly knocking him over. "I'm alive because of you. *God bless you!* What's your name?"

"I'm Jim; that's my wife Natalie. We're glad to help you. It looks like there's an Ambulance and… a Police car coming right up here." He looked all around and waved the line of cars past them so the Ambulance and Police vehicle could come right up. "You know, you're lucky you weren't the only car out here on the road, all alone at this time. It could've been bad."

"Oh, I believe in Guardian Angels. Maybe mine's here with me…"

"I believe in them, too. The cops are coming now." A policeman ran quickly up to them and asked if they were both unharmed. "We're fine, officer. Her car just broke down and somehow caught fire. I got her out of the car safely." Jim watched as he sprayed the sides of the hood with fire retardant and the only traces left were small wafts of grey smoke coming out.

"What's your name, Ma'am? I'll need to see your driver's license, please."

"Thank God I grabbed my purse as he pulled me out! I'm Ida Bonnicelli. Here's my license."

"Your name's Ida? My mother's name was Ida. I like that name." Jim smiled- then he gave *her* a hug. "I'm Jim Peterson, officer. Here's my license."

The policeman examined their faces, then their licenses, giving them both back promptly. "You sure you're O.K., Ma'am? No burns or bruises?"

"I'm fine *thanks to him!*" She looked lovingly at Jim, as he smiled back.

"We'll need to get this towed; I'm calling in a tow truck now." He glanced at Jim and Natalie. "You folks are free to go. Thank you very much for your efforts, sir."

"My pleasure. We appreciate your getting here so quickly." Jim walked over to Ida and gave her a very long hug. "You're in good hands now. We wish you all the best."

***"THANK YOU!!!"*** She waved as Jim's car pulled away toward West Chester.

"Well, *THAT* was enough excitement for one day. I'm proud of you." Natalie gave him a light kiss on his right cheek as he drove. "No getting distracted- just a kiss."

"Thanks. I *had* to stop and help her…"

"*Of course!* I believe in being a Good Samaritan. You did the right thing- and you probably *did* save her life. There's a special place in Heaven for you someday."

"Hopefully now things calm down a bit. The turn is up there, then I'll pull into the Park… or… *what's left* of the Park." The car stopped at the edge of the paved area and he saw it, the monstrous pink granite boulders standing in the sunlight. They both got out. "Well, there's a bit of debris from the storm, but it looks O.K. I like the way they positioned the blocks so you can easily view them from the road. The township did a great job cleaning up this whole area." Jim kicked away a few small branches at the base. "Everything looks good… now I'm ready for the event next week. Can't wait."

"Tom Weathersby has to get the sculpture delivered first; that's tomorrow. We already showed him the base and the way it should be pointed, so we shouldn't have to be here. I trust it'll all turn out fine." Natalie turned to walk back to the car and Jim followed close behind.

"I agree. It should be perfect. Let's head to lunch- a quick one. I love Antica's homemade pasta. It's delicious."

"Hopefully *this* trip will have no excitement." She smiled as the SUV pulled up to the restaurant.

Following their meal, they drove into their home garage and Jim thought of the old woman. Not the one they just saved… the one depicted in the painting on their Family Room wall. Walking inside, he stood right in front of it. "Hannah, you *are* beautiful. Adrian gave you a great title: '*The August Moon Lights My Way*.' You helped *so many*."

As he stood there, Jim thought he heard a very faint voice. *"As you just did, my son…"* Jim turned around quickly to see if Natalie was in the room, but no one was there. The television and stereo were off. The Family Room was completely empty. Then he gazed up at the painting again, directly at her face. *"You're the healer*. We're finally going to give you the recognition you deserve."

********************************************************************

The rustic stone farmhouse had stood for well over two centuries before Jim and Natalie approached its weathered façade, both of them awaiting the annual reenactment of the capture of Sandy Flash at the Colonial Pennsylvania Farmstead. An old man with long, silvery hair beneath his black tri-cornered hat led them along the path where they would soon unexpectedly encounter a notorious villain. Suddenly… he confronted them both.

"Stand back- **and hand me your money!**" Sandy Flash pointed his pistol directly at them, waiting for his booty.

"Oh, please, sir! Don't hurt us! Here's all the money we have." Jim handed Flash the few coins he had in his pocket, then watched him turn and run back down the path into the early Fall evening.

"That's him!" Natalie shrieked as she watched him disappear into the night. Pleasantly startled, they both ambled onto the front porch of the home and adjacent barn which were both elegantly lit by candlelight.

"Did you see that rogue, Sandy Flash?" asked a portly raven-haired matron in Colonial garb.

"See him? *He robbed us!!*" Jim yelled with a smile on his face.

"We will get that scoundrel!! There's a posse of 12 armed men on his trail right now." The woman joined two others as she went inside the farmhouse lit by candlelight, waiting for further news about the highwayman. "He'll hang for all his crimes!"

As the twilight faded to near total darkness, Jim held Natalie's hand as they crossed the rustic wooden bridge back across the creek to the parking area. "I actually wanted to thank him."

"Thank who… *for what?*"

"Sandy Flash… for leading us on this… *trail of history*…."

**Colonial era guide with lantern**

## Colonial Pennsylvania Farmstead's
## Shades of Sandy Flash event

**Entrance to 1700s Colonial Farmstead**

The notorious highwayman Sandy Flash
demanding your money

Sandy Flash makes his escape

1700s Colonial Farmstead

Continental Army soldiers attempting to capture
Sandy Flash at his mother's house

Highwayman Sandy Flash robbing patrons of a tavern

Sandy Flash is captured at McAfee's house by
McAfee and the maid

Sandy Flash is convicted and hung for his crimes; his
ghost appears in the window

# Chapter 20

The next day was dazzlingly bright, sunlight gleaming from an azure sky. Temperature was perfect: 72 degrees, a light wind, not a cloud on the horizon. Jim walked through the kitchen to see where Natalie was. "Hey hon, are you ready? The event starts in less than an hour. We need to get over there."

"I'm coming; be there in a second." Natalie's face was glowing as she came down the stairs.

"Well, you look absolutely lovely."

"Thank you. You're looking quite dapper."

"Dapper Dan, as my neighbor used to say. Like the new necktie?"

"Yes, it's got beautiful maroon and navy stripes."

"Ready to go?"

"You lead the way."

The Forester made it back up Route 52 and quickly arrived on the scene at Lenape Park. As they went over the bridge crossing the Brandywine, he could see a sizable crowd was already there. "I told *The Chester County Press* about this and also sent a note to *The Daily Local News*, *The Philadelphia Inquirer* and *The Wilmington News Journal*- so who knows? Maybe we'll get some coverage." He pulled into the lot which already had several cars parked not far from the monument, its bronze figures shining in the sun. "Look at it. Isn't it beautiful?"

"Lovely. Let's go out and see it up close."

They walked up to the massive bronze sculpture and stood about ten feet from it. "It's even more wonderful than I expected. Tom did an excellent job. Look at Hannah- ***she's radiant!*** Humphry Marshall looks very distinguished. Bayard Taylor has a book in his hands, with a 'faraway look' in his eyes, like he's longing to cross the continent and get back to Europe where he did so much exploring. ***It's superb!***" Just then he felt a hand on his shoulder.

"Hi, Jim. It's Marie, Curator from the History Center. How are you?"

"Doing well, Marie. So glad you could make it here! Looks like we're going to have a decent crowd."

"I think so. More cars are pulling in now and starting to back up on Route 52. We really thank you and Natalie for putting this together. It's a wonderful way to memorialize important people from our heritage."

"We're glad to do it." Just then he noticed Adrian and his wife coming towards them and their friend Mark who helped them with his extensive knowledge of Humphry Marshall. "Adrian… Leah… great to see you both! Mark- nice that you could come."

"I wouldn't miss this for the world." Mark gave him and Natalie a big hug.

"*Leaves are fallin' all around… The Autumn Moon lights my way.*" Jim sang the old song as Mark watched.

Mark grinned. *"I love that tune."*

"The song that helped name Adrian's painting." Jim noticed Mark nodding in approval. Then his eyes widened as he perused the parking area, which now was nearly filled. "Natalie, looks like we may have over 100 people. Maybe *much more.*"

"That's great. I see Steve here from *The Chester County Press* and a guy over there with a PRESS PASS from *The Philadelphia Inquirer*. Also someone from *The Wilmington News Journal.* They apparently got the word out to cover this and… here comes Tom."

"What a turnout! Hey Tom, great to see you! Your work is outstanding. Humphry, Hannah and Bayard are magnificent."

"So glad you like it. I'm really proud of what I was able to accomplish."

Jim looked at his watch and nudged Natalie. "O.K., I think it's time." He took her hand and stood in front of the monument as dozens of people gathered near them. He raised his arm to get the group's attention. "All right, folks. *We're about to begin.* I thank you all for coming today. My wife Natalie and I are grateful for the help of so many people who I need to mention. First, Mr. Townsend from East Bradford Township for approving the land sale… then Tom Weathersby, the sculptor for the wonderful creation he has made and Ralph Johnson at Brandywine Quarry for supplying the lovely granite boulders upon which stand three icons: Indian Hannah in the center, Humphry Marshall to her right and Bayard Taylor to her left. These three each hold a very special place in Chester County history. As you know, Lenape Park was abandoned after the flood a few years back and even though it was purchased, the owner gifted it back to the Township. I got the idea for returning it to the Lenape as I walked through Anson B. Nixon Park with Natalie and stood before the historic Kennett Beech, which was here when William Penn signed treaties with the Lenape over three centuries ago."

Jim's eyes widened as he saw the crowd growing ever larger, overflowing the parking lot area. "We also made an historic find. I bought an old map a while back and was alerted to the fact that *on back* of it before it was to be framed was the treaty Penn signed with the Lenape giving them rights to land on each side of the Brandywine, long lost and almost forgotten. We had it authenticated and… I have it here with us. I am giving this to the Chester County History Center to be part of their permanent collection and Marie here will I'm sure gladly accept it."

Marie walked right up to his side, smiling broadly. "Jim, this is wonderful! Thank you so very much. We'll definitely have this as part of our Chester County exhibit."

Jim nodded in appreciation. "If I can help just *one* person to better understand and appreciate our history, I've accomplished something worthwhile." He turned his attention back to the crowd. "Now I want to thank members of the Lenape Nation for being here today. I contacted them, alerting the tribe to the fact that my wife and I had purchased this property- called Lenape Park for many years- and intend to gift it back to them. This is where they hunted and fished and lived their lives, an area which unfortunately was taken from them so long ago. Well, we're giving it back and this deed is the official document, showing they now and forever will have ownership of this sacred land they possessed for thousands of years... and will keep for centuries to come. I'm also giving them a copy of Penn's treaty."

A man dressed in tribal gear walked to Jim's left and accepted the documents with a beaming face. "Thank you, Jim. This is a wonderful celebration- a superb gift, which our tribe sincerely appreciates. It will now be in our hands. I'm glad Indian Hannah is here to witness this." He looked up at her saying the Lenape words *"Lapich knewel." ("I will see you again.")*

Jim gazed up at Hannah as the mid-afternoon rays glimmered across her face and for a fraction of a second, as the Sun warmed her cheeks, he thought he could see her smile. He spoke out in a *booming voice* to the group: *"Hannah... welcome home."* At that moment, a beautiful white dove flew up and landed at Hannah's feet. The applause was almost *deafening*, hundreds of people clapping, cheering, whistling. One man held up a sign ***"THIS LAND IS YOURS AGAIN!"*** and blew a horn loudly in salute.

Natalie stood right beside Jim, wrapping her arms around his waist, crying as she viewed the awe-inspiring monument. Through her tears, she noticed something crawling slowly up onto the edge of the top boulder. "Hey Jim, look- ***it's a little turtle!!***"

He saw it and pressed her hand to his lips, smiling. "It's the symbol of the Lenape nation. All of them- from the past and present- ***are here in spirit with us today.***" Jim then turned back toward the sculptures, his face ecstatic as he raised his hands up and out towards them. *"Humphry... Hannah... Bayard... Thank you for everything you've done for us and for our nation. You have made America a better place."*

The scene bathed in shimmering sunlight, the crowd's ovation was thunderous all around them as the sculpted figures *came alive...*

***Humphry Marshall (1722- 1801)***

***Indian Hannah (1731- 1802)***

***Bayard Taylor (1825- 1878)***

***Three whose contributions to our heritage will live on forever...***

Lenape Chief Tamanend scupture by
Raymond Sandoval in Philadelphia

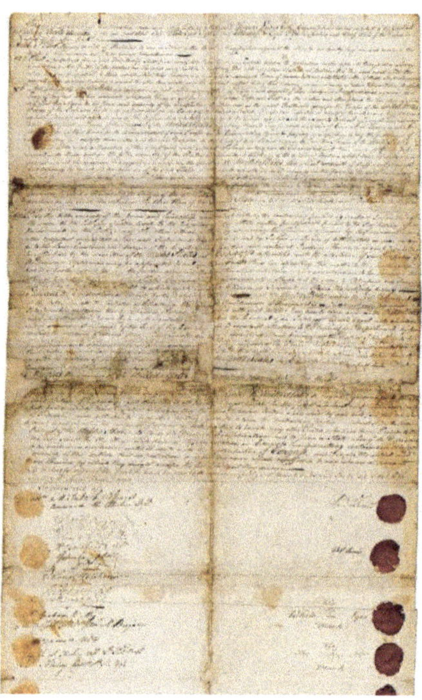

Treaty of Fort Pitt September 17, 1778- the first
treaty signed by the U S government with the
Lenape Indians courtesy National Museum of
American Diplomacy

Postcard and menu from Lenape Inn

Lenape Park sign and Indian Totem Pole

**Painting of Humphry Marshall by artist Adrian Martinez**

**Portrait of Indian Hannah titled *Walking by Light of the August Moon* by Adrian Martinez**

**Painting of Bayard Taylor as a young man**

# About the Author

Gene Pisasale is an author and historian living in Kennett Square, Pennsylvania. He has written 12 books, gives lecture presentations on special occasions and contributes a regular column titled *"Living History"* to several media outlets in the Philadelphia area. Gene earned a Master's Degree *summa cum laude* in American history from American Public University, a Master's Degree in petroleum geology from The University of Texas at Austin and an MBA Finance from San Diego State University. He began his career as a petroleum geologist in 1980, then shifted his talents to the investment industry, where he worked as an analyst and portfolio manager covering the energy/chemicals/natural resources industries for 24 years. Gene holds the Chartered Financial Analyst (CFA) and Certified Financial Planner (CFP) certifications. In 2010, he retired from the investment industry to pursue his writing career. He has presented lectures on a wide range of historical topics at venues around the mid-Atlantic region, including Alexander Hamilton's home, the *Hamilton Grange National Memorial* in New York, *Fort McHenry*, *Brandywine Battlefield Park*, *Paterson Great Falls National Historic Park*, the *Union League* in Philadelphia, *Widener University* and the *University of Delaware,* as well as for libraries, historical societies and Daughters and Sons of the American Revolution. He welcomes inquiries for book signings and special events.

Website: www.GenePisasale.com
E-mail: Gene@GenePisasale.com

# Other Books by Gene Pisasale

Vineyard Days

Lafayette's Gold – The Lost Brandywine Treasure

Abandoned Address – The Secret of Frick's Lock

The Christian Sanderson Museum: Tom Thompson Remembers

Mines and Minerals of Chester County

The Forgotten Star

American Revolution to Fine Art: Brandywine Valley Reflections

Alexander Hamilton: Architect of the American Financial System

Hemingway, Cuba and the Great Blue River

Forgotten Founding Fathers: Pennsylvania and Delaware in the American Revolution

Heritage of the Brandywine Valley

www.ingramcontent.com/pod-product-compliance
Lightning Source LLC
Chambersburg PA
CBHW041159300726
48981CB00004B/307